He highly dou...
Sofia's birth d...
body was. And...
Kaylee looked...

"If you're really Constanzia, you'll be able to prove it."

"I never claimed I was Constanzia. All I said is I thought I might be."

"Then get me your birth certificate and adoption papers."

A wariness settled over her like a second skin. "My birth certificate's at my father's house in Houston."

"Let me guess. Your adoption papers are there, too."

She hesitated, but when she spoke her voice was strong. "I guess Sofia didn't tell you?"

"Tell me what?"

"I don't have any papers because my parents never admitted I was adopted."

He let out a short, harsh laugh. "Lady, you are a piece of work."

Dear Reader,

Where do we belong? With the people who gave us life or those who happen into our lives? That was the question running through my mind when I wrote *Ordinary Girl, Millionaire Tycoon*, about a woman who believes she's finally found her place in the world.

But when that place is populated by a lottery winner who may or may not be her birth mother and the woman's over-protective step-son, matters aren't black and white. Especially when love is thrown into the mix.

Although I'm not new to Mills & Boon, I am new to Superromance. It was a pleasure to explore a deeper, richer story in what has always been one of my favourite lines. I hope you enjoy this story.

All my best,

Darlene

PS You can visit me on the web at www.darlenegardner.com.

Ordinary Girl, Millionaire Tycoon

DARLENE GARDNER

MILLS & BOON®

Pure reading pleasure™

ABOUT THE AUTHOR

While working as a newspaper sportswriter, Darlene Gardner realised she'd rather make up quotes than rely on an athlete to say something interesting. So she quit her job and concentrated on a fiction career that landed her at Mills & Boon, where she's written for Temptation and Intimate Moments before finding a home at Superromance.

Please visit Darlene on the web at www.darlene gardner.com.

To my grandmothers Rose Gorta and
Rose Hrobak, who are gone from this life but
not from my heart. I like to think these warm,
wonderful women would have enjoyed having a
granddaughter who writes about love.

CHAPTER ONE

UNTIL KAYLEE CARTER sat on the television remote and accidentally switched the channel from a *Seinfeld* rerun to the late-night news, she'd thought her mother was dead.

She picked up the remote to change the channel back, but her finger paused on the flash button when the camera panned over lush, rolling countryside that seemed to stretch for miles.

The pink-and-white blooms of apple orchards made the deep green of the grass and the azure, cloud-dotted sky even more lovely. The blossoms caused the gentle hillsides to come alive with color and touched something inside Kaylee that the city never reached, something that ached with longing.

Her modest little duplex in Fort Lauderdale off U.S. 1, which was far too close to a high-crime area where muggings and break-ins were common, seemed to fade into the background.

McIntosh, Ohio, the caption read. Named, if Kaylee wasn't mistaken, for a popular variety of red apple. The warm feelings suddenly made a bit more sense. Kaylee had been born in Ohio, although her parents had returned to their native Texas when she was only a few weeks old and she'd since moved to Florida.

The compelling face of a dark-haired, dark-eyed woman took the place of the orchard. Although Kaylee was positive she'd never seen the woman before, she seemed familiar.

The woman had a timeless quality that made it hard to guess her age. Early forties, perhaps? Her wide-set eyes and shoulder-length hair were as dark as Kaylee's own, her nose as distinctive, her olive complexion nearly as unlined except around the mouth and eyes.

The reason for those lines became evident when the woman smiled, which she obviously did often. An inner glow seemed to light the smile and radiate from her.

Kaylee leaned toward the nineteen-inch television screen, wishing she could have splurged on a bigger set. Another caption identified the woman as Sofia Donatelli, a former cook at Nunzio's Restaurant in McIntosh who'd won ten million dollars in the Ohio lottery.

"I need luck like that," Kaylee murmured.

She scrambled off the worn sofa she'd bought at a garage sale, sat cross-legged on the floor in front of the TV and turned up the sound.

An impossibly handsome reporter with a square jaw, blindingly white teeth and gilded highlights in his brown hair revealed that Sofia had become known in the Ohio Valley for her generosity since winning the prize six weeks ago.

He interviewed a young mother who told how Sofia paid for experimental surgery to help control her daughter's Tourette's syndrome and a businessman who'd gotten seed money from her to open an ice-cream parlor. The camera then switched back to a shot of Sofia and the good-looking reporter.

"You're probably asking yourself what's in this lottery bonanza for the woman who won the prize. So tell us, Sofia, what will you splurge on? A mansion in L.A.? A yacht that will take you around the world? A garage full of expensive cars?"

"What I want is something money can't

buy." Sofia stared straight into the camera, her eyes moist and glowing with an emotion so stark that Kaylee's chest tightened. "I want to find my daughter."

Kaylee's heart pounded so hard she felt it slamming against her chest wall. She edged closer to the set, afraid to miss a word.

"When did you last see your daughter?" the reporter asked.

"When she was a few minutes old. I was sixteen." Sofia smiled softly, sadly. "I thought the best thing for my baby was to give her up for adoption. I got to hold her, but only briefly. Then the nurse took her away, and I never saw her again."

"When was this?"

"Twenty-five years ago," Sofia said, "and there hasn't been a day since that I haven't thought of her."

The remote dropped from Kaylee's fingers, her heart stuttered and she had difficulty taking in enough air.

Kaylee was twenty-five. She'd never had her suspicion verified, but she'd always believed she was adopted.

It wasn't only because she was the sole brunette in a family of blondes. Quite simply, she hadn't belonged. Not in the sweltering flatlands of Houston, where she'd grown up. And not in the Carter family, where her younger sister Lilly had been the favored child.

Kaylee was the one who couldn't do anything right. She'd been expected to make straight A's, to stay away from boys, to stick to the ridiculous curfew of 9:00 p.m. and to dress like a nun, rules Lilly always managed to skirt successfully.

Kaylee hadn't been as lucky. And though she'd rebelled with a vengeance, she never had gotten up the guts to ask her mother if she was really her mother.

She'd asked her father only after her mother died suddenly of a brain aneurysm when Kaylee was in her teens. He'd never had much to say to Kaylee and didn't then, muttering that she shouldn't be ridiculous, before changing the subject.

He hadn't outright said no.

"Have you tried to find your daughter before now?" the reporter asked Sofia Donatelli.

"Many times. My stepson even hired a private investigator a few years back. But I always come up against a brick wall." Sofia talked with her hands, pantomiming the action of hitting a wall.

"Why do you think this search will be different?"

"Because I won the lottery and you put me on television." Sofia grew more animated, her hand gestures more pronounced. "There's a chance that my daughter or somebody who knows her could see this."

The reporter's forehead creased with little-used lines. "But how could anyone who sees you on television put the pieces of the puzzle together? You can't know much more about your daughter than you've already told us."

"Oh, but I do." Sofia's smile was bitter-sweet. "I wanted her to take a little bit of her Italian heritage with her so I stipulated that her adoptive parents keep the name I chose."

Kaylee's stomach seized. Her middle name was quintessentially Italian, a striking contrast to the American names of "Kaylee" and "Carter."

"What is her name?" the reporter asked.

Kaylee held her breath as she waited for Sofia Donatelli's reply.

"Constanzia," Sofia said. "Her name is Constanzia."

The breath whooshed out of Kaylee's lungs. The room seemed to tilt and her head swam so that she couldn't tell whether the sudden flickers on the television screen were due to a failing picture or her glazed eyes.

Kaylee's full name was Kaylee Constanzia Carter.

"Mommy, my tummy hurts."

The soft voice intruded into her consciousness. Her six-year-old son Joey stood in the middle of the living room. His hand rested on his Spider-man pajama top, his eyes drooped and misery clouded his cherubic face.

As she sat on the floor trying to come to terms with her shock and his sudden appearance, his color paled and his face contorted in pain. Kaylee leaped to her feet, scooped him up and reached the toilet in the bathroom the instant before he was sick.

As he retched, she rubbed his back to let him know that she was there. She felt every one of the spasms as though she were the one who was ill. When he was finally through, she ran a washcloth under the cold tap water and wiped his hot, little face. "Do you feel better now, honey?"

He nodded, but his lower lip trembled.

Thinking aloud, she said, "I knew I shouldn't have let you eat that second hot dog at dinner."

"Like hot dogs," he mumbled. He blinked hard, trying valiantly not to cry.

Kaylee's heart turned over. She gathered his small body close but still he didn't surrender to tears. Was it because he'd sensed how hard things had become for her?

Being a single mother had never been easy, but she'd had a live-in support system until six weeks ago. She'd shared expenses, childcare duties and friendship with another single mother who had a little girl Joey's age. Then Dawn met a man, took little Monica and moved away from Fort Lauderdale.

Dawn used to jokingly call Joey the man of the house. Had Joey taken that description too much to heart?

"It's okay to cry if you need to, honey," Kaylee whispered into his soft, sweet-smelling hair.

He held himself so rigidly that she thought he hadn't heard her, but then the tension left his body in a rush and, finally, he cried. Not delicate, silent tears but noisy, shuddering sobs.

Kaylee held him close, glad of the comfort she could offer.

Her son's appearance in the living room had prevented Kaylee from hearing what else

Sofia Donatelli had to say. She told herself it didn't matter. Constanzia was her middle name, not her first name. Some other Constanzia was Sofia's birth daughter.

Or maybe you are.

She shut her mind to the thought.

Still, she knew that if she'd seen the news feature years ago, she would have jumped in her car and driven through the night to Ohio in her quest to learn the truth.

But she was a mother now. She had responsibilities and one of those was to curb the rash part of her nature that had gotten her into so much trouble when she was growing up.

The notion that the lottery winner who lived in the lush Ohio Valley could be her mother amounted to nothing but a fantasy.

The sobbing, little boy in her arms who depended upon her was her reality.

CHAPTER TWO

TONY DONATELLI nearly dropped the phone.
"You did what?"

"I already told you, Tony. I let that nice
young television reporter know I'm searching for Constanzia." Sofia Donatelli made it
sound as though she'd been conversing with
a friend instead of issuing a potentially ex-
plosive announcement.

"The best part was that affiliate stations
might pick up the feature and run with it," she
continued in the same cheerful tone. "Isn't
that wonderful? That means people all across
the country might see it."

Tony's fingers tightened on the receiver. "I
thought we agreed when I was in Ohio last
month that you wouldn't give any interviews.
I thought you wanted to keep your life as
normal as possible."

"I do," Sofia said. "But I haven't had any
luck finding Constanzia on my own, and I

got to thinking that I could use the publicity to my advantage."

"Publicity isn't always a good thing, Sofia. Did it occur to you that McIntosh is about to be besieged by women who claim their name is Constanzia?"

She laughed the same laugh that had warmed him since his father had brought her into their lives. Tony had been a six-year-old boy desperately in need of a mother. His father, widowed for almost that long, had needed a wife. Sofia had only been twenty, but she'd fulfilled both roles beautifully. Tony still thought she'd given his late father far more than he'd deserved.

Tony would have gladly called her "Mom," but she'd always insisted he refer to her as "Sofia." She said she never wanted him to forget that the woman who'd given birth to him had loved him with all her heart, even if he didn't remember her.

"I hardly think Constanzias will storm the town, Tony. I only gave away the one daughter."

"And how much money have you given away since you won the lottery?"

"I really can't say."

Tony couldn't either, and that was the crux

of the problem. He'd fled the stifling environment of McIntosh for Michigan State as soon as he was old enough for college, found excuses not to come home for the summer, settled in Seattle after graduation and had only returned to Ohio for brief visits since.

Even after his father died of a sudden heart attack two years ago, Tony could justify living apart from Sofia. She was still a young woman, her life was in McIntosh and she'd visited him often in Seattle.

A one-dollar lottery ticket she'd bought on a whim after stopping for bottled water at the 7-Eleven had changed everything.

Sofia had beaten fourteen-million-to-one odds by predicting the six correct numbers in the Super Lotto. As the single winner, the ten-million dollar jackpot was hers and hers alone.

The irony that Sofia was the one who'd gotten rich quick didn't escape Tony. She'd all but supported their family single-handedly while he was growing up. His father had worked sporadically, persisting in the mistaken belief that one of his wacky inventions would make them rich.

Sofia's stroke of luck had set Tony's mind at ease about her future. Her lump-sum cash payment was just over three and a half million after federal and state taxes, enough for her to quit her job and be set for life.

But then the reports had started filtering in from his high school friend Will Sandusky, who still lived in McIntosh.

Sofia, it seemed, was a soft touch. So far she'd doled out money to a couple who planned to start a business making custom chocolates, paid off a stranger's mortgage and sent her friend on a Caribbean anniversary cruise. And now she was inviting trouble.

At this rate, she'd lose her newfound fortune before a few years were out.

Tony rubbed his forehead to ward off a brewing headache. "Sofia, you really don't see a problem here?"

"Is everything all right, Tony?" His girlfriend Ellen Fitzsimmons stuck her beautiful blond head around the door frame, her question drowning out his stepmother's reply.

She held a wine goblet in her right hand, and the overhead light caught the rich red hue of the merlot. It reminded him that he'd originally intended to break out a bottle of champagne to cap off an evening that had begun at a trendy French restaurant he'd booked a week in advance.

"Just a second, Sofia," he told his stepmother. He covered the receiver, futilely wishing Ellen had stayed in the living room. "Everything's fine, Ellen. I'll be just a few more minutes."

She hesitated, but then left the room on three-inch heels, the skirt of her dress swirling around her slender legs. Tony waited until she was gone to speak into the receiver. "I'll tell you what the problem is. Fake Constanzias who'll want a piece of your fortune."

"Tony, dear, it's not like I won a Powerball jackpot." Sofia sounded amused. "And there aren't that many women named Constanzia."

"We talked about this when the private investigator couldn't find out anything, remember? He said the adoptive parents might not have kept the name Constanzia."

"He didn't know that for sure. Besides, I have to take the chance. I don't have much information to go on."

"You're inviting pretenders."

"But I'll know if someone's trying to put one over on me. I have a picture of her in my head, Tony. When I close my eyes, I can almost see what she looks like."

Tony's head throbbed, and he rubbed his forehead with two fingers. "*When,* Sofia?

You've been looking for Constanzia since I was in college. The P.I. I hired couldn't find her. What makes you so sure she'll show up?"

"Besides the power of publicity?" she asked, then answered herself. "I have faith."

"Do you know how vulnerable that faith makes you to an impostor?"

"If it'll make you happy, dear, I'll ask Constanzia to show me her driver's license."

"It's easy to get a fake ID," he said, trying not to sound frustrated. He knew how much finding Constanzia meant to Sofia. Hell, there was nothing he wanted more for her. But if a top-notch P.I. couldn't locate her, chances were slight that a mention on a television program would. "Anybody with access to the Internet can call up a dozen sites that will do it for you."

"Oh, Tony. You're being dramatic. Do you honestly believe somebody would pretend to be my daughter just because I have a little money?"

He stifled a groan at her definition of multimillions as a "little" money. "Yes, I do believe that."

Her sigh was audible even over the phone line. "I wish you weren't so cynical, Tony."

"I wish you weren't so trusting."

"Let's not argue. I see you so seldom that even our time on the phone is precious to me. Have I told you lately that I miss you?"

"I miss you, too," he said while he faced the inevitable. He needed to go back to McIntosh to make sure a fraud didn't worm her way into Sofia's life. He felt confident he could run off most of the pretenders with a show of bluster. And as a last resort, there was always DNA testing. He took a deep breath, then forced out the words. "In fact, it's time I paid you a visit."

Even as he made the declaration, he knew he'd used the wrong word. This wouldn't be a visit, but an indefinite stay.

His stomach twisted at the thought. He'd worked hard to escape the place where the shadow of his fabulously unsuccessful father hung over him like a dark curtain.

And he'd succeeded. He made a very good living running an online security company featuring a protocol he'd developed to verify the identities of remote users. The company was so successful, the college friend he'd hired to help run the business had been pushing him to expand.

While Tony couldn't stay away from his

Seattle headquarters indefinitely, he'd been itching to take some time to redesign the company's Web site. And he could run Security Solutions from anywhere as long as he had Internet access. Including McIntosh.

"A visit from you would be lovely." Sofia paused. "As long as you realize I know you're coming to McIntosh to keep an eye on me."

"That doesn't bother you?"

"If playing watchdog is what it will take to get you here, I can live with it," she said agreeably.

He talked to his stepmother for another five minutes in which she deftly sidestepped his questions about her finances. She was especially evasive about the local financial planner she'd insisted on hiring instead of the one Tony had found for her in Columbus. One more thing to check up on, he thought.

He reluctantly rejoined Ellen in the living room when he hung up, not looking forward to the coming conversation.

She'd crossed one leg over the other, and her slim gold ankle bracelet glinted in the soft light of the living room. She gazed up at him through expertly made-up lashes. Even though her wineglass was half-full, her pink-tinted lipstick looked fresh.

"Can I top off your glass?" Her musical voice was as perfect as the rest of her. They'd been dating for seven months, ever since she'd approached him at the health club they both used. His initial impression of her, as a woman who went after what she wanted, had turned out to be correct.

"No, thanks. I need to make it an early night."

Her perfectly shaped eyebrows lifted in question. She had every right to expect that this Saturday night, as countless others before it, would end in his bed. Sundays, they usually spent together.

"Has something happened? Is that why you took so long on the phone?"

He sat down next to her on the buttery-soft leather sofa in front of a fireplace that didn't blaze and filled her in on his conversation with Sofia, ending with his plan to return to McIntosh.

"Is that really necessary, Tony?" she asked. "Sofia's forty-one. That's only fourteen years older than you. She can take care of herself."

He pressed his lips together, wondering how best to explain. Ellen would understand better if she knew Sofia, but he'd somehow failed to get them together.

"You don't know her, Ellen. She has a big heart and a trusting nature. Not a good combination for somebody who just came into millions of dollars."

"But you were just there last month."

"Last month she hadn't announced on television that she was looking for her daughter," he said.

She set her wine goblet on the glass top of his coffee table, then crossed her arms over her chest. "How long will you be gone?"

"Try to understand, Ellen." He laid a hand on her arm, which felt cool to the touch. "I need to stay as long as Sofia needs me."

"But I thought you hated McIntosh. Didn't you tell me that leaving was all you could think about when you lived there?"

Now wasn't the time to confide that even the three days he'd spent in McIntosh after Sofia won the lottery had been too long. He composed his words carefully. "How I feel about McIntosh and how I feel about my stepmother are different things."

"So you're going to let things here slide? What about expanding your company? And the house? At that price, it won't stay on the market for long."

He'd forgotten about the sprawling, contemporary house until this moment. It needed a new roof and a new heating system, but its spectacular views of the Puget Sound and the Olympic Mountains made it a bargain.

"There will be other houses," he said.

She got gracefully to her feet. Her blue eyes locked with his. "In my experience, Tony, if you don't seize your opportunities when the moment is right, you lose them."

After she was gone, Tony went into his bedroom, reached into the pocket of his pants and pulled out a small black velvet box. He snapped it open, removed an oval-cut, one-carat diamond ring and held it up to the light so that it sparkled.

He'd been carrying the diamond around for the better part of two weeks, the same length of time he'd kept the champagne in the refrigerator.

He shut the ring back in the box, opened his sock drawer and tossed the box inside next to a blank application for season tickets to the Seattle Supersonics pro basketball games. It would have to stay there until he returned from McIntosh.

THE BEAUTIFUL rolling countryside of McIntosh and Sofia Donatelli's heart-tugging plea replayed in Kaylee's mind at odd moments over the next week, but her own predicament was much more pressing.

Joey's tummy ache had not been caused by too many hot dogs but by a lingering stomach flu the pediatrician claimed wasn't serious. That was a matter of opinion.

The restaurant where she was a waitress provided a sorely deficient benefits package. Not only had she been forced to pay fifty percent of the doctor's bill out of her own shallow pocket, but she'd lost tips by staying home to care for Joey.

Not that the tips had been all that great since Dawn's departure forced her to change to an earlier shift. Even if Joey hadn't gotten ill, she needed to face the fact that they could no longer afford to live in Fort Lauderdale.

She'd spent the last few nights agonizing over where they could go. The inescapable conclusion was her father's house in Houston that she'd fled while still a teenager.

Kaylee had doubts over whether they'd be welcome, but last night she had swallowed her pride and telephoned, only to get the answering machine. So far, her father hadn't called her back.

For Joey's sake, she tried to shove aside

her worries. Her forced smile strained the corners of her mouth after she and Joey got out of the serviceable ten-year-old Honda she'd bought used five years ago.

"What do you want for dinner, sport?" she asked as she opened the mailbox in front of her duplex and took out a stack of envelopes and junk mail.

She'd picked up Joey from school ten minutes ago and worried that his color still wasn't right. Had her boss's insistence that she not miss another day of work caused her to rush his return?

"Fish sticks," he said.

She hid a groan. He'd eat fish sticks seven days a week if she let him. But at least they were cheap and easy to prepare.

"Yummy, yummy, yummy. Joey wants fish sticks in his tummy," she said, ruffling his thick hair.

He groaned. "I'm not three, Mom."

"Too bad. When you were three, you laughed at my jokes even if they were bad."

"They're bad," he agreed readily.

She covered her heart with her hand. "You wound me," she said dramatically.

Joey giggled, that high-pitched boyish noise that never failed to warm her heart.

"Got you," she said.

He giggled again. She ushered him from the mugginess of the late afternoon into the duplex, which was only slightly cooler because she kept the thermostat on a high setting during the day to save on electricity.

Had she really been living here for six years? It seemed impossible but her rapidly growing son constituted proof of how quickly the time had passed.

Still, she could barely believe that almost seven years had passed since she'd ditched her high school classes and spent the day at the mall charging purchases to the credit card she'd stolen from her mother's purse. She'd felt completely justified because her mother had grounded her for some reason she couldn't remember but at the time seemed grossly unfair.

Night had fallen when she finally returned home to find her father sitting in his favorite recliner with the TV off and the lights out. His voice had been steady when he told her he'd given up trying to track her down hours ago.

She remembered the fingernails of her right hand digging into her thigh as he went on to say her mother had collapsed that morning while waiting in line at the post office. She'd probably been dead before she hit the floor.

Following her father's lead, Kaylee hadn't cried. Neither had she told him her last words to her mother.

After the funeral, things had gone downhill fast. Without her mother around telling her what to do, Kaylee had done what she pleased. Within a month, she'd bagged her senior year and run off to Florida. Then she'd gotten pregnant.

A kind social worker had gotten Kaylee a bed in a home for unwed mothers run by a charitable organization that also helped her get her GED. If not for the stroke of fate that had landed Dawn in the same home, Kaylee would have made the biggest mistake of her life.

As the two girls had cried together over the children they'd never see grow up, somehow their tears had nourished their own emergence into adulthood. Then Dawn had come up with the radical, wonderful idea that they live together and help each other raise their babies.

And so they had, a situation that had worked out beautifully until Dawn had fallen in love. Kaylee owed Dawn more than she could ever repay so she'd tried to be happy for her. And she was. But that didn't stop her from being sad for herself.

Not because Kaylee craved a man of her own—she'd learned the hard way that romantic entanglements could cause more problems than they solved—but because she'd lost her family.

Kaylee crossed the main room to the controls on the wall, turning the air conditioning up but only far enough that they wouldn't break a sweat. She hoped.

She banished thoughts of Dawn, who she'd assured just yesterday over the phone that she was doing well, and concentrated on her greatest joy: her son.

She swallowed the sudden lump in her throat that the old memories had formed. She hadn't truly recognized how badly she'd treated her own mother until she became a mother herself.

"What did you do in school today, Joe-Joe?"

In answer, the child knelt beside the backpack he'd dumped on the floor, opened it and took out a piece of paper.

Joey was a surprisingly good artist with a keen eye for the physical characteristics that made a person an individual. He'd drawn two people holding hands, and she clearly recognized them as herself and Joey.

"Miss Jan said to draw the people in my family," he explained.

Kaylee forced herself to smile even though the starkness of the picture struck her. There was no Dawn, no Monica, no Aunt Lilly, no Grandpa Paul, no father—and no background. She and Joey existed in a vacuum against a backdrop of stark white. She searched for something positive to say.

"Is my little boy really this big already?" She tapped the picture he'd drawn of himself. His head was level with her shoulder, the size of a boy twice his age.

He rolled his eyes and affected a grown-up tone. "I'm already six years old."

"Yes, you are." She smiled tenderly, because he was growing up far too fast. "Mind if I put your picture up on the fridge?"

He shook his head, and she fastened the drawing to the refrigerator with a colorful magnet he'd painted in art class and given her for Mother's Day. It joined a gallery that included a yellow dinosaur, a purple puppy and a mystery animal with the body of a dachshund and the head of an eagle.

"Can I turn on the TV?" Joey asked.

"Go ahead, honey. But just till dinner."

Trying not to sigh, Kaylee took the pack of fish sticks from the freezer and popped eight of the frozen sticks into the oven. Then she set a pot of water to boil and found a box of macaroni and cheese in the lazy Susan.

Betty Crocker, she was not. But then she'd never paid attention when her mother tried to teach her to cook. She'd never even made a lunch to bring to school. Her mother had done that for her until high school, when she preferred to eat as little as possible and pocket the rest of the money for more important things. Like an occasional joint or the wine and beer she could talk an older friend into buying for her.

She dumped the macaroni into the boiling water, listening with half an ear to make sure the cartoon Joey had turned on wasn't geared for adults.

The irony of her life of responsibility didn't escape her. She couldn't remember the last time she'd smoked a joint, and she barely touched alcohol. She, who'd reveled in the wrong things, was determined to set an example for her son by doing the right ones.

While she waited for the macaroni to cook,

she separated her mail into two stacks. Bills in one, junk mail in another. She was almost through sorting when the phone rang.

"Kaylee, it's Lilly." Her younger sister's drawling voice, rich with the sound of Texas, came over the line.

"Lilly!" Younger than Kaylee by six years, Lilly lived at home with their father while finishing her sophomore year at Houston Community College. "How's college? Are you through with the semester yet?"

"Almost. It's exam week, and I can't wait for it to be over. Do you know how much you have to study in college?"

Kaylee barely stopped herself from lecturing her sister on the importance of a college education. Lilly was still young enough not to listen to reason, even if it came from somebody with first-hand knowledge of how hard it was to make ends meet without higher education. "What are you going to do this summer?"

"Same thing I do every summer. Work on my tan while lifeguarding at the community center," she said. "Listen. I can't talk long because I'm meeting a friend for dinner, but I wanted to let you know that Dad said you and Joey are welcome here."

Kaylee's jaw tensed. If her father really wanted her and Joey in his house, wouldn't he have called her back himself? "Did he offer, Lilly? Or did you talk him into it?"

The pause at the other end of the line was too lengthy to be meaningless. "Don't be silly, Kaylee. You know Dad. He's always been there for us."

Lilly's statement wasn't entirely accurate. Paul Carter was a dependable, hardworking plumber who'd ably supported the family. But he hadn't cared enough to intercede in the stormy arguments Kaylee had with her mother. Neither had he come after Kaylee when she'd run away to Florida. And he still hadn't seen his grandson.

To be fair, her father always sprang for Lilly's plane ticket when her sister visited them. Lilly relayed that he'd pay for their plane tickets if Kaylee and Joey wanted to visit them in Houston, but Kaylee hadn't asked and he hadn't offered himself.

"Let us know when you're coming, okay?" Lilly said. "I've got to run."

Kaylee hung up the phone, more unsure than ever that she and Joey should go to Houston.

But she had to decide something soon. Her

meager savings were dwindling rapidly. Her father would probably help her out, but she hadn't once asked him for money in six years and didn't intend to start now. If not for Joey, she'd never have asked if they could stay at his house temporarily.

She went back to sorting the mail, stopping abruptly when she came across a letter from the Florida Parole Commission. A lump of unease clogged her throat. Not bothering with her letter opener, Kaylee ripped open the envelope, pulled out a single sheet of white paper and read the bad news.

A hearing had been scheduled that could result in Rusty Collier being granted parole. The hearing was next week.

Short fingers pulled at her skirt. "Mommy, what's wrong?"

She stared down at Joey's dear, little face and tried to think. Even if Rusty did get parole, it didn't mean he would try to find them. He'd only contacted her twice since Joey had been born, then had given up when she'd asked him to stop calling.

But the very possibility that he might track them down was one more strike against Houston. Never mind that the terms of Rusty's parole would prohibit him from leaving Florida.

"Nothing's wrong, honey." She got down on her haunches and looked into his eyes. "But I have a surprise for you."

Joey brightened. "M&M's? A Matchbox car?"

She smoothed the baby-fine hair back from his forehead. It was an unusual shade. Lighter than brown but darker than blond. On more than one occasion, she'd heard it described as rust-colored. Like the hair of the man who'd fathered him.

"Not that kind of a surprise. A bigger one. We're going to have an adventure."

"Like Winnie the Pooh?"

A wave of love swept over her like a warm wind. She nodded, glad that Joey didn't yet consider the beloved character beneath his new maturity level. "Exactly like that. Is there a story called *Winnie the Pooh and the Move?*"

Skepticism replaced the eagerness on Joey's face. He shook his head.

"Well, imagine if there were such a story. Imagine if Winnie and Tigger and Christopher Robin moved."

"In the Hundred Acre Wood?"

"No. Somewhere else. Somewhere better." Ignoring his continued skepticism, she kept on talking. "It'll be fun. First we'll pack up everything, and then we'll get in the car, just you and me. We'll drive away from Florida and start over someplace else."

"When?"

"Soon. Maybe even the day after tomorrow."

Worry lines appeared between his brows. "How 'bout school?"

Kaylee hadn't thought of that and did some quick mental calculations. It was mid-May. The last day of school wasn't even two weeks away. "School's almost out for the summer, honey. It won't matter if you finish a couple days early."

Although Joey didn't frown, he didn't smile, either. "Where?"

The lush countryside that had charmed her from the television broadcast played like a travelogue through her mind. She imagined Sofia Donatelli standing among the blooming apple trees, beckoning to her with a smile and a bent finger, and made her decision.

"We're going to Ohio. A place called McIntosh."

CHAPTER THREE

MᴄIɴᴛᴏsʜ ᴡᴀs all Kaylee had imagined it would be. The gently sloping hills. The trees bursting with spring color. The open spaces. The crisp blue skies with the promise of summer in the warming air.

Everything would have been perfect if only she had a job, child care and a place to live. Friends in town would have been nice. Family would have been better.

If she hadn't panicked when she'd gotten that letter from the Florida Parole Commission, she would have formulated a better plan.

At eighteen, she'd thought it exciting to leave home for the unknown. But packing Joey and everything they owned into her car and heading for Ohio hadn't felt like an adventure. It felt like a risk.

She'd temporarily taken care of housing by getting a room at a hotel on the edge of town, but the most that could be said for it was that it was clean.

Before they could look for a more permanent place to live, she had to find work. And she needed to do it with a six-year-old in tow because there was nobody she could ask to babysit.

She pulled into a parking space on the appropriately named Main Street and got out of the car with Joey, feeling as though she'd been plopped down in the middle of a storybook.

A recent rain had wiped everything clean, causing the spring hues to seem more vibrant. The street was awash with color, the white clouds puffy overhead in a cerulean sky. They walked up a slight hill past a beauty shop, a bookstore, a general store and a shoe-repair shop while she searched for an address.

"Hey, Mom." Joey pointed a forefinger at a tall tree that sported a profusion of tiny, red flowers against its smooth gray bark. "That tree looks like it has chicken pox."

"Yeah, sport," she said. "It does."

The trees were almost always green in South Florida, the temperature forever warm, the traffic always busy. McIntosh was a welcome change. Thirty seconds could pass before a car went by, but the sidewalks, though not busy, were far from empty.

"Look at that." Joey sprang away from her, ran to the base of the tree and scooped up something. He came back to her side holding a very small squirming toad covered with warts. "Isn't he cool?"

She backed up a step. "You better put him down. He'll give you warts."

"They said on TV that's a mitt."

"A myth," she corrected. "But even if he won't give you warts, he looks like a baby. You better let him go so he can find his mother."

He rolled his eyes. "He was hatched from an egg."

Kids who watched nature shows on TV were tougher to manipulate, Kaylee thought. "Just let him go, Joey."

Joey groaned but turned away from her and scooted down. An elderly man who was passing by met Kaylee's eye and greeted her, something else she wasn't used to.

She and Joey continued walking until she found the address for Sandusky's, a small grocery store with a full-service butcher shop. The clerk at the hotel had told her that the store was looking for a cashier.

"Now remember what we talked about,

Joey." She bent down to his level. "You need to be quiet while I'm talking to the people about a job."

Joey kept by her side while she found a clerk and asked to speak to the owner. He appeared from the back of the shop a few moments later wearing a white butcher's apron that didn't detract from his appeal.

If she'd been twenty years older, she would have looked more than once. He had thick brown hair, pleasant features, kind hazel eyes and a nice smile. "I'm Art Sandusky. Can I help you?"

"Hi," she said brightly. "My name's Kaylee Carter, and I'm here about the cashier's job you advertised in the *McIntosh Weekly*."

A tremendous crash from the next aisle interrupted whatever he'd been about to say. His brows drew together. "I wonder what that was."

Kaylee looked wildly about for Joey, didn't find him and had a pretty good guess. Together she and Art Sandusky rounded the corner of the next aisle. Her son stood beside broken pickle jars and a young girl in an apron. The smell of dill and vinegar was nearly overpowering.

"What happened?" Art Sandusky asked.

"The kid asked me if I wanted to see something cool. Then he reached in his pocket and pulled out a toad." The girl shuddered. "It jumped on me."

"It didn't mean nothing by it," Joey said. The toad leaped into view and Joey scrambled away in pursuit.

The job hunt didn't go much better after that. Art Sandusky was a doll about the breakage, insisting it had been an accident and refusing to accept payment. But he'd also hired a cashier three days ago.

Kaylee's next stop was a deli-style restaurant that hadn't advertised for help and turned out not to need any. The owner probably wouldn't have hired her anyway after Joey bumped into a waiter carrying a tray of drinks. Two customers got drenched, but Joey came away dry as desert sand.

"Do you know of anyplace else that might be looking?" she asked the tired-looking man who emerged from the kitchen to clean up the mess.

"You might try Nunzio's," he said as he swished the mop back and forth. "It's the only other restaurant in town with table service."

Kaylee's palms grew damp and her heart

sped up. Her impulse had been to make Nunzio's her first stop, but she'd deliberately steered clear of the restaurant where Sofia Donatelli had once worked.

Getting established before confronting Sofia had seemed like the smartest plan, but now she needed to be a realist. She couldn't stay in McIntosh for long without a job. Applying for a waitress job at Nunzio's made perfect sense.

Her heart raced when she grabbed her son's hand, because every step she took brought her closer to the woman who could be her mother.

"C'mon, Joe-Joe," Kaylee said. "We're going to Nunzio's."

ANOTHER DAY, another impostor. This one had brought her son along.

Tony saw her as soon as he entered Nunzio's, the most logical place in McIntosh to meet with a stranger. The place not only smelled wonderful—a mouthwatering mixture of tomato sauce, garlic bread and spices—but the homey atmosphere was inviting. Checkered red-and-white tablecloths covered the booths and tables, and scenic vistas of Italy decorated the walls.

Tony had suggested meeting at three

o'clock, because it was between lunch and dinner. The only people in the restaurant were an elderly couple sitting at a corner table near the entrance, a young boy of about five or six and the woman.

The woman sat with the boy in a rear booth, although the latest in the string of females he mentally referred to as "the Connies" hadn't said anything about bringing her son.

Yesterday's Connie had been a petite bleached blonde he'd frightened off with surprising ease. When Sofia was in the restroom, he'd threatened to investigate her background for past crimes and outstanding warrants. She'd bolted when he got to the part about pressing charges against her for fraud.

Although Tony had been in McIntosh for nearly a week, this would be his first meeting with a Connie without Sofia present. He'd set this one up on the sly, wanting to spare his stepmother more disappointment.

At least this Connie looked the part.

Long, wavy hair more black than brown set off by an orangey knit sweater. Eyes he could tell were nearly that dark even from across the room. Features that didn't fit

America's cookie-cutter notion of beauty but that Tony found much more intriguing. Even the Mediterranean cast of her skin was right.

By contrast the boy looked all-American, from his tousled mop of brownish hair to his inability to sit still. The latest Connie had been smart enough to seat the boy on her side of the booth with her body hemming him in.

She looked up, and he realized he'd been staring for a good thirty seconds. Their eyes connected, and his body reacted with an unexpected tug of lust.

He frowned. The Connie was most likely married. Even if she wasn't, he had serious questions about her character. He'd place the odds of her being Sofia's daughter at a million to one. The odds were probably higher that she already knew that.

Shoving aside his momentary lapse, he walked purposefully toward her. He couldn't miss the slight widening of her eyes when he didn't stop until he reached their booth.

"I'm Tony. Mind if I sit down?"

Without waiting for permission, he slid into the red vinyl seat opposite them. Her mouth dropped open, but the little guy piped up before she could speak.

"I'm Joey." He had a chocolate milk mustache and a cowlick that caused his short hair to spring up in unexpected directions. "Wanna see a toad?"

Shock appeared on his mother's face, infusing it with life. "Joey! I thought you let the toad go."

"I did," the boy said with an unhappy pout. "But I bet I could find him again."

"I'd have liked to see him. I used to catch toads all the time when I was a kid." Tony stuck out a hand to the boy. "Is it okay if I call you Joe? You look more like a Joe than a Joey."

"Sure." The boy beamed at him, displaying twin dimples that made him look like an imp. He placed his small hand in Tony's and shook with surprising firmness. Then he grinned at his mom. "Hey, Mom, he's cool."

Tony transferred his gaze to the Connie. Her features were even more intriguing up close. Her nose was long with a little bump on the bridge, her cheekbones high, her lips full, her front two teeth separated by a very slight gap. Her lashes weren't particularly long but they were thick and as dark as her finely arched brows.

His eyes dipped to the bare ring finger of

her left hand. When they returned to her face, her midnight-dark eyes narrowed.

He got the distinct impression she didn't agree with her son's assessment of his coolness. Tough. She should understand straight off the bat that she couldn't con him.

"Let's not waste time," he said. "Tell me your story."

"Who are you?" she asked.

"He already told you, Mom," the boy interjected helpfully. "He's Tony."

"I thought Mr. Nunzio's first name was Frankie."

"It is," Tony said, wondering where she was going with this.

"If you're not the restaurant owner, are you the manager?"

"No. Why—" he began.

"Then are you hitting on me?" She looked him straight in the eyes.

So much for presenting a can't-con-me front. He thought he'd disguised that first visceral reaction, but she'd recognized it and called him on it. Damn.

"He's not hitting you, Mom," Joe said. "If he did, I'd hit him back."

"Thank you, Joe-Joe." She sent a grateful look at her son before casting a decidedly cooler one at Tony. "Look, I'm flattered. Really I am. And I don't mean to be rude, but I don't have time for this. I'm here about a job that I really need."

"Whoa." He put up a hand. "I'm not hitting on you."

"He's not, Mom," Joe agreed.

"We talked on the phone. I'm the guy you were supposed to…" His voice trailed off as a possibility occurred to him. "You're not one of the Connies, are you?"

Delicate frown lines appeared on her brow. "Excuse me?"

He rephrased the question. "Is your name Connie?"

She shook her head, her dark hair rustling. "It's Kaylee. Kaylee Carter."

"And I'm Joey… I mean Joe Carter," her son piped up.

Tony closed his eyes, winced and put a hand to his brow even as relief swept through him. "I owe you an apology. I thought you were someone else."

He started to tell her he'd been weeding through letters with his lottery-winning stepmother to decide which of the Connies could be legitimate before setting up a meet. But it suddenly seemed like too much information.

The cell phone clipped to his pocket vibrated, interrupting his train of thought. He unhooked it, checked the number and recognized it as belonging to the Connie.

"Excuse me. I've got to take this." He got up and walked to an empty booth nearby.

He felt Kaylee's eyes on him as he listened to the Connie say she'd changed her mind and didn't want to reschedule. No surprise there, considering he'd made it clear she had to get past him before she could get to Sofia.

He hung up, reclipped the phone and walked back to the booth. Kaylee watched him warily.

"I'm really sorry for the misunderstanding." He didn't sit down this time. "Let me make it up to you. Let me…"

He clamped down on his teeth before he could finish the sentence…let me take you to dinner. Yeah, like that would convince her he hadn't been hitting on her.

"…put in a good word for you with the owner."

"You know the owner?" She sounded hopeful.

"I grew up here in McIntosh so there aren't many people I don't know."

"I'm waiting to talk to him. If you could put in a good word, I'd appreciate it very much. Joey and I, we just moved here and I really need a job." She lifted her chin. "Not that I can't get one myself but a good word can't hurt."

He nodded, ready to promise her anything. Her combination of bravado and susceptibility touched a familiar chord inside him. He'd once left everything he knew behind to go off to live in a strange city. He understood what it was like to feel vulnerable.

The swinging door at the back of the restaurant banged open, and Frankie Nunzio emerged. He scanned the restaurant, spotted Tony and grinned.

A small, wiry man on the down side of fifty who moved with the energy of someone half his age, Frankie reached Tony in seconds and vigorously pumped his hand. "Hey, Tony. What? You coming in here every day now?"

"Can't stay away, but you'll be glad I came in today because I found a waitress for you." He nodded toward Kaylee. "Frankie, this is Kaylee Carter and her son, Joe. Kaylee and Joe, Frankie Nunzio."

Frankie shook Kaylee's hand every bit as enthusiastically as he had Tony's. "You're the woman waiting to see me?"

"Yes."

"Have you waitressed before?"

"I have six years of experience."

"Then I'll give you a try. I need somebody from ten to two six days a week. We're closed Sundays. Let's see. It's Friday. Can you start Monday?"

"You mean I'm hired? Just like that?"

"Think of next week as your trial run. But, hey, if you're a friend of Tony's, I'm sure you'll do fine. What do you say?"

Something wasn't right. Tony could see it in the set of Kaylee's shoulders, the slight tightening of her mouth.

"Don't you have anything full-time?" she asked.

"Not right now," Frankie said. "But the restaurant business is fluid. Something could come up. So are we on for Monday?"

She hesitated, then affixed a smile. "Yes. Provided I can find somebody to take care of my son."

"Try Anne Gudzinski," Frankie advised. "She runs a day care a couple blocks from here. After I get some papers for you to fill out, Tony can walk you over there and introduce you. Right, Tony?"

"Be happy to," he said, noting that her smile of thanks seemed distracted.

He kept her son occupied with a game of paper football while she filled out the paperwork. Tony taught Joe how to flick the "football" across the table with his fingertips.

The little boy screamed, "Score!" whenever the paper football sailed off the table and into Tony's lap, not grasping that touchdowns only counted if it barely hung over the side.

When Kaylee was finally ready to walk to Anne's day-care center, Tony could tell that something was still bothering her.

She was tall, he'd guess at least five foot nine. Her height helped her project an air of independence but again he sensed vulnerability. And damn if he didn't already like her.

An image of Ellen flashed through his mind, but he dismissed his guilt. He owed Kaylee Carter for mistaking her for someone else and acting like a jerk. He couldn't deny that he found her attractive, but his association with her was purely innocent.

Somebody grabbed his hand, but it wasn't Kaylee. Firmly holding onto his mother with his other hand, Joe launched himself in the air.

"Let's go," Joe said.

Some of the strain left Kaylee's face as

she gazed down at her son. She lifted her eyes to exchange an amused look with Tony over Joe's head.

Nothing about the moment was suggestive, but Tony again experienced that unexpected pull of desire. Normal enough. He was a healthy male, and she was an attractive woman.

It didn't mean he intended to do anything about it.

ANNE GUDZINSKI'S day-care center turned out to be a large white Victorian house with black awnings on the windows and a wide, inviting porch.

If not for the color, Kaylee thought it would have looked like a gingerbread house transported to real life.

Nothing was fanciful about how much Anne charged for child care. Anne, a pretty woman with short blond hair and so much pep she'd probably led cheers in high school, explained the cost accounted for a low ratio of children to day-care workers.

Kaylee approved of the rationale, but her wallet didn't. She'd mentally crunched numbers and worried that she couldn't survive in McIntosh on a part-timer's salary.

"Hey, Tony. Hey, Mom." Joey's excited voice

broke into her thoughts. He'd chattered nonstop during the short walk to the day-care center and it appeared as though he might keep on talking all the way back to her car. "Watch this."

Holding tightly to both of their hands, her son launched himself into the air. "I'm not a bird. I'm not a plane. I'm Super Joe."

At the apex of his jump, he let go and went airborne for a split second before landing on the ground and running ahead of them.

Tony's deep laugh shot out of him. Despite her worries, Kaylee found that she enjoyed the sound.

"Look," Joey yelled, pointing at something on the sidewalk. "A grasshopper!"

He lunged at it, missed, lunged again, missed again. There went Tony's laugh, so low and full-bodied it was capable of making a grown woman shiver.

With his height, thick black hair that sprang back from a wide forehead with heavy brows and hint of a shadow darkening his jaw, Tony had the look of a dark and dangerous man. But she already had a strong sense that impression was an illusion.

He laughed too easily and got along with Joey too well. His clothes, khakis and a navy rib-knit pullover, were casual but expensively cut.

Unlike some of the male customers who used to try to make time with her in Fort Lauderdale, he knew when to back off. He'd been about to ask her to dinner earlier, but held off.

She habitually turned down the men who asked her out and would have refused him, too. The last time she'd been on a date had been six months ago when Dawn had overheard a customer ask her out and engineered it so she could go. The man had been nice enough, but not worth the time away from Joey.

Kaylee sensed a date with Tony would be different. He was self-confident, polished and probably successful. He also possessed the most prized quality of all: he liked Joey.

It figured she'd meet him now when her life was in disarray. She had more important things to accomplish in McIntosh than indulge herself with the first hot guy who came along.

But this wasn't just any guy, she reminded herself. This was the guy who'd helped her get a job and line up day care.

"Thank you for today," she said. "I don't know what I'd have done without you."

"Don't mention it," he said, then picked up a thread of conversation Joey had interrupted earlier when he'd spotted a squirrel scampering up a utility pole. "You told me you grew up in Houston and moved to Fort Lauderdale. But you never did say how you ended up in McIntosh."

She tried not to tense up at what was an innocent question. He couldn't possibly know she was both running away from and toward something. Nobody did.

Why not tell him?

The thought popped into her head and stuck. It would be wonderful to have a confidante. To talk over the threat Rusty Collier presented with somebody who was enough of a stranger that she didn't even know his full name. To confess that she was afraid to confront Sofia Donatelli with her crazy hope. To make her feel like she wasn't alone.

Her lips parted, but then she clamped them shut. She hadn't shared her hopes and fears with Dawn, who was closer to her than a sister. She couldn't air them to a man who was still a stranger.

"We needed a change," Kaylee said.

"Do you have friends here? Family?"

A startlingly clear image of Sofia Donatelli came to mind, and Kaylee bit the inside of her lip. "I just like it here," she said vaguely.

"What's to like?"

"Are you kidding?" She swept her hand to indicate the blossoming trees, the blue skies and the wide, quiet street, then breathed deeply of the clean air scented with fragrant blossoms. "It's like a little slice of heaven."

"That's what my father used to say," he muttered, not sounding pleased.

She cut her eyes at him. "And you don't agree?"

He shrugged. "I suppose it's pretty enough, but a small town like this doesn't have a lot to offer for someone who wants to make a success of themselves."

She thought that depended on your definition of success, but asked, "Then why do you live here?"

"I don't. I live in Seattle. I'm here for an extended visit."

A bird sang, and the driver of a passing car waved in greeting. She waved back, although she'd never seen the person before in her life.

"I just got here but I already know I don't want to leave," she said. "I think I could find everything I need right here to make me happy."

She mentally amended her statement. *If* she could make enough money to support herself and Joey. Her worry came back in force. She already had doubts about her ability to stay afloat and she had yet to figure housing costs into the equation.

"Hurry up, Mom," Joey called. He'd given up on the grasshopper and stood beside the car, waiting for them to catch up. "I want to play with Attila and Genghis."

Tony raised a questioning eyebrow as Kaylee took her key chain from her pocket and remotely unlocked the car.

"Attila and Genghis are snakes," she explained, then laughed when his eyebrow raised even higher. "They're characters in his GameBoy game."

She didn't add that the game was an old one she'd picked up at a store that sold used games. So far, Joey wasn't savvy enough about what was available to clamor for new ones.

She watched her son clamber into the car, then turned to Tony. She didn't want to say goodbye. The weekend stretched ahead of her: long, empty and filled with worry. But she'd been taking care of herself and Joey for a long time. She could manage. She pasted on a smile.

"Thank you again for your help." Her feet felt glued to the sidewalk, but she managed to start to turn away.

"Wait." He laid a hand on her shoulder. His touch was gentle, certainly not firm enough to stop her, but she froze. Warmth spread under her knit sweater in the spot where his hand rested.

She gazed up at him. A cloud that had momentarily blotted out the sun drifted lazily along with the wind and cast him in a shaft of light, making him look so virile she caught her breath.

It was nearly five o'clock, and the proverbial shadow darkened his jaw. She had the insane urge to rub her cheek against the stubble, to touch his slightly fuller lower lip with her fingertips to see if it was as soft as it looked.

Because she wore a pair of clunky black dress shoes, there was no more than two or three inches difference in their heights.

If he lowered his head, or she raised hers, their lips would meet. Their eyes locked. His were a light brown that reminded her of caramel. If he tried to kiss her, she'd let him. He exhaled, and she felt his breath warm against her mouth. Her breath snagged in her lungs.

"Have dinner with me this weekend," he urged.

She didn't have to think about her answer. "Yes."

His lips curved, and his mouth, with that sensuous lower lip, moved closer.

The horn of her car blared. She jumped, banging her forehead against his nose.

"Ow," he said, his hand going to the offended body part.

"Sorry," she said, rubbing her forehead.

They both turned toward the sound. Joey sat at the steering wheel, a playful grin on his face. She waved an admonishing, unsteady finger at him. He crawled into the passenger's seat and pressed his face flush against the window so his features looked distorted.

Tony laughed his intoxicating laugh. "That must be your son's way of making sure we don't forget about him. He's invited to dinner, too, by the way."

The magic had gone out of the moment, allowing Kaylee to think more clearly. She could easily make an excuse, begging off dinner on the grounds that she'd come to her senses.

"When?" she asked.

"How's tomorrow night? At about six o'clock."

"To be safe, we should make it a little later. I'm going to call a Realtor in the morning. Hopefully Joey and I can spend the afternoon looking for a place to live."

"Why don't you hold off on making that call and let me help you find a place?"

She blinked in surprise, then realized how little she knew about him. "Are you a Realtor?"

He shook his head. "I run a company called Security Solutions."

"You're a private eye?"

He laughed, touching her arm. Her body leaned toward his, seemingly of its own accord. "It's online security. I developed a protocol that verifies the identity of remote users."

"What does that mean in plain English?"

"It means the businesses that use my protocol can be sure the information they exchange online is secure, whether it be a transaction or a business plan."

"And in your spare time, you help single mothers find places to live?"

He grinned, showing even white teeth.

"Exactly. I already told you, I grew up here. I've got connections. You can't afford to house hunt without me."

"You already know of a place for rent?" she guessed.

"I know the owner, too. Why don't I pick you up tomorrow around ten and I'll show it to you?"

The corners of his dark eyes crinkled, and she nearly staggered under the power of his smile. She could come to depend on a man like this in a hurry. Even though that would be unwise, she couldn't bring herself to refuse his help. Not when she wanted it so very much.

"All right. But I'd rather pick you up," she said. That way she'd have her car and some vestige of independence. "All I need is an address."

He gave it to her, and she committed it to memory. The horn blared again. Joey sat in the passenger seat doing a terrible job of looking innocent.

"I think the native is getting restless," she said and went around the car to the driver's side. She opened the door, then looked at him over the roof of the car and smiled. "This is crazy, but I don't even know your last name."

He smiled back. "It's Donatelli."

She might have staggered if she hadn't been holding on to the door frame. She felt like her body was on autopilot as she lowered herself into position behind the steering wheel and tried to process the new information.

Donatelli was a common Italian surname. Just because Tony shared it with Sofia Donatelli didn't necessarily mean he was the stepson she'd mentioned on the television broadcast.

But when she cross-checked the address Tony had given her in the white pages of the phone book, Kaylee already knew that Sofia's name would appear.

That meant Tony Donatelli wasn't merely a hot guy she'd met at a restaurant. He was a hot guy who could very well be her stepbrother.

CHAPTER FOUR

TONY WHISTLED to himself as he turned his rental car into the middle-class neighborhood where he'd grown up, already looking forward to seeing Kaylee and her son the next day.

He'd briefly considered asking her to dinner tonight before remembering that Sofia was planning a special meal. His stepmother seemed to think she had to make up for serving takeout fettuccini alfredo the night before, even though Nunzio's made the dish with a recipe she'd invented.

No matter. Tomorrow was soon enough.

He drove by modest brick houses with shingle roofs and yards that looked amazingly like they had twenty years ago. The Stewarts still needed to prune their trees, the Walkowskis' house could benefit from a paint job and the Pagiossis still had the best-kept lawn in town.

He didn't stop whistling until he drew even with the Medfords. Something was wrong. He did a double-take. The For Rent sign he'd seen yesterday was no longer there.

"Aw, hell," he said.

It figured that his friend Will, who happened to be a real estate agent, was out of town on a long weekend. But Sofia had contacts. Maybe she knew of another place for rent.

He parked, walked up the sidewalk and stepped over the automated doormat before unlocking the door and punching in a code to disable the new security system Sofia had installed.

All the while, he tried not to let the old memories blindside him. It was no use. They came rushing at him like a powerful wave, the same way they did every time he entered the house.

It was probably because of the silly doormat his father had invented. An elevated contraption with ground-level machinery, it was supposed to suction dirt off the soles of shoes through tiny holes in the mat. Most of the time, the holes were clogged.

Anthony Donatelli, Sr., had been dead for two years, but a part of Tony still expected him to appear and excitedly fill him in on his latest idea that would make them all rich.

The majority of the time, his father's ideas had been clunkers, but Tony had to concede his father had the seeds of a few ideas that had turned out to be moneymakers. For other people.

His father's predictions of striking it rich had been nothing but bluster. He'd always failed, either in the developing or marketing phase.

Tony used to wonder how Sofia could listen to his father blather about the Next Big Thing. He never understood why she'd cheerfully supported them while his father had dreamed away his days.

Tony rubbed at his forehead, trying to banish the memories.

"Sofia. I'm ho…here," he called.

"You don't have to break my eardrums, dear. I'm right here."

Sofia was descending the staircase dressed in a short-sleeved red sweater that complemented her Mediterranean coloring. She'd combed out her thick black hair so that it framed her face, added lip gloss to her naturally red lips and mascara to her already dark lashes. High heels worn under black slacks added inches to her height. The clothes were obviously new.

He whistled long and low. "Did I miss something? Do you have a date tonight?"

"No date." She spread her hands. "I'm running an errand, is all."

"Well, you look terrific. Like ten-million bucks."

She smiled at him and descended the rest of the stairs. Stopping in front of the mirror in the foyer, she fluffed her hair. "Charmer. Where have you been?"

He had no intention of causing her more heartache by telling her about the Connie who hadn't showed up at the restaurant. "Errands. Same as you."

"Mine won't take more than an hour. Then I'm coming straight home to cook you that special dinner."

"With the fortune you won, you should hire a cook."

She settled her hands on her hips and cocked her dark head. "I thought you didn't want me to spend my money."

"I don't want you to spend too much of your money on other people. I never said anything about not spending it on yourself."

"But I don't need much, Tony. I certainly

don't need someone to cook for me, especially because I'm no longer working at the restaurant. Then what would I do?"

"Relax? Enjoy yourself?" he suggested.

"I'll relax tonight—while I'm cooking," she said and headed for the door.

"Sofia, wait."

She turned an inquisitive look on him.

"Do you know why the Medfords' house isn't for rent any longer?"

"Why, yes." She seemed surprised that he'd asked. "They found someone to rent it this morning. Why?"

He hesitated, then figured there was no harm in telling her. "I met a single mother and her son today and told her I'd help her find a place to live."

"Is she anybody I know?"

"She's new in town."

Sofia tilted her head to the side as she regarded him. Her forefinger tapped her bottom lip. "Is she pretty?"

He squirmed under her scrutiny. "I didn't notice."

She pointed at him. "You, my son, are a terrible liar."

"Okay. Yes, she's very attractive. But it's not like that. I already have a girlfriend."

"A girlfriend, not a wife."

"Ellen could be my wife some day."

Sofia pinned him with her gaze. "I didn't realize you were serious about her."

"We've been dating for almost a year."

"Time doesn't mean anything. I once knew a man who dated the same woman for sixteen years. Then he got stuck in the elevator with a woman who worked in his office building. He broke up with his girlfriend the next day. Three months later, he was married."

"Why are you telling me this?"

"If you're having second thoughts about Ellen, it's not too late to do something about it."

"You wouldn't say that if you'd met Ellen. She's perfect. Smart, beautiful, talented, successful. Everything I could want in a wife."

"Then why do you have a date with another woman tomorrow night?"

"I already told you. She doesn't know anybody in town, so…" His voice trailed off. "How do you know I asked Kaylee to dinner? I told you I was going to help her find a house, not take her out."

She patted him on the cheek. "A mother knows what a mother knows, Tony."

He frowned, not liking the conclusion

she'd reached. Even in high school, he'd never dated two girls at the same time. His buddy Will had made that mistake when they were in the eleventh grade and wound up with a black eye, courtesy of the first girl. The second girl had convinced all her friends to give him the silent treatment.

But Tony couldn't deny there had been a moment in the street when he'd wanted to kiss Kaylee. He blotted out the memory.

"I'm only being friendly, Sofia. Kaylee's new in town. She and her son don't know anybody. I thought she could use some help, maybe somebody to talk to."

Tony certainly had questions that he'd love to get answered. Why had she arrived in McIntosh with neither a job nor a place to stay? What did Joe's father think of her relocating his son? What made her tick?

"Whatever you say," Sofia said, but in a way that told him she didn't believe his motives were as innocent as he'd portrayed them.

"So do you know of another place that might be for rent or not?"

"Not off the top of my head, but I do know the editor of the newspaper. The real estate classifieds don't come out until Sunday, but I bet he'll give me an advance copy."

Tony bent down to kiss her soft cheek. She smelled like perfume and his childhood.

"Thank you," he said. "I'm a lucky guy to have you as a mother."

Even if she had put doubts in his mind about exactly why he wanted to hang out with Kaylee.

SOFIA DONATELLI sat behind the steering wheel of her Volvo in a parking spot on Main Street with a view of Sandusky's, too distracted to enjoy the new-car smell.

She wouldn't have noticed Gertrude Skendrovich passing by on the sidewalk tightly clutching a bag from Baked Delights in one of her pudgy hands if Gertie hadn't waved enthusiastically.

Sofia waved back, sorry that the sleek blue Volvo made her so easy to spot. She couldn't regret splurging on the car. It performed splendidly in crash tests, a consideration of great importance for someone who'd lost her father in a car crash before she'd ever known him.

Gertie's smile widened, as though delighted Sofia had acknowledged her.

Sofia was neither naive nor foolish. She hadn't changed so much as the world around her had. There was no escaping that her life B.L., before the lottery, was different than it was A.L.

B.L., the curmudgeonly Gertie wouldn't have raised her head let alone her hand. A.L., she was probably trying to ingratiate herself with Sofia so she could ask for money.

Word had already gotten out that Sofia was an easy mark. Maybe that's why none of the letters the television station had forwarded from the Connies had sounded legitimate.

Tony had followed up on one of the more promising leads this afternoon, although he didn't know she was aware of that. But why not let her stepson screen the phonies? If he'd interceded before she'd met the sweet little bleached-blond impostor, she might not have cried herself to sleep last night.

She wiped away a tear, one of many she'd shed for the daughter she didn't know. She'd changed her mind about surrendering the infant while in the delivery room, but her mother said it was too late, that the adoption had already gone through.

Sofia blinked determinedly to dry her eyes. She'd think about her search for Constanzia later. Right now, she needed to find out why Art Sandusky had been avoiding her.

Wiping her damp palms on the legs of her lightweight black slacks, she determinedly climbed out of the Volvo and marched into Sandusky's. The cashier, a young woman with her blond hair in a ponytail, was new, saving Sofia from having to stop and make small talk.

The store was a grocery store/butcher shop that specialized in fine cuts of meat, which could be had at a counter that stretched the length of the back of the store.

The four aisles leading to it were narrow and packed with limited selections of bread, wine, cheese and just about every other ingredient that went into serving a nice dinner.

Sofia picked an empty aisle, which seemed the quickest path to Art Sandusky, but knew she'd made a mistake when a short, plump woman rounded the corner.

"Sofia! It's so wonderful to run into you."

"Hello," Sofia said, trying to place her. The population of McIntosh had grown in recent years to about four thousand, not so many that Sofia didn't frequently run into people she knew but not so few that she was acquainted with everyone. Since she'd won the lottery, however, it seemed that everyone knew her.

This woman was around the same age as she was. Something about her small blue eyes looked vaguely familiar.

"You remember me, don't you?" The woman fussed with her frosted blond hair. Her roots needed a touch-up. "Betty Schreiber from high school. We sat next to each other in Geometry."

The years peeled away, and Sofia recalled that Betty had been a popular majorette who'd dated a star football player and barely noticed Sofia was alive.

"I've been meaning to call you since I moved back to McIntosh," Betty said.

"When did you move back?" Sofia asked, mostly to buy time so she could figure out how to make her escape.

"Maybe five years ago," Betty said. "You know how time flies."

"Yes, I do. Listen, I'm sort of in a hurry."

"Then I should come straight to the point." Betty chewed her bottom lip, shifted her weight from foot to foot. "This is sort of awkward, but considering we were classmates, I was hoping you'd help me out."

Sofia's internal alarm sounded. "Help you out with what?"

"The transmission on my car up and died

last week. With my husband out of work—
did I tell you I was married?—we don't have
the money to fix it. It's been a real hardship."

Sofia remained silent, surprised that she
wasn't shocked. But then strangers had asked
her for money since she'd won the lottery.
Why be amazed that a long-lost classmate
was hitting her up?

"It's not like I'm asking you for a new
car. It's only a thousand dollars. If you could
find it in your heart to do this for me, I'd be
so grateful."

Sofia would be grateful if Betty got out of
her way. She reached in her pocketbook for
her checkbook. She could almost see Betty
salivate. "What service station do you use?"

"Excuse me?"

"Tell me the name of the service station,
and I'll write out the check."

Betty's face whitened but she recovered
nicely. "Surely that's not necessary. Can't
you just make out the check to me?"

"I'm sorry, but my stepson would kill me
if I did that." Sofia affected a sheepish smile
and shrugged. "He's worried that people
might try to take advantage of me. I'm sure
you understand."

"Well, uh, yes, I do." Betty seemed at a

loss as to what to say next. She brought a hand to her head. "Would you believe I don't know the name of the service station my husband uses? I'll have to get back to you on that."

Sofia nodded, careful not to encourage her. She put her checkbook back in her purse. Betty stammered a goodbye and couldn't seem to leave the store fast enough. Sofia hoped it was because she was ashamed of herself but imagined Betty would dream up some other way to ask her for money.

No matter. The woman was gone for now. Sophia walked determinedly to the back of the store, careful to not make it look like she was hurrying. She resisted the urge to take her compact from her purse and check her makeup. Tony said she looked good. She knew she looked good.

"Just do this," she whispered aloud when she was almost at the counter.

She faltered when she noticed a middle-aged man placing an order. She glanced at him long enough to ascertain she didn't know him, but the butcher behind the glass counter caught her attention.

In a white butcher's apron with his large, strong hands encased in flimsy plastic gloves, Art Sandusky wasn't trying to be noticed. He was a simple man: kind, hardworking, principled.

She'd known him since he'd moved to McIntosh and opened Sandusky's fifteen years ago. The gossip was that his ex-wife had left him for another man, something Sofia had found to be inconceivable even before she'd realized she was attracted to him.

It had happened gradually. At some point during the last year, she'd begun to remember her late husband with warmth instead of grief. She'd looked around when her teary eyes had cleared and noticed Art looking back.

He wasn't a fast worker. She'd dropped half a dozen hints before he'd asked her to the movies nearly a month ago. He'd bought her popcorn, held her hand and made her feel like a teenager. His good-night kiss had made her feel like a woman.

And then…nothing. If she didn't count the casual nod when they happened to run into each other. Yes, she'd been preoccupied after winning the lottery. But not too busy for Art.

He glanced up at her and for an instant she thought she saw appreciation gleam in his hazel eyes. But then he nodded in that impersonal way she found so maddening and finished wrapping steaks for his customer with quiet efficiency.

Most things about Art were understated. Of average height and weight, he spoke softly, smiled gently and wore muted colors. Only when she looked closer had she noticed his hazel eyes were as soft as a doe's, his brown hair luxuriously thick and his face etched with the kind of character only accomplished by years of good living.

"What can I get for you today, Sofia?" he asked when the other customer had gone, as though they'd never shared a sizzling kiss at her front door.

An explanation, she thought.

Tell him.

Her stomach rolled and pitched, a reaction she vaguely remembered from high school when faced with the cutest boy in school. She swallowed—and chickened out.

"Tony's home. I thought I'd grill some steaks to welcome him."

She never grilled steaks. She specialized in pasta dishes and could do wonders with chicken. She hazily remembered that they had a grill but wasn't sure where it was.

"I have some top sirloin on sale." He gestured to the cuts of marbled steak underneath the glass counter while she mentally called herself a coward. "Or if you want something fancier, you could go with New York strip. Or maybe the—"

"Why are you avoiding me?" she blurted out.

He blinked, frowned. "Excuse me?"

Her heart raced and her stomach churned. What was it about this man that made her feel so gauche and unsure of herself? She'd been married and widowed. She'd worked in restaurants, where she was used to handling men with ease and humor. With Art, she had trouble forming a sentence.

"At the store last week, you turned down another aisle when you saw me coming. And at the post office the week before that, you couldn't leave fast enough when I got there."

His soft eyes slid away, then back. "I don't know what you're talking about."

She swallowed again but the action did nothing to get rid of the lump in her throat. "I had a nice time when we went out. I thought you did, too."

"I did," he confirmed in that same maddeningly calm voice.

She ignored the butterflies that fluttered

unhappily in her gut. "Then why haven't you called me?"

His Adam's apple bobbed. "I've been busy."

The universal cop-out line of men everywhere. All the breath left her lungs. She'd been so sure an explanation existed for his sudden chill and now one occurred to her. He didn't want to date her again.

"I've been busy, too." The corners of her mouth felt weighted by lead, but she forced herself to smile.

A customer—somebody else she didn't recognize; thank goodness—got into line behind her. Art glanced over her shoulder, then met her eyes, but barely.

"How about those steaks?" Art said. "Can I pick you out two nice top sirloins?"

Sofia willed her lips not to tremble. "You know what, I've changed my mind. I think I'll make Tony a nice lasagna instead."

His eyebrows drew together, and his expression appeared pained. She waited, hoping he'd say something to stop her from leaving.

"I'll see you around then, Sofia," he said.

She nodded, turned and walked blindly down a mercifully empty aisle for the exit. If there'd been a bed in sight, she'd have thrown herself down on it and cried.

"Mrs. Donatelli." A petite woman with salt-and-pepper hair appeared from an adjacent aisle, flagging her down before she reached the exit. Sofia recognized her as a teacher at the local high school. "I'm Mary Winters. I taught English to Tony years ago."

Not trusting her voice not to wobble, Sofia said nothing.

"I'm heading up a charity drive to fight illiteracy, and I was wondering if you could—"

"I'm sorry, but I can't do this right now," Sofia said and banged through the door to the street.

Everybody wanted something from her, it seemed, except the one man to whom she'd gladly give her heart.

CHAPTER FIVE

KAYLEE MOVED around the cute little two-bedroom, one-bath house as though in a trance. And maybe she was, because she'd been with Tony for half the morning and had yet to come clean about why she was in McIntosh.

"You can move in tomorrow if you like it. All I'd need is first and last months' rent plus a security deposit," the owner offered. He was a kindly, white-haired gentleman named Mr. Stanton who reminded her of her maternal grandfather, who used to slip her five-dollar bills on the sly. She needed a whole lot more than five dollars now.

"What do you think, Kaylee?" Tony prompted.

She thought matters had quickly spiraled out of control. She was inside a house she couldn't afford with a man who didn't know she'd come to McIntosh to meet his stepmother.

After confirming the relationship by consulting the phone book Kaylee found in a dresser drawer in her motel room last night, she'd dialed the listed number, intending to invent an excuse for why she couldn't meet him. An operator's recorded voice had come over the line, informing her that the number had been changed and was now unlisted.

Resigned to meeting Tony this morning as planned, she'd spent a restless night during which she'd decided to immediately tell him she suspected she could be his stepsister.

Except he'd been waiting for them in the driveway, and the moment of truth had been easy to put off. Worse, she hadn't been able to resist asking him about his childhood.

He'd soon gotten around to telling her about Sofia, although he hadn't mentioned the lottery. Tony said Sofia had constantly surprised him when he was growing up. Presenting him with a congratulatory balloon for making the honor roll. Driving him to Cincinnati to see a ball game on his birthday. Baking him a chocolate cake for no good reason.

His friends, he said, used to wish she was their mother. Even with a full-time job, she'd been a tireless volunteer: room mother, religious-education teacher, team mom.

The more he talked, the more she'd ached for her fantasy of having Sofia for a mother to become reality.

"Kaylee?" Tony's voice again. He repeated, "What do you think?"

She could tell what Tony thought. Joey's impression wasn't hard to figure, either. He was swinging from an old tire that hung from the sturdy branch of a grand oak tree around back.

"I need to think about it," she told him, then addressed Mr. Stanton. "Can I get your phone number so I can contact you later?"

"Don't think too long. The classified ad will be in the newspaper tomorrow, and I figure I'll get plenty of interest," he said before shuffling off in search of pen and paper.

Tony regarded her closely. "If you're worried about the upfront cost, we could ask Mr. Stanton if he'd be willing to waive the security deposit."

Kaylee felt her face heat. She'd taken another look at her finances before they'd started their search and the rent she could afford to pay was distressingly low.

The reality was that she'd let her heart rule her head. Again. She'd rushed to McIntosh, which was no more affordable than Fort

Lauderdale. Not on a waitress's salary with child-care costs thrown into the mix.

She needed to relocate to a bigger city where better-paying jobs and housing choices were more plentiful. Even then, she'd probably have to advertise for a roommate to share expenses.

"Kaylee, how does that sound?"

She bit her bottom lip while she resigned herself to confiding in him about her financial problems. If she didn't, he'd keep on showing her places she had no prayer of renting.

"That won't help." Kaylee squared her shoulders but couldn't meet his eyes. "I can't afford to live here."

He was silent for a moment. "Doesn't Joe's father pay you child support?"

"He's not in the picture," she said evasively, hoping he'd take the hint and leave the subject of Joey's father alone.

"Then let's ask Mr. Stanton if he'll lower the rent."

Kaylee shook her head. "He wouldn't be able to lower the rent enough."

Tony started to say something else but then Mr. Stanton reentered the room and handed her a piece of scrap paper.

"Here's my number," he said. "I don't have one of those cell phones but the grandkids bought me an answering machine last Christmas so you can leave a message if I'm not in."

Kaylee thanked him and gathered up Joey. Tony was a strong, silent presence at her side. He'd probably never had money problems in his life.

Because Tony knew McIntosh better than she did, he'd insisted on driving that morning. She settled uncomfortably into the passenger's seat, loathe to start a conversation.

What could she say that wouldn't sound like she was asking for a handout? And, oh, Lord, she'd shrivel up and die if he offered her money.

"That house was nice, Mom," Joey piped up from the backseat. "Did you see how high I went on the swing? And I found a beetle in the yard."

"Lots of backyards have beetles, Joe-Joe," Kaylee said.

She wondered why he didn't answer until she heard the beeps that signaled he'd turned on his GameBoy.

She tried to admire the colorful spring blossoms on the passing trees, but her eyes burned with embarrassment. The silence, though, was worse. She started to wish that Tony would say something. Finally, he did.

"How did you manage things in Fort Lauderdale?"

"I shared a duplex with another single mother. She worked days. I waitressed nights. Between us, there was always somebody home to watch the kids. It worked out great until she moved in with her boyfriend."

"Is that when you decided to come to McIntosh?"

He was fishing, no doubt trying to discover how she'd come to be in McIntosh without a job and so little money. Recognizing the perfect opening for her confession, her breathing grew short and her palms dampened.

"Yeah!" Joey suddenly yelled from the backseat.

Kaylee whirled to find Joey staring down at his GameBoy, a rapt expression on his face. He glanced up at her.

"I just beat level six, Mom. I've never done that before."

She nodded and tried to look appropriately impressed before gathering her courage and turning back around.

She couldn't put it off any longer. She had to tell Tony why she was in McIntosh.

She'd been so preoccupied that it came as a surprise to see they were already back at Sofia Donatelli's house. A woman was emerging from a Volvo parked in the driveway.

"There's Sofia." Tony's voice held a smile as he pulled his car behind the Volvo. "I'll introduce you."

Kaylee couldn't speak. She couldn't move. She could hardly breathe as she stared transfixed at the woman from the television broadcast.

Sofia Donatelli moved toward the car with an easy grace, and everything about her seemed more vivid than it had on television. Her hair was a darker brown, her smile warmer, her eyes softer.

Tony hopped out of the car, then opened the door to the backseat, rousing Joey from his GameBoy-induced stupor. Feeling as though she were moving in quicksand, Kaylee opened the passenger door and got out of the car.

"Who do we have here?" Sofia smiled at Joey, and it struck Kaylee that grandmother and grandson could be seeing each other for the very first time.

Her eyes misted as Joey puffed out his

chest and stood at his full height, which wasn't even four feet tall. "Joe Carter," he said. "I'm six."

"Pleased to meet you, Joe." Sofia shook his hand formally, then swung her gaze to Kaylee. "And I bet you are…"

Their eyes linked, and Sofia's voice trailed off. Wonder seemed to fill her expression, which Kaylee felt sure was reflected on her own face. As though by design, both women walked to the front of the car until they were separated by only a few feet.

"You're here because you saw me on television," Sofia announced in a voice filled with awe.

A shiver ran down the length of Kaylee's body. She wanted to agree but couldn't nod her head or find her voice.

"No, Sofia." Tony appeared behind his stepmother, standing half a head taller although Sofia was nearly Kaylee's height. "This isn't one of the Connies. This is Kaylee Carter, the single mother I told you about."

Sofia's expression clouded, and her head shook from side to side. She didn't take her eyes from Kaylee. "Is that true? Your name isn't Constanzia?"

Kaylee tried to convey with a look at Tony

how sorry she was, then breathed deeply of the blossom-scented air and said the words bound to change the rest of her life.

"I go by Kaylee Carter," she said, then rushed ahead, "but my full name is Kaylee Constanzia Carter."

SOFIA HELD BACK the tears, determined not to let anything obscure her vision of the young woman.

She'd held her baby only briefly before a stern-faced nurse had swept the crying, dark-haired infant from the delivery room, but she'd had plenty of years to imagine what her daughter might look like.

She'd envisioned her as a chubby-cheeked toddler, a long-legged girl, a spirited teenager and a lovely young woman. The woman stood in front of her now, and it was like looking at the picture in her mind.

Her hair was as dark and thick as Sofia's own, her eyes the same shade of dark brown that Sofia saw in the mirror. She was tall but didn't slouch. Someone, probably her adoptive mother, had wanted her to be proud of her height.

She was beautiful in the way real women were beautiful. She hadn't had a nose job to get rid of the interesting little bump on her nose. Orthodontia hadn't corrected the very slight, very charming gap between her front two teeth. And she wore very little makeup, not that she needed any.

Sofia knew she should say something, anything, but was afraid she might start crying if she did.

"I don't believe it." Tony didn't sound the least big choked up. He sounded livid. "You used me to get to my stepmother."

"No, I didn't," Kaylee denied. "I meant to tell you."

"When?" he asked harshly.

"The when doesn't matter, Tony," Sofia interjected. "All that matters is that she's here now."

"Don't jump to conclusions, Sofia." He placed himself protectively between her and Kaylee. "You know as well as I do that the chances of her being your daughter are low."

Sofia raised her chin, not wanting to listen to her stepson. After the recent false alarms and so many years of disappointment, she needed this time to be different.

"When's your birthday?" Sofia asked, holding her breath as she waited for the young woman's answer. The day she named was within a week of when Constanzia had been born, a discrepancy that was negligible.

"Show Tony your driver's license, Kaylee." She forced herself to use the name the young woman went by instead of the name she wanted to call her: Constanzia.

Kaylee hesitated only slightly before digging her wallet from her purse and flipping to her driver's license. His lips set in a stubborn line, Tony gave it a good, hard look. Sofia didn't have to see the license to know the name on it read Kaylee Constanzia Carter and that her birthday was when she said it was.

"That proves nothing," Tony bit out. He glared at Kaylee, which Sofia wanted to apologize for. "Kaylee told me she's from Houston. How could a family in Texas end up with your baby?"

Before Sofia could propose a scenario, Kaylee said, "My grandmother moved to Cleveland when she remarried. She wouldn't leave Ohio when she got sick so my parents moved north to take care of her. She died right before I was born."

"That doesn't prove anything, either." Tony set his jaw. His eyes blazed. "There are records we can check. Until we see those, Sofia, you shouldn't talk to her."

"It never hurts to talk, Tony."

"That might have been true before but since this lottery business…"

The young boy—Joey, Kaylee's son, quite possibly *her grandson*—tugged at Tony's sleeve, cutting off the spate of angry words. Tony looked down at the boy, who was gazing up at him with somber eyes.

"Tony, why are you mad?"

Sofia watched the anger gush out of him. Her Tony, with the big heart that he tried to hide, had always been a sucker for the little ones. His expression returned to its normal placid lines, and he patted the boy's head with a gentle hand.

"I'm not mad, Joe. I'm just not sure that your mom is…related to my mom."

"Oh," said Joey, then, "Can I play in the backyard? I saw a tree house."

"That tree house belonged to Tony when he was your age, dear." Sofia's heart jumped to her throat when Joey raised his excited eyes to meet hers. He was a fine boy, full of life and energy, the way Tony used to be. "Tony, will you show Joey the tree house so Kaylee and I can talk?"

He set his jaw in a stubborn line, and Sofia realized he was reluctant to leave her alone with the stranger who was already so familiar. "I don't think—"

Sofia stood directly in front of him and peered into eyes she wished weren't so troubled. Didn't he understand that having Kaylee here was nothing short of miraculous? "Please, Tony."

Joey tugged at his hand. The sun shone on the boy's eager young face, highlighting a sprinkling of freckles across his nose. "Yeah, please, Tony. Please, please."

Sofia had to say this for her stepson: he knew when he was defeated. The rest of the fight went out of him. After a last worried look at Sofia, he let Joey lead him into the backyard, leaving her alone with Kaylee.

The tall, dark-haired young woman's expression no longer mirrored her own. She looked pained.

"What is it, dear?" Sofia asked.

"There's something I should tell you up front. I don't have proof that I was adopted. My parents never admitted it to me. It's just a feeling I have."

Sofia's breath caught and for a moment she felt light-headed. She'd become well versed in the legalities of adoption over the years.

Ohio law required attending physicians to file original birth certificates with the state's health department. When a child was adopted, the original record was sealed and a new certificate issued listing the adoptive parents as though they were the biological parents.

Although the certificate of adoption wasn't a public record, the index of all registered births that occurred in Ohio was.

The P.I. Tony hired four years ago hadn't been able to find Sofia's name in the index. Neither could he locate records at the private clinic in northwestern Ohio where Sofia remembered giving birth; they'd been destroyed in a flood during the 1980s.

He'd interviewed doctors and nurses who had worked at the clinic twenty-five years ago, but none remembered Sofia or her baby or knew why the original birth certificate hadn't been filed.

The most likely theory, that the clinic had been involved in black-market adoptions, hadn't seemed plausible because of the clinic's sterling reputation.

But, still, the P.I. had told Sofia that it was

likely her Constanzia didn't have official adoption papers.

It was on the tip of Sofia's tongue to tell Kaylee that the lack of papers made her more likely to be Constanzia instead of less, but she held back the information. She'd eventually tell Tony, though. Not tonight, but later when he was more open to reason. That might help to convince him.

"Sometimes feelings are enough," Sofia said.

She blinked back the happy tears that threatened to overflow and had to stop herself from rushing forward and enfolding the young woman in her arms.

She'd waited twenty-five years to hold her again. She could wait a little longer.

Especially because now, at long last, it appeared as though the wait was finally at an end.

SOFIA WAS looking at her the way Kaylee had always wanted her mother to look at her.

Her eyes were round and soft, her mouth curved in a smile, her expression full of wonder instead of disapproval. After the things Tony had told her about Sofia, it wasn't hard to imagine that her lap would have been always available, her arms always open.

Kaylee's throat closed and her eyes blurred with tears. It should have felt weird to find herself face-to-face with the stranger who might be her mother, but it didn't.

It felt like she had been given a second chance to get things right.

Only the specter of Tony stalking off to the backyard dampened the momentous occasion. She cleared her throat, feeling as though she owed Sofia an explanation for his outburst.

"I wasn't trying to hide anything from your stepson. Honestly, I wasn't. I was waiting for the right moment to tell him, but I waited too long."

"Don't mind Tony." Sofia waved a hand in his direction. "He's very protective, but he wants me to be happy. He'll come around."

Kaylee wasn't so sure but refused to focus on the only dark spot in a meeting that had already brightened her life. Still, she felt compelled to stick up for him. "I don't blame him for not wanting you to get hurt."

"I just met you, Kaylee, and I already know one thing about you." Sofia paused, gifting her with that smile that was as brilliant as the sun. "You would never deliberately hurt me."

Warmed by the words, Kaylee smiled back. Sofia took both of her hands, melting Kaylee's heart as well. Kaylee wanted to launch herself into Sofia's arms, but she felt Tony's disapproval even though he wasn't in sight. He already didn't trust her. She was loathe to give him more ammunition.

"Tony's right about one thing. We shouldn't jump to conclusions," Kaylee said, but her mind leaped ahead of her anyway. This was very possibly the woman responsible for giving her life. "I don't have my birth certificate. I left home about seven years ago and never needed it. But I'll get a copy."

"That sounds like a plan." Sofia squeezed Kaylee's hands. "But right now, I'd love for you to come into my house so I can find out all about you."

Kaylee started to smile her consent, but discovered she was already smiling. Sofia kept possession of her hand, an act she might have regretted when Kaylee stepped on the doormat. The contraption roared to life, star- tling Kaylee so much she squeezed the older woman's hand. Hard. "What's it doing?"

"Suctioning the dirt from the soles of your shoes," Sofia said, laughing. "I should have warned you."

Kaylee started to ask where she'd gotten such an odd doormat, but forgot about the device when she walked into a home as warm and open as Sofia.

Sunlight streamed into the rooms, causing the soft colors to seem more inviting. Kaylee's gaze took in the large oak table in the kitchen and the cozy fireplace in the family room. Her parents' house in Texas was decorated in warm tones, browns and beiges mostly, but her mother had been a neatnik who insisted everything had a place.

Sofia's home was casually rumpled. The shelves were full of knickknacks, available surfaces piled with papers and the furniture worn around the edges despite the fact that Sofia had plenty of money to buy new things. But Kaylee liked the house exactly how it was.

Sofia led her into the roomy kitchen with counters crammed with appliances, then let go of her hand. She bustled about, offering Kaylee a glass of lemonade and instructing her to wait in the family room.

Kaylee wandered into another cozy room with sliding glass doors that led to a wooden deck. The backyard was visible beyond the deck. Tony stood with his hands resting on his lean hips, gazing unhappily at the house. Kaylee squirmed, although sunlight probably prevented him from seeing inside the house. She didn't relax until he climbed the ladder, most likely to join her son in the tree house.

She sank into an overstuffed tweed sofa facing the glass doors just as Sofia came into the room carrying a plate of what smelled like homemade chocolate-chip cookies.

Kaylee studied her, trying to decide if they looked alike. Nearly as tall as Kaylee and every bit as dark, Sofia's features were more rounded. But Kaylee thought they shared other facial traits, such as long noses and mouths with corners that turned up slightly.

Sofia set the cookies down on a coffee table, inviting Kaylee to help herself. Kaylee bit into one of the sweets, experiencing a pang of loss. Her mother used to make chocolate-chip cookies, too.

"I'll come straight to the point." Sofia perched on the end of her seat. "What makes you think you could be my daughter?"

"This is going to sound strange," Kaylee said, then hesitated.

"Go ahead," Sofia urged. "You can tell me anything."

Kaylee had never opened up readily to strangers, but found that she believed Sofia.

"All my life, I've felt like I was searching for something, but I never knew what," she said, then told Sofia about how she'd happened to see her on television. "The countryside gripped me first, but I could reconcile that because I was born in Ohio. But then I saw you, and somehow I just knew."

"Knew what?" Sofia prompted when she lapsed into silence.

"I knew this is where I belong. In McIntosh. With you." She whispered the last two words, afraid to say them too loud. But Sofia looked as though she…understood. "I tried talking myself out of what I'd felt. But I dreamed of you, and it seemed like a sign that I should come to McIntosh."

She hesitated, tempted to tell Sofia about how news of Rusty Collier's impending parole board hearing had hastened her decision. But that was a story for another day.

"I thought I might feel differently when I got here, but the feeling only got stronger," she finished, then gave a self-deprecating shrug. "I know it doesn't make any sense."

"It makes a lot of sense." Sofia reached across the short distance separating them and squeezed her hand. Her eyes were moist. "Go on. I want to know everything about you."

They talked for fifteen more minutes, covering Kaylee's parents' move back to Texas when she was barely a month old, the birth of her sister Lilly and her lifelong feeling that she didn't fit in.

They also discussed her mother's early death, although Kaylee didn't have the courage to tell Sofia what a sorry excuse for a daughter she'd been.

Sofia told her that she'd lost touch long ago with the boy who'd fathered Constanzia, but it wasn't the boy who interested Kaylee. It was Sofia.

When a movement outside the glass doors caught her eye, Kaylee knew their private time together was over. Tony climbed down the tree house ladder, then hovered protectively nearby while Joey followed suit.

"It looks like Tony's about to decide we've had enough time together," Kaylee said.

"This isn't nearly enough time." Sofia echoed Kaylee's thoughts. "Tell me, did you have any luck finding a place to rent?"

This morning's disappointment came crashing back. Kaylee hadn't wanted to face reality. Not yet. But Sofia's question forced her hand. "No, we didn't. I'm afraid Nunzio's will have to find somebody else to fill the lunch shift. Joey and I have to relocate to a bigger city."

"No," Sofia exclaimed, her expressive face stamped with dismay. "Is it only because you can't find a place to rent? Is that why you think you have to leave?"

Kaylee hesitated, loathe to tell Sofia she couldn't find an *affordable* place to rent, just as she couldn't find a job that paid enough. She'd be horrified if Sofia thought she was angling for a handout.

"Yes," she said. "That's why."

Sofia clapped her hands. "Then I have a wonderful idea. My basement's not fancy, but there's a room with twin beds and a full bath down there. It would be perfect for you and Joey."

Tears gathered in the backs of Kaylee's eyes, and she felt her shoulders shake as she tried to hold them back.

"Kaylee." Concern laced Sofia's voice. The older woman rose to come sit beside Kaylee on the sofa, where she stroked her arm. "What's wrong?"

Kaylee's mother had been dead for nearly seven years, the length of time she'd lived away from family. She couldn't find the words to explain how much she'd missed having a mother willing to take on her problems. Or to express what it meant to have another chance to nurture that precious relationship.

"Nothing's wrong," Kaylee said. "I would love to live here. But only if you agree to let me pay rent."

Sofia's budding smile disappeared. "I'm a millionaire. I don't need your money."

Kaylee met her eyes. "I need to feel like I'm not taking advantage of you."

Her sincerity must have communicated itself to Sofia, because the other woman released a sigh. "It's a deal, but I don't want you to pay me a penny more than you can afford."

Kaylee caught sight of Tony striding toward the house, and some of her euphoria faded. He'd be furious when he discovered the arrangement. But she couldn't refuse, not when refusing would mean leaving McIntosh and Sofia.

"Deal," she said and stuck out her right hand.

Ignoring it, Sofia wrapped her in a hug. Sofia's hair smelled of chocolate-chip cookies, her arms spoke of acceptance and unconditional support.

Kaylee realized in that moment she'd brave anything for this second chance at a mother's love.

Even Tony Donatelli.

CHAPTER SIX

THE TIRES on Tony's rental sedan screeched when he turned from the main road into the parking lot of the McIntosh Hotel. He cut his speed and strove to get both the car and himself under control.

He'd barely been able to keep his temper below the boiling point since Sofia had told him Kaylee and her son were moving in the following afternoon.

She'd waited until Kaylee had gone, no doubt anticipating his reaction. No amount of reasoning could get her to reconsider. She claimed the issue wasn't whether Kaylee was her daughter. It was that Kaylee needed a place to live.

Sofia was kindhearted enough to help a stranger, but Tony knew she didn't think of Kaylee that way. With nothing more than a feeling to back it up, his stepmother was already leaning toward believing that Kaylee was her long-lost daughter.

Tony needed more than a feeling.

His impatient gaze took in the misnamed McIntosh Hotel. It could more accurately be called a motor inn. Sixteen drive-up units arranged in a semicircle flanked a modest-sized office.

The streetlights bordering the parking lot didn't emit enough light, still, the place looked shabby. The exterior needed a paint job, the windows on each unit a good scrubbing and the doors sturdier locks.

The crime rate in McIntosh was low, but Tony had skimmed the weekly newspaper when he'd last been in town and noticed a fair number of break-ins. If he remembered correctly, one of them had been at this hotel.

What was Kaylee thinking to stay here? He didn't want her in his stepmother's house, but it would be better for everyone involved if she went back to where she came from.

From where Kaylee's older-model Honda was parked, he determined that she and Joe were staying in unit nine. He pulled his car next to hers, cut the headlights and jumped out.

Pushing aside his concern, he rapped sharply

on the door to unit number nine. The door opened a crack within seconds, and Kaylee peered out. She wore a crimson robe, the color of which complemented her skin tone. Her long hair wasn't completely dry and her face was scrubbed clean. Who went to sleep that early?

"I came to—" he began.

"Shhh, Joey just fell asleep," she whispered and then he understood. She didn't bed down at barely half past eight. Joe did.

He kept his tone low. "I need to talk to you."

Her brow crinkled, as though he'd requested her right arm. "Now? Can't it wait until tomorrow?"

Tomorrow, she'd be entrenched in his step-mother's house. Tomorrow, it would be far more difficult to extract her.

"It can't wait," he said.

"Just a minute." She closed the door in his face. One minute passed, then two. He'd begun to suspect she'd stood him up when the door opened and she slipped out into the night. She'd changed into blue jeans, tennis shoes and a pale yellow sweatshirt and had a wholesome beauty he didn't want to acknowledge.

"Before you say anything, I owe you an apology," she said. "I should have told you who I was. I meant to. But at first I didn't know you were Sofia's stepson. After I found out your last name was Donatelli, I couldn't find the right moment."

As far as apologies went, this was a pretty one. She met his eyes and looked appropriately contrite. He would have fallen for her act yesterday, but not today.

He couldn't deny she and his stepmother were of a similar physical type but her deception made it likely that she was an opportunistic fortune hunter.

To think he'd planned to call Mr. Stanton and offer to pay the upfront costs so Kaylee could afford to rent that house. Hell, he'd been prepared to write an additional check covering the yearly difference in how much the place cost and how much rent Kaylee could afford.

"I didn't come here for an apology," he said. "I came to let you know where I stand."

Before he could make his point, she shivered and hugged herself. No wonder. She hadn't thought to wear a jacket even though the temperature had dipped into the fifties when night fell. With a sigh, he shrugged out of his jacket.

"Take this." He draped it around her shoulders without waiting for permission.

Her hair smelled like flowers and she felt surprisingly delicate.

His body reacted, and he jerked backward, annoyed at himself. When he spoke, his voice sounded harsh.

"I don't want you moving in with my step-mother. Call her tomorrow and tell her you've changed your mind."

She tilted her head so they were nose to nose. "I haven't changed my mind. Joey and I are moving in tomorrow, exactly like I told Sofia we would."

His jaw clenched and he went into the same spiel that had worked on the bleached-blond Connie. "I won't let you take advantage of her. I'll run a background check on you and find out if you have a criminal background or an outstanding warrant."

"Go ahead," she said through gritted teeth. A muscle twitched in her jaw. "I don't have anything to hide."

"I won't let you off the hook easily," he continued in the same fierce voice. "If I find out you're scamming my stepmother, I'll make it my mission to see you prosecuted. You won't see a penny of her money."

She drew back and gazed at him out of round eyes she'd managed to infuse with hurt. "That's insulting. I'm not after Sofia's money. I came here for the truth."

He had a moment's remorse, then hardened himself against her. "That won't work this time. I won't let you go through me to get to my stepmother."

"Is that what you think I did? Softened you up to make it easier to swoop in and get to her money?"

"Didn't you?"

Her jaw firmed, and her eyes glittered. "If I'd known what a jerk you were, I wouldn't have spent time with you for all the money in the world."

He felt the insult like a slap. "Acting in my stepmother's best interest doesn't make me a jerk."

"You're acting in your own best interest. Maybe you're the fortune hunter. Maybe you don't want to share your inheritance with anyone else."

Sofia had offered Tony a cool million after winning the lottery. He'd refused it, stressing that he wanted her to save for her retirement.

"You don't know what you're talking about," he retorted.

"Neither do you. You know nothing about me. How dare you pass judgment on me."

Her chin lifted and a storm brewed in her eyes. If she could feign outrage this convincing, he understood how she'd fooled Sofia.

Hell, he'd started to experience a sliver of doubt. The bald fact was that Constanzia existed. He highly doubted that Kaylee was Sofia's birth daughter, but somebody was. And he had to admit Kaylee looked the part.

"If you're really Constanzia, you'll be able to prove it."

"I never claimed I was Constanzia. All I said is I thought I might be."

"Then get me your birth certificate and adoption papers."

A wariness settled over her like a second skin. "My birth certificate's at my father's house in Houston."

"Let me guess. Your adoption papers are there, too."

She hesitated, but when she spoke her voice was strong. "I guess Sofia didn't tell you?"

"Tell me what?"

"I don't have any papers, because my parents never admitted I was adopted."

He let out a short, harsh laugh. "Lady, you are a piece of work. I expected adoptees to claim to be Constanzia. But I never thought somebody who hadn't been adopted would have the nerve to show up in McIntosh."

"I didn't say I wasn't adopted," she snapped. "I said my parents never admitted it."

"Then let's get them on the phone right now and ask them."

"My mother died seven years ago," Kaylee said, "and my father won't talk about it."

"Ask your father again."

She shook her head. "It wouldn't do any good."

"That makes an awfully convenient reason you can't provide proof of your claim."

"I already told you. I'm not claiming anything," Kaylee insisted. "I'm merely exploring a possibility."

"Then explore it somewhere other than my stepmother's house." He stepped toward her, but she didn't back away. Her scent surrounded him: a lightly scented shampoo, soap and female.

"No," she said.

He felt his pulse jump. "You do understand that I'm living there, too. That I'll be watching you."

He watched her now and saw her pupils dilate and her breath hitch. It was cold enough that he could see their breath, which mingled in the air between them and charged it with awareness.

His body tightened, his blood rushing to his groin. His eyes dipped to her lips. Damn it. Despite everything, he wanted to kiss her. She shivered, and he thought she wanted that, too.

His resolve to not fall under her spell weakened. He was about to reach for her to satisfy them both when she said, "Is that all? Because I'm c-c-cold."

Her words hit him like a bitter wind. Of course. Her wet hair. The chilled air. His jacket hadn't been enough to keep her from the dropping temperature.

He backed up abruptly, then swept his hand to indicate the door. She whipped off his jacket, practically throwing it at him, then turned and crossed the threshold.

"If you hurt my stepmother," he said softly to her rigid back, "I'll make you regret it."

Her body went still but she didn't turn. "If your stepmother knew you were here right now, that's what would hurt her."

She slipped inside the hotel room without another word. He stood in the gloom for a moment, feeling the same way he had when he'd discovered she'd duped him.

He felt as though she'd punched him in the gut.

Despite what she'd said, he wasn't about to let her take advantage of his stepmother. Even if she had a nearly irresistible allure and the cutest kid this side of the Mississippi.

She'd fooled him once, but it wouldn't happen again. He waited until he heard the snick of the lock being engaged, then walked to his car, already planning his next move.

He'd hired a private investigator once before to find out what he could about Sofia's lost daughter. Now that Kaylee had arrived in McIntosh with her far-fetched story, it was time to give that P.I. another call.

If nothing else, he could locate a copy of her birth certificate and grill her father about whether or not he and his wife adopted a baby girl born in Ohio twenty-five years ago.

KAYLEE SAT cross-legged on the thin spread of the hotel room bed, considering her options while Joey flipped the channels of the small television.

"Why aren't any cartoons on?" he asked.

"It's Sunday morning, Joey. Most people are in church."

"Why aren't we in church?"

Good question. She tried to set a good example by taking him whenever she could. She'd been tempted to accept Sofia's offer to attend mass that morning with her and Tony, but Kaylee hadn't thought she could endure an hour of his silent disapproval.

"We'll go to church next week after we get settled," she promised.

"But won't God be mad at me for this week?" His eyes turned round and earnest.

"You can't drive, Joey. If God got mad at anyone, it'd be me. But He understands how hard it is to move somewhere new."

Joey flopped down on the bed, reminding her of one of the creepy crawlies he was always picking up. He couldn't remain still. "Are we staying here?"

"I already told you we're moving into Mrs. Donatelli's basement today."

"How about Texas? And Aunt Lilly's house?"

"We changed our plans and came here instead, remember?" She made herself smile. "I think McIntosh is a beautiful place. Don't you?"

"It's okay." He flopped onto his stomach and turned back to the television, obviously bored with the conversation. He clicked the remote until he found a nature show about snakes.

He slid to the end of the bed, his attention captured as a man with an Australian accent crawled under a house to give viewers a close-up view of a venomous brown snake.

"She's gorgeous, but don't do this at home, kids," he warned. "A bite from one of these little beauts could be deadly."

"Cool," Joey breathed.

Kaylee sighed. Just what she needed. A crazy man feeding Joey's obsession with anything that crawled, crept or scurried. Still, she couldn't bring herself to turn off the show. Not when his attention was so thoroughly captured.

She rubbed her eyes, a reminder that she'd had trouble sleeping after Tony's visit. It was lunacy to be attracted to him, but that didn't seem to make any difference. Her body hummed with sexual awareness whenever he was near. It didn't help that she could tell he wasn't immune to her, either. Last night he'd nearly kissed her, for the second time.

She sighed. What Tony had almost done wasn't the only thing that had kept her awake. A voice in her head had kept replaying something he'd said.

Ask your father again.

As much as she hated to admit Tony was right, that's what she should have done before coming to McIntosh. If she hadn't been adopted, she wasn't Sofia's daughter. Period.

It seemed so simple, but in reality it was anything but. She hadn't seen Paul Carter since leaving Houston and had only talked to him on the phone two or three times. Those had been brief conversations where they'd said nothing of consequence before he handed the phone off to Lilly.

Kaylee leaned against the bed's headrest and tipped back her head, but no answers were written on the ceiling. Only Paul Carter had those.

She got off the bed in search of her purse and dug the calling card she'd bought at a local discount store from her wallet. Bracing herself, she picked up the phone.

Her fingers hesitated on the number pad. Sunday morning. Her father wasn't a church-goer. He would be up and around, possibly sitting in the kitchen drinking coffee and reading the morning paper. He'd answer the phone.

Squaring her shoulders, she punched in the numbers and waited while the phone rang once, twice, three times. She was prepared to conclude he wasn't home after all and hang up when her father's deep voice came over the line. "Hello."

She took a deep breath. "Hello, Dad. It's Kaylee."

Silence, followed by, "Your sister's been worried about you."

She hesitated, but not because she felt guilty for worrying her sister. She did. But it hurt that he hadn't said he'd been worried, too.

"That's one of the reasons I'm calling," Kaylee admitted. "Joey and I aren't coming to Texas, after all."

No response. No inkling he was disappointed that he wouldn't lay eyes on her after seven long years. No expression of regret that he wouldn't meet his grandson. Not even any curiosity about where she was or why she wasn't coming.

"I've, um, worked something else out," she said.

"Your sister will want to know where you are."

Moisture gathered in her eyes, but she blinked it back. "We're in Ohio."

"Ohio." He repeated the state's name as though he'd never heard it before, but didn't ask where in Ohio. He didn't even ask why they were there.

"Is there a number where she can reach you?"

"No number." Kaylee didn't have a cell phone because she couldn't afford to pay another bill every month, and she didn't know the number at Sofia's. Not that she'd give it to him. She'd decided to leave her location vague in case Rusty got paroled and tried to find them. "You can tell her I'll be in touch in a couple of days."

"I will."

She'd always found it difficult to talk to her father. It was a hundred times harder over the phone. "How have you been?"

"Fine. Lilly's grades were very good this semester."

Kaylee experienced a stab of pride at Lilly's academic achievements but at the same time her heart sank. With her father, it had always been about Lilly.

It was a natural time to end the conversation, but she had yet to broach the most important topic. She couldn't think how to ease into her question so she chose the direct approach.

"Dad, did you adopt me?"

Another silence, this one much longer than

the previous ones. She heard her own shallow breathing over the voices on the television.

"Who have you been talking to?" he finally asked.

She placed a hand over her heart, where she felt a physical ache. Would she finally, after all these years, get the answer to the question that had clouded her childhood?

"I haven't been talking to anyone. It's just something I've always wondered about."

"Why?" His voice was clipped.

"Because I don't look like anyone in the family. You and Lilly are blond and blue-eyed. Mom was, too."

"Genetics isn't an exact science."

"I know that," she said, frustrated that he wouldn't give her a straight answer. She thought about asking him to mail her birth certificate but reconsidered. She could always get a copy from the state of Ohio. "Can't you tell me anything?"

"There's nothing to tell," he said, but she sensed from the waver in his voice that he was lying.

He ended the conversation abruptly, leaving Kaylee holding the receiver and listening to the dial tone. Her head swirled with questions, one of them paramount.

Was Paul Carter's refusal to talk about whether she was adopted proof that she wasn't the blood child of the parents who'd raised her? Or that she was?

WHILE TONY had been growing up in McIntosh, Sofia had seen to it that Sundays were special.

It had been the only day of the week that she didn't work, and she'd made sure nobody else did, either. His father hadn't minded. After wasting the week fooling around on one of his useless inventions, his father had acted as though a day off was his due.

So they'd all gotten up early for church, then Tony and his father read the Sunday newspaper at the kitchen table while Sofia whipped up something delicious for lunch.

What they did in the afternoon hadn't mattered as long as they did it together. Sometimes they went into town for a movie. Other times they stayed home playing board games. Or drove into the country and went on a hike.

The tradition continued until Tony turned

thirteen and could no longer stomach watching his father relax after he'd essentially done nothing all week.

Sofia couldn't force him to participate, but she hadn't abandoned the tradition. She'd claimed it was too important to let die.

So Tony wasn't surprised after lunch when Sofia objected to him shutting himself in his room to get some work done.

"I'm not on vacation, Sofia," he said. "I have a business to run."

"I know that, dear. But it's Sunday. Kaylee and Joey are moving in today. I hoped you'd be around to welcome them."

"After last night, that would be hypocritical."

Sofia's eyes narrowed. "Last night? What happened last night?"

Tony hadn't meant to tell her, but now couldn't avoid it. "I went to her motel and asked her not to move in."

Sofia's hand flew to her throat. Her dark eyes glittered, reminding him of Kaylee's glare the night before. But Kaylee's prediction of how Sofia would react to his visit had been off. Sofia wasn't hurt. She was angry.

"How dare you, Tony Donatelli. You had no right to interfere like that."

Tony shook his head. "I love you, Sofia.

That makes it not only my right but my responsibility to protect you from people trying to take advantage of you."

Her eyes had softened when he mentioned love but were glittering again by the time he finished his sentence.

"You don't know that Kaylee is taking advantage of me."

"Then why is she moving into your house when she can't provide a shred of proof that she's your daughter?"

"She's going to get a copy of her birth certificate."

"A birth certificate that has no mention of your name."

"You know as well as I do that couples are issued new birth certificates when they adopt." She paused. "Did you know her parents never told her she was adopted?"

"She told me that last night," he admitted.

"It fits with what the private eye told us about something about Constanzia's adoption being odd," Sofia continued. "Maybe that's why Kaylee's parents kept the truth from her."

"And maybe Kaylee wasn't adopted," he bit out. "Have you thought about that?"

She glared at him and he wondered how he could possibly get through to her. Sofia was far from stupid, but she had the distressing habit of seeing only what she wanted to see. Why else would she have supported his deadbeat father all those years?

"You're as stubborn as they come," she said angrily. "That makes it hard to talk to you sometimes."

He ran a hand over his lower face and deliberately lowered his voice. "Look. I know you want Kaylee to be Constanzia. But you have to go into this with your eyes open. You're a rich woman now. You can't trust everybody."

"I trust you, Tony." The anger had also gone from Sofia's voice. "All I'm asking for is the same courtesy."

He sighed. "I've always trusted you, Sofia. It's other people I don't trust. Everybody wants something from you. It even happened after church this morning."

Father Evans had nearly tripped over his robes in his haste to intercept Sofia and ask if she could find it in her heart to donate more money to the church.

Sofia crossed her arms over her chest. "Summer's coming, and the church needs a new air conditioner."

"But what did the priest do with the money

you already donated? You didn't ask him that."

"You have to take some things in life on faith, Tony. Father Evans is the leader of the parish, so I have to trust he'll do the right thing with my donations."

"It's the wrong time for you to take anything on faith. Especially Kaylee Carter."

"You're not listening, Tony. We don't always see most clearly with our eyes. Sometimes it's more important to trust what we see with our hearts."

Tony got ready to make another objection but knew it would be useless. Neither did he think it was the time to break it to Sofia that he'd hired a private investigator to look into Kaylee Carter's background.

Sofia might be willing to blindly believe whatever Kaylee told her, but that didn't mean Tony had to go along.

"My heart is the reason I'm in McIntosh with you, Sofia."

His stepmother's expression softened, and she shook her head while she regarded him. "It's no wonder I can never stay angry at you."

"Good," Tony said, "because you're the last person I want to argue with."

The tinny strains of "Yankee Doodle Dandy"

suddenly filled the house. The musical doorbell was a legacy from Tony's father, who'd claimed he'd come up with the idea until discovering that somebody else had registered the invention with the U.S. patent office.

Sofia walked over to his bedroom window, which overlooked the street. He'd raised the blinds that morning to let the sun stream into the room.

A smile curved her mouth before she said, "That must be Joey ringing the bell. Kaylee's just coming up the walk now."

He stayed at his desk. "Then you'd better answer the door."

Sofia walked to the head of his room, then hesitated. "Are you sure you won't come down?"

She looked so hopeful that he couldn't bring himself to outright refuse. "Tell you what, if she needs help lugging heavy things from her car, give me a shout."

That was the very most he could offer.

Nobody shouted for him over the next hour, probably because Kaylee had arrived with few possessions.

He watched her from the window, careful to stay far enough back that she couldn't see

him. Her long, wavy hair was loose, and she
wore jeans and a gray sweatshirt.

Although she and Joe came with an as-
sortment of suitcases, she'd brought little
else from her previous life. A couple of pil-
lows, some boxes of what might have been
books, a Wiffle bat, a blanket.

Were the rest of her things in storage or did
she really have so little? What kind of life had
she led that she could fit everything she
owned into a compact car?

Apparently finished with unloading, she
shut the trunk of her Honda, then started back
toward the house.

A gust of wind rustled the stately dogwood
in the front yard, dislodging a shower of
white blossoms when she was halfway up
the sidewalk.

They fell around her like snowflakes, landing on her clothes, kissing her face, catching
in her hair. She lifted her arms to her sides
and raised her face to the bright blue sky, a
delighted smile curving her lips.

His breath caught, and he took a step
closer to the window. She looked like one of
those figurines caught in a snow globe. Like
innocence and beauty.

The door to his bedroom banged open.

He jumped back from the window, feeling like he'd been caught doing something he shouldn't.

He scowled at the thought and turned to the intruder, who had committed the true wrong.

Six-year-old Joe came to a screeching stop. He wore a red T-shirt depicting crawling spiders and the words Jeepers Creepers. He covered his mouth with his tiny right hand and gazed at Tony with huge eyes. "Uh-oh."

Tony's annoyance fled. "Hey, Joe. What are you doing up here?"

The boy slowly let his hand drop from his mouth. "Explorin'. What are you doing?"

"Working," Tony said, although that wasn't entirely accurate. He'd grown tired of Web site redesign about an hour ago and had been playing around on an idea for an educational video game.

Joe ventured over to his computer screen, which showed rocky outcrops, thorn bushes and thickets adjoining open plains. In the foreground was a yellow-maned lion. "Whoa, that's cool," the boy said.

"Yeah?" Realizing he had the perfect test

subject at his disposal, Tony joined Joe at the computer. "I'm thinking I could turn it into a video game. Whoever's playing could help the lion hunt for food, shelter, water, that kind of thing. I'd have different animals, like a monkey in the jungle or a polar bear in the Arctic."

Joe leaned closer to the computer. "It'd be more fun to be the animal."

From the mouth of babes. Of course. Pretending to be an animal would be tremendous fun for a kid. Ideas swarmed through Tony's mind along with a title for the game. Creature Features.

"Could I try it when you get it working?" Joe asked.

"Absolutely." Tony would like nothing better.

"Remember when I told you I was explorin'?" Joe said, executing a lightning-quick change of subjects.

"Yeah?"

"I found a bunk bed," Joe said in a rush. "It's way cool."

"I always thought so," Tony said slowly. The sturdy oak bunk bed was the centerpiece in what had been Tony's boyhood bedroom. Although Tony now slept in the queen-size bed in the guest room when he visited, he still had a soft spot for the bunk bed.

Joe gazed up at him with pleading eyes. "Do you think I could sleep in the bunk bed?"

Tony's impulse was to refuse. He hadn't been able to stop Sofia from inviting Kaylee and Joe into her home, but he sure as hell could make sure they didn't get the run of the house.

"I don't think…"

The boy's expression fell, and Tony's voice trailed off. Kaylee and Joe had already moved in. What did it really matter where Joe slept?

"It's not my house, Joe. So it's not up to me. But I bet my stepmother wouldn't have a problem with it."

His eyes brightened, as though lit by a one-hundred watt bulb. "Really?"

"Really."

As abruptly as Joe had entered the room, he exited.

"Guess what?" Tony heard him yell at the top of his lungs. "Tony said I could sleep in the bunk bed."

Tony groaned, then closed the door to shut out the replies. If he weren't careful, Kaylee would think she was also welcome upstairs.

An image of the way she'd looked on the sidewalk, with the blossoms falling around her like snowflakes, crowded his mind. She'd look even better in his bed, with her dark hair against the white sheets.

His body hardened, and his groin tightened. He closed his eyes, willing his body back under control before he went to work implementing Joe's ideas into his video game.

It was going to be, he thought, a very long month.

CHAPTER SEVEN

WHEN KAYLEE was very young, her mother had insisted their family of four sit down to dinner each night. She'd seen to it that they minded their table manners, ate at least two vegetables and shared what had happened during their day.

Kaylee had wrecked the tradition when she turned thirteen.

At first, she'd refused to say anything. When her mother tried to engage her, she got defensive so that more than one meal had ended in a screaming match.

Kaylee had escalated the situation by staying out past dinnertime. Most nights, she'd scrounged something from the refrigerator and ate it standing up at the sink.

"You're a million miles away, Kaylee," Sofia said from across the table. "What are you thinking about?"

Kaylee brought herself back to the present

and looked around the dining room table. Sofia, sitting to her immediate right, was smiling bemusedly. Across the table, Joey was digging into a piece of the chocolate cake Sofia had made that afternoon especially for him. Tony was regarding her warily over the lip of his coffee cup.

"I was thinking this was nice," she said. "My family used to eat together when I was a girl, and I've missed it."

That was the truth. She'd always liked the family dinner. She still couldn't say why she'd sabotaged it.

Tony set down his coffee cup and pinned her with a look. "This isn't quite the same thing. We're not family."

Energy crackled between them, charging the air with awareness. She thought of how she'd nearly kissed him the day they'd met, how she'd wanted to kiss him even after he'd accused her of trying to con his stepmother.

No, they weren't related. They had no common blood, no common ancestors. If they had been related, Kaylee wouldn't feel this tingling awareness every time she looked at him.

"I wish you wouldn't say such things, Tony," Sofia admonished. "As a favor to me, can't you keep an open mind?"

The obstinacy Kaylee read so visibly in Tony's expression waned. He clearly hated to disappoint Sofia. It made Kaylee like him a little more.

"You've always told me that being skeptical was a good thing," Tony said.

"I told you that because you hung around with that rascal Will Sandusky. He was always making up some story or other. About seeing a UFO land in the apple orchard. About bench-pressing five hundred pounds. About half the cheerleader squad asking him to the prom."

"That last one was true." A corner of Tony's mouth quirked, making him look less severe. "He said yes to three of them."

"I don't remember that," Sofia said. "What happened? Surely the girls found out about each other."

"Yes, they did. The three of them got so mad they all cancelled on him."

Kaylee leaned forward, intrigued by the story. "So he sat home alone?"

Tony smiled, seeming to forgot his antagonism toward her. "Are you kidding? Will went stag and spent the night on the dance floor cutting in on other people's dates."

Kaylee laughed, thinking that Will was

somebody she'd like to meet. Her hair fell into her eyes and she tucked the heavy mass behind her ears, wishing she'd tied it back.

She suddenly realized that she and Tony were the only ones laughing. Sofia stared at her as if she'd seen a ghost.

"Sofia?" She turned toward the older woman and took her hand, which felt cold to the touch. "Is something wrong?"

Sofia kept staring, not into Kaylee's eyes but at a point somewhere to the left of them. Her face had gone pale.

"Sofia?" Kaylee prompted. "What is it?"

"Your…earring. It's unusual."

Kaylee fingered her left earlobe, tracing the outline of one of the small golden cubes. She wore earrings most of the time even though her hair habitually covered them. She hardly thought there was anything special about the pair she wore tonight, however.

"Thank you." She peered more closely at Sofia. "Are you sure that's all it is?"

Sofia seemed to snap out of her trance. She slipped her hand from Kaylee's and patted her on the back of the hand.

"It's been an emotional day," she said. "Have I told you how happy I am to have you and Joey here?"

"A couple of times," Kaylee said. Sofia had even made dinner an event, preparing a chicken dish from a personal recipe that had won Nunzio's acclaim and desire to serve it in the dining room. "We're just as happy to be here."

Kaylee glanced at Tony, expecting him to make some wry comment. His bottom lip curled, but he remained silent.

"Mmm-mmm good," Joey announced with a happy, cake-stained smile. He was clearly oblivious to the tension at the table. "They say that about soup on TV, but they should say it about cake."

Sofia smiled indulgently. "I'm glad you liked it, Joey. Maybe tomorrow you can help me make donuts."

He screwed up his little face. "You don't make donuts. You buy them. At the store."

"Somebody has to make those donuts the store sells."

"Is that what you do? Are you a donut-maker?"

Sofia laughed. "I only make my donuts for special boys. Ask Tony. I used to make them for him all the time."

"Cool," Joey said. He looked like a choc-olate-covered imp. The cake wasn't only around his mouth, but on his hands.

"You need a bath, Joe-Joe," Kaylee said.

Sofia rose and started to collect dirty dishes. "After I clean up, Kaylee, I'll show you where we keep the bath towels."

"Oh, no you don't. You cooked, so Kaylee and I will clean up." Tony took a plate from his stepmother's hand. He looked pointedly at Kaylee. "Isn't that right, Kaylee?"

"Absolutely." She met the challenge in his eyes, silently conveying she wasn't afraid to be alone with him. "Joe-Joe can wait a little longer to take a bath."

"If I run his bath, he won't need to wait," Sofia offered.

"Great idea." Tony addressed Joey. "You'd like that, wouldn't you, Joe?"

Joe made a face. "Don't like taking baths."

"You'll like the bathroom downstairs," Tony said. "You can turn the water on and off by clapping."

"Cool." Joey jumped from his chair and sprinted down the stairs with Sofia in pursuit.

Kaylee rose to help Tony clean up. "Will Joey really be able to turn on the water by clapping?"

"Yep."

"I've never seen anything like that in stores."

Tony picked up another plate and went into

the kitchen, tossing over his shoulder, "That's because it isn't in stores. My father invented it."

Kaylee picked up some dishes and followed him. "It should be in stores. It's a good idea."

"You won't say that after you drop something in the bathroom and the water turns on." He rinsed the plates, opened the door to the dishwasher and stacked them inside before reaching for the glasses she carried.

By silent consent, Kaylee cleared the table while Tony loaded the dishwasher. The dozen little trips back and forth gave her time to think about his father the inventor, who'd also come up with the automated doormat.

"It seems like your father had some good ideas," she remarked as she set an empty bread basket and the rest of the chocolate cake on the counter.

A plate in hand, he paused to give her an inscrutable look. "There's a difference between a good idea and a successful idea."

"Didn't he get any of his ideas developed?"

He turned on the faucet, and the sudden gush of water seemed unnaturally loud while she waited for him to finish rinsing the plate.

"Developed, yes." A muscle in his jaw

tensed, and she wondered why. "Success-fully marketed, no."

"But—"

His eyes bore into hers. "I didn't arrange for Sofia to help with Joe's bath so we could talk about my father."

She felt her spine stiffen and knew her re-prieve had come to an end. "If you're going to say you don't trust me around your step-mother, don't waste your breath. You've al-ready made that clear."

"I want you and Sofia to take a DNA test."

She blinked, wondering why such a logi-cal solution hadn't occurred to her.

"I did some research on the Internet this morning," he said. "The tests are 99.9 percent accurate. We could go to a lab in person or have them send us a specimen collection kit. All you'd have to do is swab the inside of your cheek. Either way works for me, but I'd prefer going to a lab."

His account meshed with Kaylee's knowl-edge of DNA testing, which scientists had refined so it was nearly infallible. Such a test would prove conclusively that Sofia was her mother.

Or that she wasn't.

He leaned back against the kitchen counter

and crossed his arms over his chest. Distrust came off him in waves. "So what do you say? Will you do it?"

She chewed on her lower lip, already fearful of discovering that the wonderful woman she was starting to love didn't belong to her.

"Kaylee?" he prompted harshly. "Yes or no?"

She delayed her answer by asking, "What did Sofia say?"

"I haven't asked her yet. Before I mentioned it, I wanted to get your agreement." He paused significantly. "Do you agree?"

Kaylee swallowed, knowing she could only give one answer. "Yes."

His dark eyebrows raised.

"You thought I'd say no, didn't you?" She shook her head. "I'm still not sure what I did to make you so suspicious."

"You're kidding, right?"

She put her hands on her hips. The dishwasher was beside the sink, across from a row of cabinets that effectively hemmed Kaylee inside the same cramped space Tony occupied. "No, I'm not."

"So you're still denying you used me to get to Sofia?"

"Yes! I met you by chance. I didn't know who you were."

"Then why did you flirt with me?"

"You thought that was flirting?" She didn't try to curtail her hot burst of anger. "That wasn't even close."

She closed the short distance between them, looked at him from under her lashes and rubbed his bottom lip with two of her fingertips. His eyes darkened, and a pulse jumped in his jaw.

"What are you doing?" he asked, but didn't back away.

She trailed her fingers across the full length of his lip, along his slightly scratchy jaw and down his throat before letting her palm rest against his rapidly beating heart. She brought her face close to his, so he'd be able to feel her warm breath against his mouth. His clean scent mingled with the aroma of herbs that still hung in the kitchen.

"This," she said huskily and brought her mouth within an inch of his, "is flirting."

She was about to pull back when his hands gripped her upper arms, holding her in place. Triumph had risen inside her when she witnessed the effect she had on him. Now that triumph faded, because he had the same physical effect on her.

"Things have changed," he whispered, and she felt his warm breath tease her lips, "because this time I'm not going to fall for it."

She wrenched away and retreated until her back was up against the far counter, which was still only six feet from him. Her chest heaved up and down, and she felt as breathless as if she'd just finished running a race.

"I'll make you a deal," she blurted. "You stay out of my way, and I'll stay out of yours."

He shook his head. "Can't do it. Not when you're living in Sofia's house. I told you I'd be watching you, and I will be."

"I've already agreed to the DNA testing. What more do you want?"

"I want the results," he said. "The sooner, the better."

The tread of footsteps intruded into the silence, forewarning them of Sofia's arrival into the kitchen. "Do you mean you two aren't done cleaning up yet? Joey's already bathed and ready for bed."

"We were talking," Tony explained, still staring at Kaylee. She stared back. He might be able to kick up her heart rate, but she wouldn't let him intimidate her.

"I heard you say something about results." Sofia grabbed a kitchen sponge and started swabbing down a counter. "The results of what?"

"The DNA test Kaylee's agreed to take," Tony said. "It'll tell us conclusively whether you and she are mother and daughter."

Sofia stopped wiping. She gave her stepson an unreadable look before smiling warmly at Kaylee. Kaylee couldn't help thinking her smile would be decidedly cooler if the test came back negative.

"Thank you for agreeing to the test, Kaylee," she said. "But it won't be necessary."

Tony's head snapped around. "What are you getting at, Sofia? Why won't it be necessary?"

"Because I'm not taking any test." Sofia covered her heart, which couldn't possibly be beating as rapidly as Kaylee's. "I have all the proof I need right here."

TONY DRUMMED his fingertips on the table at Nunzio's, trying not to let it rankle that Kaylee wouldn't look at him.

She'd nodded in his direction when he'd entered the restaurant, then proceeded to ignore him even though he'd requested to be seated in her section.

She greeted most of her other customers as lifelong friends instead of people who'd probably come into Nunzio's because they were curious about the woman claiming to be the lottery winner's daughter.

He'd heard that business had been booming at lunch in the three days since Kaylee had started work.

He drummed his fingertips again, realized it was something he tended to do when anxious, and put his hands in his lap.

Kaylee had responded to his promise that he'd be watching her by keeping out of his way. He'd been busy this week working on Creature Features and finishing up the Security Solutions Web page redesign, but she had little to say to him when they met up at Sofia's sit-down dinners.

Her coolness shouldn't have bothered him.

Yet it did.

She was a few tables from him, one hand cocked on her hip, pad in hand, laughing at something Charlie Marinovich said. Charlie Marinovich!

Two grades ahead of him in high school, Charlie had been a member of the chess club and the Young Republicans. Now he ran McIntosh's weekly newspaper with such little humor that the publication didn't carry the comics.

Kaylee wouldn't smile at Tony, but she found Charlie funny. Her head was thrown back, exposing the lovely line of her neck, her full lips parted to show the charming little gap between her front two teeth. Her…

"Hey, buddy. Good to see you."

Tony's head jerked up. Will Sandusky, all six feet four and two hundred plus pounds of him, slid into the booth.

"Whoa," Tony said. "Did you get scalped?"

Will brushed the top of his flattop with a careless hand. His brown hair was cut even shorter on the side, a look he hadn't been sporting when he and Tony got together the previous week. "Jackie thought it'd look good this way."

"Jackie Westgard?" Tony named a girl Will had briefly dated when they'd been classmates at Michigan State.

"Not Jackie Westgard. Jackie Bowden."

Tony screwed up his forehead. "Who's she?"

"Somebody I met a couple years ago when I went to a Reds game in Cincinnati."

"If you've kept in touch this long, it must be serious."

Will grinned, his blue eyes lighting. "Hell, no, it's not."

He stated the denial with such good humor that even Jackie Bowden would have a hard time taking offense. Will oozed charm, which had helped him to become a successful McIntosh Realtor.

Of all the people Tony had grown up with, Will was the only one with whom he kept in touch. They'd been close as kids and became closer after they'd both landed at Michigan State, Tony on an academic scholarship and Will on an athletic one.

When Will had blown out his knee and his chances of an NFL career in his junior year, Tony had helped him work through the disappointment. Now that Tony needed advice, Will was the one he'd called.

Edie Markowitz, a plump, middle-aged waitress who'd worked at Nunzio's for more than a decade, sauntered up to them.

"Hey, Tony, Will. What's shaking?" It was her standard greeting, for which she never seemed to expect a reply. She gestured to their unopened menus. "Let me know when you're ready to order."

Tony frowned. "Isn't this booth in Kaylee's station?"

She nodded. "Yep. But she asked me to take it."

"Could you ask her to take it back?" Tony smiled to remove the sting from his words. "You know how I feel about you, Edie, but I brought Will in here so I could introduce him to Kaylee."

"Sure thing, Tony."

Tony watched her approach Kaylee, who looked decidedly unhappy when Edie indicated their booth.

"What's going on, buddy?" Will asked.

Tony had specifically requested a back booth to minimize the chances of them being overheard, but he still lowered his voice. "I told you last night on the phone. I want your impressions on Kaylee."

"So the tall brunette is the woman everybody's been talking about?" Will gave a low whistle. "You didn't tell me she was a looker. Or that she doesn't like you."

Irritation bubbled inside Tony. He barely resisted warning Will he'd contract whiplash if he craned his neck any more. "She doesn't like hearing my suspicions."

"Nah. I'd say it's you she doesn't like. Although accusing her of trying to bilk Sofia probably had something to do with it."

Tony opened a menu and thrust another at a grinning Will. The sooner they decided what to order, the sooner Kaylee would have to wait on them. After they closed the menus, she approached the table with obvious reluctance.

She'd pulled her dark hair back in a long ponytail that drew attention to the oval shape of her face and showcased her distinctive features. Will was right. She was a looker.

"I'd like you to meet a friend of mine, Kaylee." Tony indicated Will. "This is Will Sandusky. Will, Kaylee Carter."

"Nice to meet you," Kaylee said politely.

Will shook her hand, conveying appreciation with his eyes. "The pleasure's all mine."

Tony had seen Will greet women the same way a hundred times. The result was a smile, a blush, a nervous laugh. Those reactions had never bothered Tony before. They did now.

"Are you related to the man who owns Sandusky's?"

"Art's my uncle, but I'm not in business with him. I'm a Realtor. So come see me if you need anything." Will bestowed the full force of his smile on Kaylee, nearly blinding Tony in the reflected glow of white teeth.

"We're ready to order," Tony cut in, trying not to sound as grumpy as he felt.

Kaylee turned to business, writing down their selections on her pad, then picking up the menus and departing without meeting Tony's eyes once. Watching her go, Tony frowned. The frown deepened when he noticed Will also watched her.

"So, tell me," Tony said. "Do you think she looks like Sofia?"

Will kept his eyes on Kaylee, who'd stopped at Charlie Marinovich's table. Once again, she was laughing.

"I see a general resemblance," Will said slowly. "Similar coloring, similar face shape." He smiled wide and warm. "Sofia must have been a real beauty when she was younger."

"Cut it out, Will."

Will's eyes snapped to his.

"Just tell me whether you think they could be mother and daughter," Tony said.

"Yeah, I do. But my opinion doesn't matter. Neither does anyone else's. Get her to take a DNA test and you'll have the facts."

"Sofia refuses to submit to one," Tony responded. "I've been trying to get her to change her mind for days, but she won't listen."

"Why not?"

"She says it's not necessary. Hell if I know why."

"That makes it harder." Will put his elbows on the table and leaned forward. "Tell you what. I'll ask Kaylee out and give you my impressions about whether she's on the up-and-up."

It was a reasonable suggestion. Will was single, and Kaylee was free. But Will was also the biggest hound dog Tony knew.

"Or not," Will said, and Tony realized his expression must have given away his thoughts. "I didn't realize you felt, uh, territorial."

"I don't," Tony denied quickly. Too quickly. Ah, hell. "It's just that you're right. Opinions aren't facts."

"Then hire a P.I.," Will suggested. "You did that a couple years ago, right? Although it seems to me he didn't find out much."

"He didn't. No birth certificate with Sofia's name as mother. No records at the private clinic where she gave birth. No evidence that anybody who worked there was involved in anything illegal."

"The records at the clinic were lost in a flood, right?"

"Yeah," Tony said. "The original birth certificate should still have been on file at the Department of Health but it wasn't. The P.I. thinks there was some record-keeping mistake."

"How about Sofia's mother? Couldn't she have helped?"

Sofia and Angela Crenna had been in contact only sparingly before his father's death. They'd been rebuilding their relationship since Angela had showed up at the funeral, but Tony gathered it was a slow process.

"Angela claimed her memory wasn't what it used to be," Tony said, recalling what had been in the P.I.'s report. "She wasn't any help."

"I think hiring the P.I. again is worth another shot. He could look into Kaylee's background, tell you whether it's possible she's Sofia's daughter."

Tony took a swig of water. "I'm way ahead of you. I already rehired him. He found Kaylee's Ohio birth certificate on file and confirmed she's who she says she is. She was born in the right month and year, although a couple days after Sofia delivered."

"Couldn't her date of adoption be on the certificate rather than her date of birth?"

"Possibly. But her mother's dead and her father isn't talking. Unless he provides information about the adoption—the date, the county where it took place, the agency that handled it—Kaylee can't petition the court to unseal her records. And we can't know for sure whether she's Constanzia."

"That's a tough situation."

"The whole thing smells funny to me," Tony said. "Kaylee's broke, and Sofia's rolling in money. Why else does she show up now?"

"Because she wants to connect with her birth mother?" Will suggested.

Tony scowled at him. "You're the one who convinced me everybody in town is after my stepmother's money."

"You convinced yourself of that, buddy," Will said. "I think the people here feel a sense of, well, kinship with Sofia. They think her good fortune is their good fortune."

"It's not," Tony said shortly. "Hell, her own mother won't accept money from her. Why should her neighbors?"

"Let me get this straight. Sofia's mother won't accept her money or talk about the adoption?" Will rubbed his forehead. "Something strange is going on there."

"I've always thought so," Tony admitted.

"I always thought Angela had to know more than she was saying."

"You should go see her. She might talk to you."

"That's not a bad idea." Tony tapped his chin while his brain raced. He barely knew Sofia's mother, but she'd been friendly enough when they'd met. He didn't think she'd be averse to a visit.

His train of thought halted abruptly when he spotted Kaylee heading their way carrying plates of food. His eyes drank her in, but she avoided looking at him when she set down his meatball sandwich and Will's pasta. She smiled at his friend. "Anything else I can get for you?"

"Those smiles are enough. They brighten up the place."

Kaylee's smile grew broader, but this time she glanced at Tony. "It's not hard to smile at someone who smiles back."

She left the table. Feeling censured, Tony glared at Will. "Do you have to flirt with every woman you come across?"

"It's not me you have to worry about, buddy," Will drawled.

"What are you talking about?" Tony asked irritably.

Will inclined his head in Kaylee's direction. Tony turned to see her rip off a sheet from her pad and hand it to the newspaper editor.

"I think Kaylee just gave our old pal Charlie a phone number where he can reach her," Will said.

CHAPTER EIGHT

KAYLEE ALLOWED Sofia to guide her down the main street of McIntosh, not that she had much choice. The older woman's arm was securely linked with hers, and she showed no sign of stopping.

"I can't believe you won't tell me where we're going," Kaylee said.

Sofia didn't even break stride. "I already told you. It's a surprise."

Kaylee giggled, something she couldn't remember having done in a very long time. She couldn't recall the last time anyone had surprised her, either.

Sofia had been waiting for her that afternoon when the lunch shift ended, easing the band that had started to form around Kaylee's heart.

Tony's presence at the restaurant, in the company of the good-looking guy he'd obviously brought along to check her out, had unsettled her.

How was it that she could crave the sight of him and dread it at the same time? She'd thought her attraction would die a swift, natural death in light of his suspicions, but that hadn't happened.

The fear that he'd convince Sofia to send her and Joey packing hadn't stopped her foolish heart from racing whenever he was nearby. At the moment, however, Sofia had such a firm grip on her arm it didn't seem as though she'd ever let go.

"I'm too old for surprises."

"Nobody's too old for surprises," Sofia said and cheerfully greeted an elderly woman who was passing by. The woman started to say something, but Sofia kept walking and talking. "Besides, you need to let me spoil you. That's what I'd have done if you'd grown up in McIntosh. Ask Tony."

"Speaking of Tony, he and his friend Will had lunch at Nunzio's today."

"Will the thrill." Sofia slanted her a twinkling look. "That's what the ladies in McIntosh call him. He's dated most of them. Did he ask you out?"

Kaylee shook her head. "No, but Charlie Marinovich asked for my phone number."

"Ah, our esteemed newspaper editor. Did you give it to him?"

"Yes, but I'm not sure I want to go out with him."

"He's a better bet than Will the Thrill although lacking in the hunk factor." Sofia's eyes sparkled. "I personally think you should date Tony."

"Tony! He doesn't even like me."

"Oh, really?" Sofia's dark eyebrows rose. "I think the problem is that he likes you too much."

"Liked," Kaylee corrected. "Past tense. He changed his mind."

"He'll change it back. He's a good man, my Tony. Hard-headed as a statue. But a good man. Smart, too. Which is why he'll eventually realize you're a much better match for him than that woman in Seattle."

A chill settled over Kaylee like a blast of cold air from a freezer. "Tony has a girlfriend?"

"I knew it!" Sofia beamed, telling Kaylee she hadn't hid her displeasure at the thought of Tony's girlfriend very well. "I knew you liked him, too."

"Liked," Kaylee repeated. "But that was

before he came up with the Great Conspiracy Theory. Don't go getting any thoughts about us."

"A mother can dream, can't she?" Sofia put an abrupt end to the discussion by coming to a stop and announcing, "Here we are."

Here was a storefront with a red door and the image of a woman's splayed, long-fingered hand stenciled on the window under flowing script that read Nails R Us.

"Surprise," Sofia said. "We're getting manicures and pedicures."

Kaylee reigned in her rush of pleasure. "But I'm supposed to pick up Joey at day care within the hour."

"I called Anne and she has no problem keeping him later today. Anne understands the importance of having pretty nails."

"But don't you think it's a bit…frivolous?"

"Frivolous?" Sofia shook her head. "Of course not. It's our right as women to feel good about our hands and feet."

"So this is something you do all the time?"

Sofia looked sheepish. "It's something I've started doing since I won the lottery. Before then, I didn't have the time or the money."

That sentiment, Kaylee understood. She looked down at her own nails, which were unpainted and not quite uniform, and felt a little thrill at the prospect of pretty nails.

"I've never had a manicure before," she confessed, "let alone a pedicure."

"Then it's only right that I'm the one to make sure you get them."

Sofia grabbed her hand, and Kaylee felt the connection as though bound to the other woman by a rope. Sofia hadn't spoken the words, but Kaylee heard them as clearly as if she'd shouted them: *Who better than a mother to introduce her daughter to the perks of being a woman?*

"Come on," Sofia said. "Let's make up for lost time."

KAYLEE COULDN'T STOP staring at her fingernails. The nail technician who'd given her a French manicure had been a miracle worker. She'd not only brushed the tops of Kaylee's nails with white polish but expertly extended the color down her cuticles. The result were nails that looked longer and hands that appeared slimmer. Kaylee wished she were wearing sandals because her feet looked just as good.

"Thank you," she told Sofia as they walked

toward the day care. "This is the nicest afternoon I've had in a long time."

"Me, too," Sofia agreed. "Next time we're going shopping. I want to do all those things we missed out on."

An alarm rang in Kaylee's ears. She belatedly recognized the distant sound as a police siren, but the timing of the noise couldn't have been more appropriate.

"We need to be careful, Sofia. We're not sure we're related." Kaylee wanted to leave it at that, but her conscience got the better of her.

She now had a copy of her birth certificate, thanks to her sister Lilly, who'd sent it by courier after Kaylee learned it would take too long to get one from the Ohio Department of Health. But the birth certificate yielded no clues, and there was no point petitioning the court to unseal an adoption record she couldn't prove existed.

She took a deep breath, released it slowly and said something that was long overdue. "I think we should have that DNA test."

"And I don't." Sofia's chin had a stubborn tilt. "We feel like family. We don't need anyone's stamp of approval."

"But Tony—"

"Let me worry about Tony," Sofia interrupted. "I've been doing it for…"

Sofia neither finished her sentence nor her next step. She stopped so abruptly that Kaylee passed her by. She doubled back, noticing that Sofia stared transfixed at a point up ahead.

Kaylee followed her gaze. Mr. Sandusky had exited the front door of his store. He walked slowly in their direction, his eyes riveted on Sofia. Kaylee tried to call up his first name, which she was pretty sure started with an A. Adam? Aaron?

"Art," Sofia said softly when he reached them.

Yes, Art. That was it.

"Sofia," the man replied, just as softly.

Kaylee waited for one of them to say something else but neither seemed capable of more speech. Her gaze ping-ponged from Sofia to Art and back again. What was going on?

"Hello, Mr. Sandusky," Kaylee said. "Remember me? I came in your store to ask about a job."

"I'm so sorry, Kaylee." Sofia clutched Kaylee's arm with her newly beautiful nails, her grip unnaturally tight. "I should have introduced you. This is Art Sandusky. Art, Kaylee Carter."

Art smiled at her with his eyes as well as his lips and shook her hand. His grip was warm and firm. "Call me Art. And I do remember you. Your little boy was the one with the toad."

Kaylee grimaced and turned to Sofia to explain. "Joey smuggled it into the store. He showed it to a girl stocking pickles. She screamed and broke three jars."

Kaylee expected Sofia to say something. Anything. But the older woman couldn't seem to do anything but stare at Art.

"I wish you'd let me pay for the damage," Kaylee said.

Art winked at her. "Nonsense. It was worth three broken jars to have some excitement around the place."

Again Kaylee waited for Sofia to interject herself into the conversation. Again, she didn't.

"I'm working the lunch shift at Nunzio's," Kaylee told him. "The next time you come in, your meal can be my treat."

His eyes fell on Sofia and held. "Enjoying the recipes Sofia came up with is enough of a treat."

The silence descended once more, and then he bowed slightly and formally. "Good afternoon," he said and walked away.

Sofia turned and watched him go with a wistful expression.

"You like him," Kaylee said when he was out of earshot.

Sofia shrugged, but it was an affected shrug. "He's a very nice man."

"Not to mention rich in the hunk factor," Kaylee added.

A red flush started at Sofia's neck and spread upward.

"What's going on between you two?" Kaylee asked.

"Nothing." Sofia sighed heavily as she resumed walking. Kaylee fell into place alongside her. "That's the problem."

"Then why don't you ask him out?"

"We've already been out. About six or seven weeks ago."

"Didn't you have a good time?"

"We had a wonderful time, or at least I thought we did." Sofia's lips tightened but Kaylee still saw them tremble. "It took us hours to finish dinner because we had so much to talk about. At the movies, we held hands. He made me feel like a teenager."

Kaylee could easily believe that. When the two of them had been struck speechless at the sight of each other, she'd been reminded of a pair of teens.

"What happened next?" Kaylee asked.

"I already told you. Nothing."

Kaylee frowned. Something didn't compute. The chemistry between the two of them had almost ignited the sidewalk. "I don't understand."

"I don't, either. I kept waiting for the phone to ring or for Art to come by the restaurant, but there was nothing. So I finally got up the courage to ask him what was wrong."

"Well," Kaylee prompted impatiently, "did he tell you?"

Sofia shook her head.

"You know what I think you should do? I think you should ask him out."

Sofia gazed at her with apprehension. "I couldn't."

"Why not?"

"Because…" Her voice trailed off. She clasped her hands together, which seemed to be shaking. "Because I just couldn't. I know it's silly. I've been married and widowed. But something about him makes my tongue twist."

"You've got a crush," Kaylee said, squeezing her arm. "A crush does that to people."

"An unrequited crush."

Kaylee doubted that was the case. Her guess was that Art Sandusky was as entranced with Sofia as she was with him.

She lapsed into silence as she walked alongside Sofia to the day-care center, using the same route she and Tony had taken a few days before. Kaylee's tongue hadn't been tied but it had felt like a dozen fluttering butterflies inhabited her stomach.

No, she admonished herself. She wouldn't think about Tony and the confusing feelings he aroused. He had a girlfriend, and she needed to figure out a way to bring Sofia and Art together.

After a moment, she had it. She smiled to herself at the prospect of banishing the sadness from Sofia's eyes. She'd never tried to matchmake before. But for Sofia, she'd do anything.

Even if it involved asking Tony for help.

TONY SNAGGED a beer from the refrigerator, uncapped it and took a pull. He heard the liquid sliding down his throat, a testament to how quiet the house was.

It was a false quiet. Sofia had left for a night of cards with her friends hours ago, but Tony wasn't alone in the house. Joe was asleep upstairs in the top bunk bed, and Kaylee was downstairs, staying out of his way.

He stood beside the basement door, keeping very still while he tried to figure out if she were watching television. He didn't hear anything but the hum of the refrigerator.

Even if he had heard the TV, it wasn't as though he'd go downstairs and ask to join her. He moved away from the door, then just as quickly moved back. His hand fastened on the doorknob.

He could let her know she didn't have to stay downstairs when Sofia wasn't home, that he didn't have a problem with her making herself comfortable on the main floor. His hand slipped from the knob before he could turn it.

What was he thinking? If she were asleep, he might frighten her. If she weren't, he was asking for trouble. Despite his doubts about her, he couldn't deny that he found her physically attractive.

He frowned, feeling vaguely disloyal to Ellen. Not that distance had made his heart—or Ellen's—grow fonder. The opposite seemed to be happening. He'd tried calling Ellen out of duty earlier, only to find her not home for the second straight night. He hadn't bothered trying her cell. She hadn't bothered to call him since he'd arrived in McIntosh.

But there were better reasons than a girlfriend he was growing apart from to steer clear of Kaylee. He didn't trust her, and she didn't like him.

He wandered outside onto the wide porch overlooking the empty street and sat down on the wicker rocking chair. Thursday night at nine o'clock, and it was so quiet he could pick out the distant hoot of an owl and hear the buzz of insects attracted by the porch light.

If he'd been in Seattle, he'd probably just be arriving home now. More often than not, he and Ellen dined out after work. Afterward she liked to have a nightcap at one of the bistros scattered throughout the downtown area. Or stroll through an art gallery, take in a basketball game or see an art flick. The choices were endless.

Rare was the night he sat on his balcony. He had better things to do. Here in McIntosh, he didn't.

The sound of the screen door opening shattered the silence. Kaylee stepped onto the porch. He didn't know whether she could see him in the darkness so took the opportunity to look his fill.

Her wavy, black hair spilled down her back, making him itch to run his fingers through it. Her blue jeans and sweatshirt weren't provocative, but he liked the way the jeans outlined her curvy rear end and could imagine what her body looked like under the sweatshirt. His body tightened. Feeling uncomfortably like a voyeur, he knew he had to announce himself.

"I didn't know you were still awake."

She didn't jump at the sound of his voice but ventured toward him, not stopping until she reached the porch rail across from the rocking chair. "It's too early to go to sleep yet. Not when there's so much to see."

He gazed into the street, but it was still empty. He heard dogs barking, but they weren't visible. Most of the neighbors had their porch lights on, not yet having retired for the night, but they illuminated nothing of interest.

"I don't see anything," he said.

"That's because you're not looking in the right place." She tipped her head back, and her long hair tumbled farther down her back. "Isn't it beautiful out here?"

Her skin appeared unusually pale in the moonlight. Her profile looked like one of those carvings done by an exceptionally talented artist, with loving attention paid to her long, elegant nose, small chin and high forehead.

She was the one who was beautiful.

"Before Joey and I moved to McIntosh, I never knew the sky could be full of light. On a cloudless night, it looks like Christmas up there. No matter the time of year."

He rose from the wicker chair, joined her at the railing and lifted his gaze. Without the artificial lights of the city or a layer of smog to diffuse the stars, they twinkled above like thousands of tiny lights.

He blinked. Never before had he thought of something as simple as a star in such a fanciful way.

She brought her gaze back to earth, turned and balanced against the railing so that she faced him. "As beautiful as it is, I didn't come out here tonight to stargaze."

The pulse in his neck jumped. Had she been thinking along the same lines as him? That Joe was asleep, Sofia would be gone for a few more hours and they were alone. Together.

"Why did you come out here?" he asked, hardly daring to hope.

"I wanted to talk about Will Sandusky."

Something hot, unfamiliar and feeling suspiciously like jealousy gripped him. He'd gotten Will to agree not to pursue Kaylee but hadn't considered that Kaylee might want to pursue Will.

"You're on your own there." He tried to hold the jealousy at bay, but it hummed to life, like an electrical wire. "I'm no matchmaker."

"You think I want you to set me up with your friend?" She straightened from the rail, her posture rigid and indignant.

"Don't you?"

"I can get my own dates, thank you very much."

"After seeing you go to work on Charlie Marinovich, I believe that one," Tony huffed.

Her lips tightened, and she settled her hands on her hips. "What's that supposed to mean?"

He'd been out of line. He knew that. She hadn't done anything more provocative than smile at Charlie. Marinovich had done the rest himself. If she'd smiled at Tony that way, he'd have acted the same as the editor. Hell, he had. He scratched his head. "I'm sorry. I shouldn't have said that."

"That's right. You shouldn't have," she said tartly. "Charlie's a nice man. I'm sure *he* would have told me if he had a girlfriend before asking me to dinner."

Tony stiffened, feeling like she was flinging guilt instead of words. "I asked you and *Joe* to dinner," he corrected, but it was a flimsy excuse and he knew it.

"It doesn't matter," she said, shaking her head.

But somehow he knew that it did matter, that she deserved an explanation. But how could he explain without admitting that Ellen had been far from his thoughts at their first meeting? Tony had been so drawn to Kaylee that all he'd thought about was getting to know her.

"I came out here to talk about Will," she continued, "not about you and me."

"What about Will?" he asked, bracing himself. She might not want him to fix her up, but she could need him to supply Will's phone number.

"I'd like you to talk him into helping me set up Sofia with his uncle."

If she'd claimed her goal was to set up his stepmother with Will himself, Tony wouldn't have been more surprised. "Are you talking about Art Sandusky, the man who owns the store?"

"Don't tell me you haven't noticed Sofia has a thing for him?"

"I can't say that I have," he replied while mentally reviewing what he knew about Art Sandusky. The grocer had moved to town while Tony was still in grade school, so that must have been fifteen years ago. He seemed to remember Will mentioning that his uncle was divorced and had settled in McIntosh to be near family.

"It's true," Kaylee said. "They went out a month or so ago, and Art's been acting strange ever since. But he's attracted to her, too. I can tell."

"I'm not clear on what you want Will to do."

"I need Art to be at Nunzio's tomorrow night at seven o'clock. All Will has to do is get him there, and I'll take care of the rest."

"Exactly how will you do that?"

"I'll get Sofia there. When we run into Will and his uncle, I'll suggest the four of us have dinner together." Her expression grew animated, and again it struck him how attractive she was. He wouldn't call her pretty. Her beauty was of the classic variety, the kind that didn't fade with age. "Or if Will has something else to do, he doesn't even have to come. He can arrange to meet his uncle, then call the restaurant to say something came up. Once I have Sofia and Art at the same table, I can get called away myself."

After the interest Will had expressed in dating Kaylee, Tony felt sure his friend would take part in her plan. The problem was that Tony didn't want him to.

She stopped talking abruptly. "What's the matter? Don't you like the idea?"

Before Tony could think up a response, she grimaced and shut her eyes. "I can't believe how insensitive I just was. I owe you an apology."

He blinked. "For what?"

"For not realizing you might not be ready for Sofia to date." She reached out and touched his hand, immediately infusing him with warmth. "How long ago did your father die?"

"Two years, but you're way off base," Tony said. "After putting up with my father, Sofia deserves to be happy."

She took her hand away, and he felt the loss. Her head tilted. "Wasn't Sofia happy with your father?"

"How happy could she have been with a man who didn't do anything more productive than sit in the basement and dream?"

The moment the question was out, he wanted it back. His feelings about his father were still so raw that he typically changed the subject whenever anyone mentioned him, as he had a few nights ago in the kitchen. Most people loved their parents unconditionally. He did not.

"Didn't your father have a job?"

He didn't pick up any disapproval in her question, which may be why he answered it. "He had a lot of jobs, none of which he kept. What he had were ideas about how to get rich."

"Like the automated doormat and the faucet that turns on by clapping?"

"Not to mention the alarm clock that blares every time a snore gets above a certain decibel level."

Kaylee winced. "If I snored, I'd rather go the homeopathic route."

"Exactly."

"But the automated doormat isn't a bad idea."

"Neither were the disposable camera or the textured teeth wipes, but somebody else developed those first," Tony conceded. "One thing I learned about ideas is that you have to follow through by developing the invention. Then you have to find an investor willing to back you."

"I take it your father never did those things?"

Tony placed his hands on the rail and turned his eyes to the star-filled sky. His father had been gone for two years, but Tony still hadn't forgiven him for what he'd put their family through. "He tried. Hell, he probably hit up every businessman in McIntosh. It was damn embarrassing."

"I can understand that."

He turned to look at her. He couldn't completely make out her eyes in the dark, but he knew they were full of empathy, like her voice. He felt her presence like a blanket that had wrapped him in understanding.

She didn't take her eyes from his, seeming to be waiting for something.

His hand lifted, but he clenched his fingers into a fist when he realized he'd been about to touch her cheek. It was foolish to think anyone could understand how humiliating it had been to be the son of such a colossal failure.

Why, he wondered, had he told her the story?

"When I was in Sandusky's the other day, Art told me he wanted my advice on what kind of computer to buy," Tony announced.

She blinked, and he read the confusion in her eyes at his abrupt change of subjects. "I'm sure you'll give him good advice."

"I can tell him I'm ready to talk computers," he said. "You don't need Will. I'll ask Art to dinner."

She laid a hand on his arm. "Really?" Her appreciation was obvious, even in the darkness. "That would be great. Thank you."

He liked the feel of her hand. Too much. The awareness that was always there between them flared, intensified by the night. She must have felt it, too, because she took her hand away. Their eyes met, and he imagined he saw an invitation in hers. But maybe that was only because he wanted it to be there.

"I just have one question," he said.

She nodded, and he wondered what she would say if he asked if he could kiss her. Yes, he thought. She'd say yes.

But he couldn't betray Ellen that way. Neither could he start something with Kaylee when he was so unsure of her. He searched her eyes, looking for clues as to what kind of person she was.

"Why are you going to all this trouble to set up Sofia with Art?" he asked.

He could tell by her expression that it wasn't the question she'd been expecting. She took her time answering.

"Because Sofia deserves to have her dreams come true," she replied softly.

After she'd gone, he sat in the darkness for a long time. She'd seemed sincere, both when she'd listened to him talk about his dead father and in her desire to help Sofia hook up with Art Sandusky.

Was that an act? Another way to weasel into the family's good graces?

Tony scowled, because she hadn't seemed as though she were acting. The more time he spent around her, the more genuine she appeared. He reminded himself that Kaylee wasn't the roadblock in the DNA testing. Sofia was.

But what if his instincts were wrong? What if Kaylee's little-miss-matchmaker routine was all part of an elaborate act to get to Sofia's millions?

Tony decided on the spot to pay a visit to Sofia's mother in Columbus the next day. Will could be right. Angela might have information she hadn't been willing to share with his private investigator.

The chill finally chased him inside, but Tony couldn't be sure if the cold was due to the night or apprehension at what kinds of answers Sofia's mother might have.

CHAPTER NINE

SOFIA'S MOTHER lived in a working-class section of Columbus that Tony should have found familiar. Her house was the house where Sofia had grown up, the place where Angela Crenna had spent all of her adult life.

Tony had never been there before.

He'd seen Angela in person exactly once and that had been at his father's funeral. He'd been too young to remember but had heard that she hadn't even come to the wedding when Sofia married his father.

Glancing at the printout of the directions he'd gotten from the Internet, he turned at a red light and followed a narrow road to the bottom of a slight hill and a block populated by small houses with compact yards.

He checked the address he'd copied from Sofia's address book and pulled to the curb in front of a tiny white house that no one would guess belonged to the mother of a multimillionaire.

Sofia had confided that Angela didn't want her money any more than Tony did. Judging by the state of her property, the difference was that Angela needed it.

His cell phone rang before he could get out of the car. He flipped it open, immediately recognized Ellen's number and admitted to himself that he'd rather Kaylee was calling.

"How are things in McIntosh?" Ellen asked after they greeted each other. "More importantly, when will you be back?"

"I'm not sure." His gaze traveled over his step-grandmother's property. The trees needed to be pruned and the house painted. "I have to stay here a while longer."

"You realize that I'm not sitting at home waiting for you?"

"I figured that out when you weren't home the last two nights I called." The gutters along one side of Angela's house sagged, he noted.

"Aren't you going to ask where I was?"

He squinted to get a better look at the roof. It didn't seem to be in very good shape, either. "I'm sure you'll tell me if you want me to know."

"I was out both nights with Mark McBride. You remember Mark, don't you? He runs an art galley over in Pioneer Square."

The mention of the other man transferred Tony's attention from the roof to the phone call. He knew exactly who she was talking about. Mark McBride had never tried to hide his interest in Ellen, but Tony hadn't known she returned it.

Neither had Tony realized that the thought of Ellen dating Mark wouldn't trouble him.

"Are you saying that you want to stop seeing each other?" he asked, finding that prospect didn't bother him, either.

"Heavens, no. You know how I feel about you, Tony. You're the most delicious man I've ever met. I wouldn't hesitate to accept if you wanted to put a ring on my finger."

He thought of the small velvet box back home in his dresser drawer and hardly remembered why he'd thought he wanted to give it to her.

"But you've got to understand that I have no intention of sitting home alone while you're doing whatever you're doing in McIntosh," she continued.

"I'm taking care of my stepmother."

"And I'm taking care of myself. When you

get back to Seattle, you can make up your mind whether you want to take care of me. I won't pin all my hopes on a man who isn't ready to settle down."

"Ah," Tony said as understanding dawned, "so this is about me not putting a bid on that house."

"That's only a symptom of the problem, Tony."

"I wasn't aware until now that we had a problem," Tony said almost to himself while he wondered how he could have missed the signs.

She was silent for a moment. "Let me know when you're back in Seattle. Better yet, give me a call when you decide what it is you want."

Before he could tell her not to wait by the phone, she hung up. He clicked off his cell. He already knew he wouldn't be calling Ellen anymore, something that would have seemed inconceivable two weeks ago.

But two weeks ago, he hadn't yet met Kaylee, who was the reason he was here in Columbus.

Turning his thoughts back to Angela Crenna, he got out of the car and walked up the cracked sidewalk, climbed two worn steps to the tiny porch and rang the doorbell.

The volume on the television inside the house was turned up loud enough that he could hear the sound of a day-time game show. He caught snatches of words. *A new car! Pick the right number and the prize will be yours. Showcase Showdown.*

Thirty seconds passed. He rang the doorbell again, waited, then opened the screen door and pounded sharply on the inner door. Another fifteen seconds went by before the door swung open.

An elderly woman wrapped in a black shawl gazed up at him. When he'd seen Angela at his father's funeral, her hair had been dyed black. The roadmap of lines on her face, however, were the same.

She peered at him, her eyes narrowed. "Tony Donatelli? Is that you?"

"It is, Angela."

She opened the door wide, fear stamped on her aged features. "Is Sofia okay?"

"She's fine," he said quickly, realizing he should have said so immediately. "Couldn't be better."

Her shoulders sagged with relief. She smiled, taking years off her age, which he knew to be seventy-seven. She'd given birth to Sofia, her only child, when she was thirty-five.

"Come in. Come in." She stepped back from the door, gesturing him inside a stale-smelling house that could have used more light.

She turned off the television, had him follow her to a cramped kitchen, poured him a glass of unsweetened iced tea, sat down across from him at a table for two and got to the point. "Now suppose you tell me why you're here."

"It's about Constanzia," he said.

Angela grew very still, but her expression didn't change.

"Did you know that Sofia went on television and announced that she was searching for her?"

The old woman gave a barely perceptible shake of her head.

"She got a lot of letters from young women claiming to be Constanzia, especially at first. They've trickled off, but I'm still afraid someone will take advantage of her. I need your help to make sure that doesn't happen."

"Me?" She pointed at her chest with a gnarled finger. "How can an old woman like me help?"

"I'm trying to gather as much information

as I can about Constanzia and her adoption. So far I've only heard Sofia's version of the story."

Her expression turned guarded. "What did she tell you?"

"That she was sixteen when she got pregnant by a high school classmate. That you sent her to live with distant relatives in upstate Ohio until she came to term. That she delivered the baby at a private clinic and held her for only a few moments. That it broke her heart to give the baby up for adoption."

"It was only me and her, and she was just sixteen. I did what I thought was best." Angela's voice sounded beseeching, as though trying to convince him of that.

Tony knew Sofia wasn't convinced. She'd dutifully finished high school but her resentment at her mother had mushroomed, eventually resulting in an estrangement that had lasted twenty years.

"I need to know if you remember the name of the doctor who delivered Constanzia," Tony said. "Or the name of the adoption agency or attorney who handled the details. Anything that could help me weed out an impostor."

Angela shook her head, then stared down

at the table. "I already told you. I'm an old woman. My memory is bad and gets worse every year. I don't remember anything but the name of the clinic."

Tony already knew the name of the clinic. He also knew Angela would say no more, though he tried asking her the same question phrased half a dozen different ways.

He finally gave up, asked after her health and spent the better part of an hour filling her in on how Sofia was handling her sudden wealth before telling her he had to get back to McIntosh.

"Tony." Her voice stopped him when he was halfway down the sidewalk. He turned back to find her standing on her porch, looking even older than her considerable years. "You never told me if anybody showed up in McIntosh after Sofia went on TV?"

"A few women did," Tony said, "but I'm only worried about one of them. A young woman named Kaylee Carter and her six-year-old son. They're living in Sofia's basement."

"Does Sofia think this woman is her daughter?"

Tony tried to read Angela's expression, but couldn't. "I think she does. I suggested a

DNA test, but Sofia claims she doesn't need one."

When it became obvious that Angela wouldn't comment further, he took his leave. But he couldn't shake the impression that Angela knew much more than she was willing to tell.

ANGELA SHUFFLED back into the house after watching Tony's car drive away and sank miserably into the sofa. She cradled her head in her hands, remembering with vivid clarity Sofia's anguished cries when the nurse took away her newborn.

Angela hadn't wanted her daughter to hold the baby at all. She'd thought the separation would be easier if Sofia had no time to bond with her infant, but the soft-hearted nurse hadn't heeded her wishes.

As the subsequent weeks and months passed and Sofia became a shell of the happy, vibrant girl she'd been, Angela had blamed the nurse.

She gradually realized the nurse hadn't been at fault, that Sofia had forged a bond with her baby while the little girl grew inside her. By then, it was too late to do anything about it. The baby was gone for good, and

Angela's relationship with her daughter was destroyed.

She squeezed her eyes shut, hating herself for telling Tony she didn't remember a time she could never forget.

But if she had revealed what had really happened and the news got back to Sofia, her daughter would never speak to her again. Angela had endured years of Sofia's silence. She didn't think she could survive it for the rest of her lifetime.

She ran a hand over her face, trying to decide the right thing to do. If she opened up the hornet's nest that was the past, she could probably find out where Constanzia had gone and who had raised her.

After another hour of agonizing, Angela rose slowly and painfully from the sofa, her arthritis once again acting up. Going to her bedroom, she dragged a little-used suitcase from a far corner of a closet. Then she started to pack.

The task would probably take her the rest of the day, but that was okay. She was an infrequent driver, too nervous to start on a two-hour trip when darkness would fall in a little more than three. Tomorrow morning would be soon enough to set out for McIntosh.

She might be able to get the answers she needed with a phone call, but a visit to McIntosh could accomplish the same thing. Surely she'd be able to tell if the young woman in her daughter's house was really Constanzia.

And if she couldn't, she'd have to tell the truth. If she could muster up the courage to do so.

NO MATTER how hard she tried, Kaylee couldn't stop the grin that kept creeping onto her face. The thought of pushing Sofia and Art Sandusky together and letting the laws of attraction take over was too delectable.

"What are you up to?" Sofia asked her.

It was a few minutes before seven on a surprisingly uncrowded Friday night at Nunzio's, and Sofia sat catty-corner from her at their table for four. They were finally alone after walking a gauntlet that included two requests to Sofia for monetary help, one for a start-up business and another for an insurance payment.

"I'm not up to anything." Kaylee tried to sound appropriately innocent but her grin broke free once more.

"I'll figure it out eventually." Sofia waved

a hand as though she wasn't concerned. "It has something to do with the restaurant. Nobody works the lunch shift five days in a row, then gets a babysitter on the fifth so they can come back to the restaurant for dinner."

"I did," Kaylee said. "I like it here."

"That may be true." Sofia wagged a finger at her. "But you're up to something."

Kaylee had deliberately chosen a seat that enabled her to see the entrance to the restaurant. The trick was not to make it obvious that she was watching the door.

Sofia swiveled her head. "Why do you keep looking over there?"

Frankie Nunzio, who had been moving from table to table playing the solicitous host, waved and headed their way. He wore an all-black ensemble and a huge grin.

"If it isn't two of my favorite ladies." He included Kaylee in the greeting, but picked up Sofia's hand and kissed the back of it. "Can't stay away, can you, Sofia?"

"I can't, but it seems other people can." She swept her hand to indicate the half-full restaurant. "Where is everybody?"

"This is about as busy as it gets. We're still pretty full at lunch, especially this week when everybody and their brother wanted to

Take a look at what's on offer at
www.millsandboon.co.uk

Pure reading pleasure

My Account / Offer of the Month / Our Authors / Book Club / Contact us

All of the latest books are there PLUS

- Free Online reads
- Exclusive offers and competitions
- At least 15% discount on our huge back list
- Sign up to our free monthly eNewsletter

- More info on your favourite authors
- Browse the Book to try before you buy
- eBooks available for most titles
- Join the M&B community and discuss your favourite books with other readers

get a look at Kaylee. But business at night has dropped off since word got around that you're not in the kitchen anymore."

"But the food's just as good as it was when I worked here," Sofia said.

"That's not what I hear. We're using the same recipes, but the customers say they taste different." He screwed up his face. "I think it's because you used to improvise."

"Improvisation is the joy of cooking," Sofia said.

"If you ever want to come back, there's a place for you." Frankie frowned. "But with all the money you have, I can't see that happening."

The middle-aged waitress who'd embraced Sofia when they'd arrived at the restaurant beckoned to Frankie. He extended his apologies and then bustled away to see what she needed.

"I figured out what you're up to," Sofia said triumphantly after he was gone.

Kaylee's gaze shot to the entrance of the restaurant, expecting to see Tony and Art Sandusky but they'd yet to arrive. Where were they?

"You and Frankie arranged for me to be at the restaurant on a slow night to show me how much Nunzio's wants me back," Sofia said smugly.

Kaylee gave Sofia her full attention while she tried to figure out what had led her to arrive at that conclusion. "It hadn't occurred to me that you wanted to return to work. Do you?"

Sofia played with the end of the cloth napkin on her dinner plate. "You mean you didn't set this up?"

"No. But you didn't answer my question. Do you want to come back to Nunzio's?"

"Tony would never let me hear the end of it," she said. "He says I should be enjoying my windfall."

"So why aren't you? I've lived with you for almost a week and you don't act like a lottery winner. You don't buy anything."

"I bought a new car and some new clothes," Sofia said. "I paid off my credit cards and I'm contracting with a company to put new windows on the house."

"You could buy a new house."

"I don't want a new house," Sofia said, throwing up her hands. "I like my old one just fine."

She'd apparently liked her old job just fine, too. "I don't get it," Kaylee said. "If money doesn't mean that much to you, why did you play the lottery?"

"It was a whim," Sofia said. "But I'll never regret it, because the biggest payoff wasn't the money. It was finding you."

The look on Sofia's face was so tender that Kaylee's eyes misted. It reminded her of the way the mother who raised her used to look at her. But then Kaylee had become hell to live with and she'd never seen that look again.

"Sofia, Kaylee. What a surprise running into you two here."

Kaylee's head lifted at the sound of Tony's stilted, unsurprised voice. He and Art Sandusky stood at the head of the table, with Art shifting uncomfortably from one foot to the other.

"Oh, my gosh. Look, Sofia. It's Tony and Art." Kaylee attempted to inject surprise into her voice. "Will wonders never cease?"

Ack. Why had she said that? At least Tony had enjoyed it. Amusement danced on his dark, handsome face.

"As luck would have it, we have two extra seats at our table." Kaylee fought not to close her eyes at the horror of having just said "as luck would have it." She never talked like that. "We'd love for you to join us."

"That'd be great. Wouldn't it, Art?" Tony pulled out the chair next to Kaylee's and sat down, giving Art no choice but to take the seat next to Sofia.

Kaylee exchanged a conspiratorial look with Tony, finding that she liked the twinkle in his eyes much more than the suspicion that usually dwelled there.

"It's so nice to see you again, Art," Kaylee said. Although the grocer looked nearly as self-conscious as Sofia, he kept stealing peeks at her. "Isn't it nice to see him, Sofia?"

The warmth that had been in Sofia's eyes before the two men sat down was gone, replaced by disbelief. And panic. Kaylee definitely saw panic.

"Very nice," Sofia murmured.

Art finally discovered his voice. "The pleasure, of course, is mine."

He sounded wonderfully old-fashioned, which Kaylee found to be extremely charming. Sofia apparently did, too, judging by the dull red flush that had spread across her cheeks.

Kaylee's intention had been for all of them to have dinner together, but it suddenly seemed to her that four was very much a crowd.

"Oh, my goodness. I just remembered I left my curling iron on." Kaylee tried to sound appropriately concerned. "I'm afraid it might burn down the house."

Tony chuckled softly under his breath, and she nudged his knee sharply with hers.

Sofia didn't laugh, but started to gather her purse and pull on the pretty blue sweater Kaylee had encouraged her to wear. "I'll drive you home so you can turn it off."

"I couldn't inconvenience you that way, Sofia," Kaylee said hurriedly, then realized she'd painted herself into a corner. By now Art must have realized she hadn't driven to the restaurant. Nothing could be done about it now. She had to forge ahead. "Tony will drive me. Won't you, Tony?"

Sofia crossed her arms over her chest like a mother who had caught a child in a lie. "Or you could take my car keys and drive yourself."

"I couldn't do that." Kaylee searched her brain for a plausible excuse, but she hadn't tried to deceive anyone since her teens. Lying convincingly was a lot harder than she remembered. "I'm not a very good driver," she blurted out finally. "You can't trust me with your car."

Before anybody could dispute her totally erroneous claim, Kaylee got to her feet. She directed a pointed look at Tony, who was struggling not to laugh. She held her head regally high. "Are you coming, Tony?"

"I sure am." He got to his feet, a smile creasing his lips, a chuckle in his voice. "I don't want to miss what you're going to say next."

CHAPTER TEN

SOFIA COULD FEEL herself slipping down in her seat, the better to hide under the table. She made herself straighten and looked Art in the eyes. Despite this being one of the most mortifying moments of her life, she noticed that they were exceptionally nice eyes. Wide-set, hazel, nonjudgmental.

"If I had a hood, I'd pull it over my head," she said.

"I'm glad you don't." Those eyes crinkled at the corners. "Because I like what I see."

She felt her blush deepen and brought a hand to her face in a useless attempt to ward off the heat.

Art had said similar sweet things on their one and only date, but then he'd pulled his disappearing act. She couldn't permit her heart to get the better of her head.

"Thank you for saying that, but I still need to apologize for Kaylee. I'm not sure why she did this…" *Liar, liar,* a voice inside her head screamed. "…but I'd understand if you didn't want to have dinner with me."

"Of course I want to have dinner with you," Art said, but they both knew there was no "of course" about it.

The pain in her palms eased, and she realized she was no longer digging her newly manicured fingernails into her skin.

"You do realize Kaylee and Tony aren't coming back?" Sofia asked, providing him with another chance to back out.

He nodded. "I realize that."

"What you might not realize is that girl's going to get a piece of my mind when I get home tonight."

His eyebrows arched. "Then Kaylee is living with you. I'd heard as much, but didn't know if it was true."

"It's true," Sofia said. "But why would you hear anything about Kaylee and me?"

"Are you kidding? Since you won the lottery, you've become a bona fide celebrity. Everybody in McIntosh is interested in anything to do with you."

She frowned. "I get more attention now than I ever did, but I hadn't realized people talked about me."

"Believe me, they do. Now that Kaylee's arrived, there's more talk than ever."

"What are they saying?"

He shrugged. "It depends on the source. Most say she's the daughter you gave up for adoption. But there are those who think she's taking advantage of you."

"Kaylee would never do anything like that," Sofia said sharply. "She's not that kind of person."

"What kind of person is she?"

"The kind any woman would love to have as a daughter," Sofia said. "People think that my lucky day was when I won the lottery, but it was really when she and her son came into my life."

"I don't think you're the lucky one." He let his eyes rest on her. "I think Kaylee is."

Sofia melted, right there in the middle of the restaurant where she'd spent so many of her adult years. He continued to stare at her until everything inside her turned to mush.

And quite suddenly she knew that she wouldn't yell at Kaylee when she hunted her down tonight.

She'd kiss her for being thoughtful enough to set up what could turn out to be one of the best nights of her life.

KAYLEE HURRIED Tony out of Nunzio's, alarmed by the silent shake to his shoulders. The instant they cleared the restaurant, a great gale of laughter escaped from his lungs.

"Oh, my gosh. Look who's here. Will wonders never cease." He imitated some of her more choice expressions, then held his side as he doubled over.

Kaylee propped her hands on her hips and tried to look stern, but managed to keep a straight face for about two seconds before she joined in the laughter.

"Look who's talking," she said through her giggles. "You're a terrible actor."

"I'm a terrible actor?" He shook his head, wiping tears from the corners of his eyes. "What about you?"

"What about me?"

He fingered a springy strand of her long, dark hair. "Doesn't your hair have a natural wave?"

"Yes," she admitted.

"Then what do you need a curling iron for?"

She grimaced and bit her lip, which seemed to amuse him even further.

"I couldn't think of another excuse," she said.

He let loose another laugh. "You don't even have a curling iron, do you?"

"No," she admitted, and they grinned at each other. A week of distrust fell away, and it seemed to Kaylee they were back at the point they'd started.

She gestured at the restaurant. "You do know that we can't go back in there."

"You're afraid you might die of embarrassment?"

"Actually," Kaylee said, grimacing dramatically, "I'm afraid Sofia might kill me."

Tony tapped his chin. "That presents a problem. It's dinnertime, and I'm starving."

At the mention of his hunger, Kaylee's stomach rumbled noisily. "I'm hungry, too."

He cut his eyes at her stomach, grinned and said, "No kidding."

She covered her stomach with one hand, curiously not self-conscious. But maybe that was because she was beyond embarrassment after what had happened in the restaurant.

"Should we go back to the house and make something? I don't need to pick up Joe-Joe for a couple more hours, but we could stop and get him along the way."

He shook his head. "It would take too long to go to the house and make something. Let's go to the deli around the corner."

Kaylee made a face. "That's too risky. Sofia and Art might finish dinner early and spot your car."

He scratched his head as though puzzling something out, then turned mock-innocent eyes on her. "Yeah. Can't have them figuring out you didn't really think you left your curling iron on."

His smile took the bite out of his sarcasm, but she wouldn't have been offended anyway. She was starting to be able to tell when he was teasing.

She punched his arm lightly. "That's true. I do have appearances to keep up."

She wasn't sure what had precipitated the change between them, but could feel that something was different. Whatever it was, she vastly preferred it to the chilly coexistence they'd endured for the past week.

"Let's live dangerously." He grabbed for her hand. Warm shivers danced up her arm, growing even warmer when he smiled. "Let's go to the deli and eat those sandwiches really fast."

She let him lead her down the street, finding the main part of town just as charming at night as it was during the day. Even more so, considering she and Tony were no longer at odds.

"I've got a better idea," she said the moment it popped into her head. "Let's get the sandwiches to go."

"To go where?" Frown lines appeared on his forehead. "There aren't that many interesting places in McIntosh to go."

"I disagree," she said. "I can think of one place where I'd love to eat those sandwiches."

"Where?"

"If you hand over the keys to your car after we get our food, I'll surprise you."

The face he turned to her was innocence personified, but he couldn't fool her. She'd seen that same look on her son's face after he'd secretly stuffed his pockets with caterpillars.

"I don't know whether I'd trust such a rotten driver with my car, even if it is a rental."

She stuck out her tongue. He laughed again, and she found herself looking forward to what promised to be a very interesting evening.

TONY STOOD beside the car Kaylee had parked on the shoulder of the narrow, little-traveled road, holding their bag of takeout food as Kaylee trespassed on private property.

"You want to eat here?" he asked dubiously. "In the apple orchard?"

She spun around, her arms outstretched. "Why not here? It's gorgeous. The perfect place for a picnic."

Tony had never associated Olney's Orchard with perfection. The family-owned business, located about five miles from the heart of McIntosh, had been in operation for as long as Tony could remember.

While a teenager saving up for college, Tony had gotten seasonal work at the twenty-acre orchard picking apples. Mr. Olney hadn't used harvest machinery, afraid the technique would cause too much damage to his precious fruit.

Tony still remembered Mr. Olney's rules to pick by: Lift and twist the apple. Don't pull off the spur. Don't grasp the apple too tightly. Don't drop it into the bucket too roughly.

Trying not to bruise the things while protecting the buds for next year's crop had been pure drudgery.

Working the orchard had been strictly a fall activity. He'd never given the place a second thought when springtime rolled around. He did now, trying to see what Kaylee saw.

The apple trees snaked up and over the rise in a dozen uniform rows, their pink-and-white blossoms shining in the light of the moon and the stars.

He supposed springtime in an Ohio apple orchard would be gorgeous to a woman who'd lived the past seven years in a place with no discernible seasons.

His eyes drifted back to Kaylee. She'd ventured deeper into the orchard, too far away from him to clearly see her features. But the full moon shone on her, making a silhouette of her body.

Her head was thrown back, exposing the graceful line of her neck and long, curly hair. Her light jacket billowed slightly in the wind. His eyes traced the fullness of her breasts, the flare of her hips, the length of her legs.

Awareness surged through him, energizing his body. He'd thought he had this unwise attraction under control. Now he knew he'd thought wrong.

"Aren't you going to join me?" she called. "I've picked out the perfect spot for our picnic."

He slowly swiveled his head, his gaze taking in row after row of apple trees. The distant headlights of a car traveling the main road that led back to McIntosh materialized, then disappeared. The edge of the grove would be visible to the driver, but not the gravel access road where Kaylee had parked.

The terrain was too hilly to afford a view of what was beyond the rise, but Tony knew the Olney family homestead was about a mile away. It consisted of a large Victorian house positioned beside an outbuilding where old man Olney sold cider and various kinds of apples—Jonagolds, Red and Yellow Delicious and McIntosh, to name a few—to walk-up customers during the fall.

Nobody was traveling the gravel road leading to the house tonight. Tony suspected that nobody would. He was well and truly alone with a woman he'd be smart not to touch.

"Come on," she urged.

His feet wanted to move, but his brain held him back. He couldn't tell her he was reluctant to join her because he didn't think he could keep his hands off her, so came up with another reason. "You do know this is private property."

"You say you know everybody in McIntosh. If we get caught, surely you can talk the

owner into not having us arrested for trespass-
ing."

She had him there. Old man Olney might
not be understanding about interlopers on his
property in the fall and late summer when his
trees were laden with apples. He'd look the
other way in the spring, when there was nothing to steal but blossoms.

"Okay, you win," he said, venturing forward.
"Where is this perfect spot you've picked out?"

"Right here." She sat down precisely
where she was, on the soft earth beneath a
blossoming tree. She didn't seem to care that
they had no picnic blanket and that she'd
probably get grass stains on her khaki pants.
"What could be more perfect than here?"

He was sure that in the daylight it would
look like an ordinary patch of grass, but the
moon and the stars cast it in a silvery glow.

Shaking his head at the fanciful thought,
he lowered himself to sit beside her, opened
the oversized brown paper bag and handed
out the sandwiches.

"I love picnics," she said after they'd eaten
in companionable silence for a few minutes.
"No matter what you're eating, the food always tastes wonderful."

They'd both opted for ordinary selections—turkey clubs, potato chips, cans of juice. He'd eaten the same kinds of food dozens of times, but mentally conceded that tonight's meal was exceptionally good.

The flavors seemed richer, the smells more appetizing. He could have attributed his enhanced senses to the novelty of a nighttime picnic, but knew the real reason was the company.

"I wonder how things are going with Art and Sofia," she said after she'd eaten the last bite of her sandwich. "From what Sofia told me, things had been awkward between them lately."

"There's always hope." He took a swig of juice. "Look at us."

She started to deposit their trash in the paper bag. "I did notice that you're not your usual snippy self tonight."

He let out a short breath. "You think I'm snippy?"

"Oh, yeah." She put down the bag and awarded him her full attention. "And defensive. And protective. But I can't fault you too much for the last one, because it's easy to see how much Sofia means to you."

He stopped himself from telling her he was still trying to persuade Sofia to take the DNA test. He didn't want his lingering doubts to get between them tonight, especially because his private investigator had yet to find any skeletons in Kaylee's closet.

It was starting to appear as though she might be exactly who she portrayed herself to be: a young woman searching for the truth about her birth.

But why exactly was she searching when she couldn't be sure there was anything to find? Had there been something lacking in her childhood that had spurred her to question who she was and where she belonged?

She'd told him about her move to Fort Lauderdale, but she'd said precious little about growing up in Houston aside from intimating that her father was hard to talk to.

"What was your mother like?" he asked her.

He thought for a moment that she'd retreat into herself, but then she answered, "She was strict and so controlling that I felt like I couldn't breathe. She had so many rules it made my head spin."

"Then you were sheltered?"

She laughed, but the sound held no humor. "I didn't say I followed the rules. When she said I couldn't date, I asked out the boys.

When she talked to me about the evils of alcohol, I got drunk. When she grounded me, I snuck out the window. I did everything I could think of to make her life miserable."

"Why?" he asked.

"At the time, it was because I thought she was too strict. But now that I'm a mother myself, I can see how fine a balancing act raising a child is. I'll probably make some of the same mistakes she did."

"Everybody makes mistakes," he said.

"Not Sofia."

"She thinks she did. She thinks she should have given me a greater appreciation of the place where I grew up so I would've stayed."

"If you can't see the beauty in McIntosh, that's not her fault. It's yours." She breathed in the clean, night air. "How could you not love it here?"

"Because I know there are better places to live. Like Seattle, for instance."

She tucked her legs under her. "Then make me understand what's so wonderful about your life in Seattle."

She gazed at him expectantly and he realized she'd effectively turned the conversation away from herself. Again.

"Start with your company," she suggested.

"You said it was called Security Solutions, right?"

He sighed in defeat and answered her. "That's right. I started out small, just me and a guy I went to college with, but we're up to ten employees. Nick, my college buddy, has an MBA in business. We've gotten so successful that we're turning away business."

"Have you considered expanding?"

"That's what Nick wants to do. He's lobbying for us to open branch offices in different parts of the country."

"What do you want to do?"

"I'm not sure," he said. "I like the idea that the company is becoming so successful but the thought of overseeing such a large enterprise would mean longer hours and more headaches. So far I've held off deciding which direction to take. I've had too many other things to think about."

She was much better at listening than she was at sharing. She maintained eye contact as he talked to show she was interested. She didn't interrupt, waiting until he paused before saying anything at all.

"Like what?" she asked.

"Like Sofia winning the lottery, for starters," he said, "but I've also been looking to buy a house."

"Where do you live now?"

"In a condo in a downtown neighborhood called Belltown. It's become the place to be, which means it's hard to find a parking spot and it's noisy well into the night."

"I can understand why you'd want to move, then. Have you found anything you like?"

"My Realtor showed me a place a couple of weeks ago overlooking Puget Sound that was perfect."

"When will you know if the owner accepted your bid?"

He frowned. "I didn't put in a bid."

"Why not?"

He started to blame his unexpected trip to McIntosh, but the reason suddenly seemed weak.

"It could be because living in downtown Seattle is so convenient." He didn't think that was the answer, either, but provided a feasible line of reasoning. "There's tons to do. Restaurants, plays, pro sporting events. I'm thinking about getting season tickets for the Sonics, but I haven't gotten around to it yet."

"That seems to be a pattern with you."

"What do you mean by that?" He heard the edge in his voice.

"I'm sorry. That was out of line. Forget I said that."

"No. Go on. Tell me what you meant."

She exhaled slowly before she answered. "I just meant that you seem to have put a lot of things on hold."

"Are you implying I don't know what I want?"

She lapsed into silence, providing him with the answer. A lock of hair had fallen into her face. He brushed it back, letting his fingers linger on her cheek.

"You're wrong." He rubbed her bottom lip with the pad of his forefinger. "Right now I know exactly what I want."

He lowered his head and kissed her, the way he'd wanted to kiss her since he'd first spotted her at Nunzio's.

He would have drawn back at the first sign that she didn't welcome his kiss, but she sighed and leaned into him. Her hand rested on his chest, where he could feel his heart beating hard.

She tasted sweet, like the apple juice she'd drunk with their picnic dinner. She'd said she ordered it because no other beverage seemed appropriate for a picnic in an apple orchard.

He cupped the back of her neck and coaxed open her mouth, wanting to get to the sweetness inside. The moment his tongue touched hers, the kiss changed. Innocence fled, replaced by a hot, licking sensation that flared deep inside him.

He deepened the kiss, wanting more of her. She returned his passion, stroke for stroke, caress for caress.

Her hands pushing against the plane of his chest came as a shock, but he couldn't ignore the message she was sending. He immediately drew back, reluctantly lifting his mouth from hers.

"Stop," she said weakly, unconvincingly.

But stop was one of those magic words, second only in importance to "no." His father hadn't taught him many things, but he'd taught him that.

He dropped his hands from her hair and put space between them, waiting for her to explain.

"You have a girlfriend," she said. "Sofia said you've been dating her for almost a year."

After their phone conversation earlier that day, Tony no longer considered Ellen his girlfriend. Even if she held out hope that things would eventually work out between them, he was free to see other women. Ellen certainly made it clear she was seeing other men.

He frowned as snatches of the conversation with Ellen returned to him. Ellen had intimated that he didn't know what he wanted, the same as Kaylee had.

But he did know. He wanted it all: A successful career, a beautiful wife, a nice house. And he wanted to keep on kissing Kaylee, exploring the passion that had sprung between them.

If he told her about breaking up with Ellen, that might be possible.

But what then? How could he and Kaylee build a relationship when he wasn't ready to concede that her appearance in his stepmother's life was innocent?

Even if it was, Tony's life was in Seattle. Kaylee had already given her heart to McIntosh. Better to let her think he and Ellen were still together.

"Yeah." He was loathe to outright state that Ellen was his girlfriend so phrased it a different way. "Ellen and I have been dating for almost a year."

She got up abruptly, dusting stray bits of dirt and grass from her pants. Her head was turned away from him when she said, "Then it's better that we pretend this never happened."

She preceded him back to the car, and his eyes dipped to the sway of her hips. He could feel the imprint of her lips on his mouth, and his jeans still felt far too tight.

And he knew there was no way in hell he'd ever be able to pretend he'd never kissed her.

THE EASY CAMARADERIE that she'd unexpectedly shared with Tony was gone, erased in an instant by that sizzling kiss.

Kaylee tried to be angry at him, but she couldn't. She'd known he had a girlfriend. Known, too, that he didn't trust her. She was as much to blame for what happened as he was.

After they stopped at Anne Gudzinski's to pick up Joey, the silence that had descended upon them grew a little less deafening. Joey slept the entire way home, the only sounds in the car the even ins and outs of his breathing.

Kaylee would have awakened him when they got to Sofia's house, but Tony wordlessly overruled her. He'd lifted her son into his arms and strode with him to the top bunk in his old bedroom, in much the same way that he'd carried Joey from Anne's house to his car.

Joe-Joe's head rested trustingly on his shoulder, as though he knew that Tony would never drop him.

Would Kaylee have had the same sense of tranquility if she'd chosen a better man to father her child? She shoved the thought from her mind.

Joey wouldn't be Joey if she'd made a different choice, and she could never regret giving birth to him.

And Tony...well, Tony was about as available to her as the man in the moon.

"I should get him into his pajamas," she whispered after Tony had pulled off Joey's tennis shoes.

"Leave him," Tony whispered back. "It won't hurt him to sleep in his clothes for one night."

She examined Joey's sweet, exhausted face and had to agree. Anne said he'd been full of energy earlier, dashing from one end of her yard to the other in mad pursuit of fireflies. The activity had obviously worn him out.

Kaylee preceded Tony into the hallway, and he softly closed the bedroom door on her sleeping son. Kaylee could see Sofia's bedroom from her vantage point. The door was open, the room dark, which meant she must still be out with Art.

Kaylee was happy for her but nervous for herself. If Sofia had been home, the temptation to linger with Tony in the dimly lit hallway wouldn't be an issue.

"Thank you," Kaylee said.

"You don't have anything to thank me for."

"Yes, I do," she said. "You got Art to the restaurant. You bought me dinner. You helped me get Joey to bed."

"Think nothing of it," he said.

"But I do." She touched his arm and knew immediately that she'd made a mistake.

The awareness that had crackled between them all night blazed to life. Their eyes locked, and her insides turned to liquid. Now that she knew what it was like to kiss him, she wanted to kiss him again. And again.

But she knew that she shouldn't.

She lifted her hand, breaking the connection. "Well, good night."

"Good night," he said, but didn't move. The air around them still seemed charged.

Gathering her resolve, she determinedly broke eye contact. She turned away as casually as she could, slowly and surely increasing her distance. She was halfway down the stairs when she heard the door to his room close.

Once she was on the main floor, she leaned her head back against the wall. Another minute alone with him in that darkened hallway and she would have kissed him and damned the consequences.

She heard a key turn in the front door and straightened, instantly shelving her problems. Sofia was home.

She peeked around the corner of a wall into the foyer, half-expecting to see two people instead of one. But Sofia was alone. Her expression was difficult to decipher. She didn't look happy. She didn't look sad. She looked…confused?

Disregarding that Sofia might be miffed at her for her clumsy matchmaking, Kaylee went immediately to her side. "Sofia? How'd it go? What happened between you and Art?"

Sofia met her gaze straight on, but it seemed to take a few seconds for her focus to kick in.

"I'm surprised you have the courage to

show your face after the stunt you pulled, young lady."

Sofia sounded so much like a mother as she scolded her that Kaylee felt a little burst of happiness, but she was wise enough to hide it.

"I'm sorry, Sofia, but it was obvious that Art feels the same way about you as you do about him. I thought all he needed was a little nudge."

"I wouldn't be so sure of that." Sofia averted her face and kicked off her shoes before trudging into the kitchen and setting her pocketbook on the table.

Kaylee trailed after her. "What do you mean by that? What happened tonight?"

Sofia sank heavily into one of the kitchen chairs. Her face crumbled. She'd given birth at such a young age that she was still an attractive, vibrant woman, but tonight she looked like she'd aged ten years. "I don't know."

"How could you not know?" Kaylee checked the glowing numbers of the clock on the microwave. "It's after ten o'clock. You and Art can't have been eating dinner all this time."

"We weren't." Sofia's smile was tremulous. "It's such a gorgeous night that after dinner we walked around McIntosh and talked."

Kaylee could relate to that. The beauty of the night had also seduced her, conning her into believing that she and Tony were a couple.

"Talking is good." She pulled out the chair closest to Sofia, sat down and took her hand. It was cold. "Very good. What could be bad about talking?"

"Nothing. It was wonderful." Sofia's expression turned dreamy. "We talked about books and movies and family and, well, everything."

"So when are you going to see him again?"

"That's the thing. I don't know. He didn't say anything about getting together again."

"Did you?"

Sofia nodded. "A movie's opening next weekend that I'd like to see. I asked if he wanted to go with me, but he said he didn't like the actor."

"Maybe he doesn't." Kaylee rubbed her hand.

"Then why didn't Art kiss me?" She sniffled, and Kaylee knew they'd reached the crux of the problem. "He walked me to the door, shoved his hands in his pockets, said good-night and left."

"You could have kissed him."

"Not unless I jumped him! On the way to the house, Art didn't come within six feet of me."

That made no sense. The attraction that crackled between Art and Sofia was so tangible it was almost visible. Something was going on with Art, but Kaylee couldn't figure out what.

Sofia sighed, obviously realizing that Kaylee couldn't offer fresh insight. She turned over her hand and squeezed Kaylee's, as though Kaylee was the one who needed commiseration.

"Enough about me. I want to hear about your night. What did you and Tony do after you turned off that curling iron you don't have?"

Kaylee grimaced. "I was afraid you saw through that story."

In answer, Sofia gently tugged on a strand of Kaylee's curly hair, just as her stepson had done earlier. "So what did you do?"

"We got take-out sandwiches and ate them at Olney's Apple Orchard."

For the first time since Sofia came into the

house, she smiled. "Then you two are getting along better?"

"Yes," Kaylee said, remembering the kiss. "I guess we are."

Sofia's pleasure at her answer was written all over her face. Kaylee briefly considered warning her not to jump to conclusions but changed her mind. A warning might prompt Sofia to ask more questions, and Kaylee didn't want to field questions about exactly what she and Tony had done at the orchard.

"Oh, I almost forgot," Sofia said, reaching for her purse. "There's something I meant to give you tonight at the restaurant."

She removed a small jeweler's box from her purse and set it on the table in front of Kaylee.

When Kaylee hesitated, Sofia urged, "Go ahead. Open it."

Kaylee flipped open the box to a stunning emerald-cut sapphire flanked by tiny diamonds and set in a hand-crafted platinum ring. Her breath caught at the beauty of the stone.

"The jeweler told me that people in the Middle Ages believed that sapphire rings protected the wearer from harm," Sofia said. "What do you think?"

"I think it's beautiful," Kaylee breathed. She took the ring out of the box and held it up to the light to better admire the rich blue color of the stone. "But I can't accept it. It's too valuable."

"Weren't you the one who told me that I should spend my money?"

"On yourself. Not on me."

"But giving you this makes me happy, and I can tell you like it."

"I love it," Kaylee admitted. "But not because it's beautiful. Mostly I love it because sapphire is the birthstone for September."

"That's why I got you a sapphire, and that's why you're going to keep it. Now try it on," Sofia said, sounding like bossy mothers everywhere.

When given a direct order like that, Kaylee couldn't refuse. She didn't even want to. She slipped the ring onto the fourth finger of her right hand. The fit was perfect.

"Thank you," she told Sofia.

Sofia rose, then bent over and kissed Kaylee softly on the forehead. "Thank *you*. You're the daughter I always wanted."

A wave of love swept over Kaylee. Despite her uneasiness over the high cost of the ring, she couldn't part with it now, not when it came from Sofia's heart.

She sat at the kitchen table for a long time after Sofia went upstairs, acknowledging that she'd fallen hard for the mother. That wasn't the scary part.

The scary part was that she was also falling for the son.

CHAPTER ELEVEN

THE SPUTTERING SOUND of a car engine caused Tony to pause in writing the code that would enable his Creature Features monkey to peel a banana.

He sat at his laptop, waiting for the car's ignition to catch and its engine to roar to life. Silence. Followed by the engine turning over again, followed by more silence.

But he'd already heard enough to determine that the malfunctioning car was in the driveway below his window, where Kaylee had parked her Honda last night.

"Come on," Tony urged the car. "Start."

The engine stammered weakly one more time.

"Ah, hell."

Even if Sofia knew squat about cars, which she didn't, she'd already pried Joe away from the video-game system she'd bought him yesterday and took him to the park.

The only person home to help Kaylee was Tony.

Cursing under his breath, Tony pushed his chair away from the computer, rose and looked out the window. He'd been right. The inoperative car was Kaylee's.

As he watched, she got out of the Honda, propped up the hood and bent at the waist to peer at the engine.

Tony had an excellent view of a nicely rounded rear end and long, beautiful legs left bare by her blue-jean skirt. Attraction rocketed through him, the same way it had last night.

He acknowledged that attraction was the reason he'd avoided her this morning, but there was no avoiding Kaylee now. Not if she was going to get to work today. From the sound of it, her car wouldn't get her there.

She was so absorbed in examining the engine that she didn't appear to hear him come out of the house.

"Want some help?" he asked when he was in the driveway.

Her head jerked up, and their eyes met. He felt the same way he did every time she looked at him, as though an invisible wire was pulling him inexorably forward.

He held both her gaze and his ground.

After what seemed like an eternity, she blinked and the spell was broken.

"I'd love some help," she said. "How much do you know about cars?"

"I can change a tire and check the oil, but that's about it."

Her face fell and he experienced a pang of regret that he didn't know more, but he'd viewed books and not mechanics as his way out of McIntosh when he was a teenager.

"Then I'm better qualified than you are to figure out what's wrong," she said, "and I think my problem's the electronic ignition."

He peered over her shoulder at the engine. "Why do you say that?"

"Process of elimination. It can't be the battery, because the engine's turning over. That leaves the ignition system. It's supposed to create a spark to ignite the fuel-air mixture. That's obviously not happening."

He was impressed. "You sound like you know what you're talking about."

"I worked with a waiter in Fort Lauderdale who used to be a mechanic," she said. "I paid attention when he tuned up my car."

"Was this a guy you dated?"

He wasn't sure why he'd asked. It wasn't any of his business, and there was no reason for her to answer. But she shook her head, seemingly not offended.

"He was a friend who knew I couldn't afford to take my car to the shop." She grimaced. "But there's no getting around that this time. It figures that on top of everything else I have to be at work in twenty minutes."

"I'll drive you to work," he offered. "Then I'll call a tow truck. One of Will's cousins is a mechanic. His name's Bob Jones. He'll give you a fair price."

She chewed on her bottom lip, as though coming up with cash while living with a millionaire actually worried her.

Was this some sort of trick? Sofia would gladly give Kaylee the money for the repair. Hell, his stepmother would probably buy her a new car.

But if Kaylee were telling the truth about being in McIntosh to learn about her birth instead of to dig into Sofia's deep pockets, the possibility existed that she had too much pride to ask for a handout.

"Come on," Tony said. "If we don't leave soon, you'll be late for work."

She grimaced. "I hate to put you out. I know you're working."

He'd been playing. Creating the world of

Creature Features was too enjoyable to be called work. But her comment reminded him that he could stand to put in a couple of hours on Security Solutions business.

"The work isn't going anywhere," Tony said. "It'll be there when I get back."

"In that case, thank you," she said, a sentiment she repeated before they'd traveled a mile in his car.

"It's nothing," he said. "Just a ride into town."

"When you're a single mother, it makes a world of difference to have somebody you can count on to give you a ride into town." She settled back against the car seat and released a breath. "Since Dawn moved out, I haven't had that."

"Don? Is he Joe's father?"

"It's spelled *D-a-w-n*. She's the single mother I used to live with. I think I mentioned her before. We were roommates until she fell in love and moved out."

"Why didn't you live with Joe's father?"

She didn't answer for a moment. "We didn't have that kind of relationship."

The brevity of her answer didn't discourage him from remarking, "You must have been pretty young when you had Joe."

"Nineteen's not that young," she said.

"It is when you're away from family and friends."

"That was my choice," she commented. "I was the one who dropped out of high school and left home in the middle of the night."

Taking that morsel of information together with what she'd told him at the apple orchard about her strict mother, Tony began to form a picture of her childhood.

"Was this before or after your mother died?"

"After," she said. "My mother used to watch me so closely, I doubt I could have gotten away before."

The restaurant came into view, effectively ending the conversation although there was plenty more Tony wanted to know. Unlike the other times they'd talked about her past, he sensed that this time Kaylee would have answered his questions.

He pulled to the curb, keeping the engine idling.

"I'll pick you up when you get off work at two," he said.

"You're a lifesaver." She opened the passenger door, then reached across and touched him. "I can't tell you how much I appreciate it."

A flash of blue on her hand caught his eye. He looked closer and saw that it was a sapphire surrounded by tiny, brilliant diamonds.

"That ring? Is it new?"

She hesitated. "Sofia gave it to me last night."

A warning flared in his mind. He had a fair idea of what rings cost after shopping in the Seattle jewelry stop where he'd bought the diamond for Ellen. He'd place the price of this one at upward of two or three thousand dollars.

"I thought all you wanted from Sofia was a chance to learn the truth." He kept his tone casual but his body tensed as he waited for her answer.

"The sapphire's my birthstone." Kaylee's dark eyes appeared earnest when they met his. "I wouldn't have accepted the ring otherwise."

He read sincerity on her face and tried to view the gift from her point of view. If she were Constanzia, a birthstone ring from Sofia would carry sentimental value. Besides, the cost of the ring would hardly put a dimple in Sofia's bank account.

"I can understand that," he said.

She beamed at him, the smile lighting up

her entire face, before she left the car and hurried into Nunzio's. He watched her go, absurdly pleased when she glanced back at him over her shoulder before disappearing inside the restaurant.

He turned the car around and started to drive back to Sofia's house, his mind on getting Kaylee's car towed.

He stopped at a red light at the corner of Main and Fifth, and his gaze drifted lazily over a smattering of Saturday afternoon shoppers.

One man, taller and thinner than everybody else, stood out. It was Jim Elliott, the CPA he hadn't wanted his stepmother to hire as her financial planner.

Tony had tried to set up a meeting with Elliott as soon as he'd arrived in McIntosh, only to discover that Elliott had just embarked on a two-week vacation.

Tony watched as Elliott unlocked the door of his office and disappeared inside. The traffic light turned green, and Tony pulled his car over to the curb. Now that the CPA was back in town, Tony didn't want to wait another minute to talk to him.

The business hours printed on the CPA's office door clearly stated that his office was closed Saturdays, but Tony let himself in the unlocked door.

No receptionist was on duty to stop him from walking past the stately waiting area to a small office with the door standing open. Jim Elliott was inside, shuffling through papers piled on a mahogany desk.

He was middle-aged, married, childless and sang in the church choir. Sofia had made Tony aware of that last fact because she seemed to think a man's good character was more important than his experience. Tony didn't agree.

"Hey, Mr. Elliott," Tony said to announce himself.

Elliott looked up from his paperwork, seemingly nonplussed by an unexpected visitor. "Tony. I didn't know you were in town."

"I got here almost two weeks ago. I tried to make an appointment to meet with you, but you were on vacation."

"I'm still on vacation, if you can call traveling to California to find a nursing home for my wife's mother a vacation. Personally, I think I need a vacation from my vacation."

"I can relate." Tony never considered a trip to McIntosh a vacation, either. "Do you have a minute to talk?"

A guarded expression descended over his face. "I came in to catch up on my mail, but the office won't be open until Monday. If you want to hire me, it'll have to wait until then."

"This isn't about me. It's about Sofia."

Elliott's lips pursed. "I was afraid it might be. But you must realize there's a confidentiality issue here. I can't discuss my clients."

"Then don't discuss specifics. The reason I'm back in McIntosh is that I'm worried about my stepmother, Mr. Elliott. Every time I turn around, I hear of her giving money to somebody or other. I want to know she has a plan in place for her future."

Elliott folded his hands in front of him. "Have you asked Sofia about this?"

"She tells me everything is under control," Tony said. "Between you and me, I want to know if it is. Surely you can tell me that much."

Elliott ran a hand over his forehead and blew out a breath. "I shouldn't tell you this. And I wouldn't if I wasn't worried myself. The truth is that I'm not sure if everything is under control."

Tony folded his arms over his chest and

waited for Elliott to continue, bracing himself to hear bad news.

"Things started out promising enough. She did everything I advised—set up a trust fund, named a beneficiary, bought extra life insurance, had a home-security system installed, got an unlisted phone number." Elliott ticked off the points on his fingers. "She was agreeable when I suggested she not make any major decisions about what to do with her money for ninety days. That was so she didn't do anything rash she might later regret."

"That all sounds good to me," Tony said. "But you implied that something's gone wrong."

Elliott sighed again, and Tony sensed him waging an internal struggle over how much to reveal.

"I wouldn't be here if I didn't care about Sofia, Mr. Elliott," Tony said. "I want her to make investments that will provide for her financial security."

"I want that, too." Elliott hesitated, then continued. "And that's why I'm worried. My assistant kept me up to date when I was in California. Most of your stepmother's money is liquid. She's not supposed to be making decisions on how to spend it, but she is."

"She's not spending on herself." Tony stated the obvious.

"No, she's not. But she's making regular withdrawals so the money has to be going somewhere. If I were you, Tony, I'd make very sure somebody's not taking advantage of her."

THE CPA'S WARNING reverberated in Tony's head hours later when he was back at his computer. He'd been working on Creature Features, but for once the video game couldn't hold his attention.

His conversation with Jim Elliott had proved that Tony was right to be worried. The cool three and a half million that Sofia had brought home after taxes was in danger of disappearing.

Tony had heard of a study estimating that a third of lottery winners eventually ended up bankrupt. The tendency was to keep the money in easily accessible bank accounts instead of building financial security with growth accounts and variable annuities that kept down the tax burden.

Sofia should be aware of the importance of financial security. She hadn't had any when Tony's father was alive and feeding her the load of nonsense about how he'd strike it rich one day, while the family barely scrimped by on Sofia's earnings.

But what exactly was she spending her winnings on? Sofia had been frustratingly closemouthed about her finances since his arrival in McIntosh.

He thought of the expensive ring on Kaylee's finger and the pricey video game system Sofia had bought for Joe. The purchases were insignificant for someone who had won as much money as Sofia, but they could indicate which way the wind was blowing.

He checked his watch, confirming that he didn't need to pick up Kaylee for another hour. He saved a screen full of coding, glanced at the corresponding jungle scene that had transformed his computer into a child's paradise and exited the application.

Then he opened his Internet browser and typed in the name of the business in Columbus that specialized in DNA analysis. Its Web page stated that the lab preferred subjects swab the inside of their cheeks to provide samples, but closer reading revealed alternative ways to collect DNA.

Tony phoned the lab to confirm the validity of his plan. Five minutes later, he picked up a hairbrush from the counter of the down-stairs bathroom that Kaylee and Joe used.

Carefully selecting brunette strands with the roots intact, he dropped them into a plastic bag with a Ziploc top. He closed it, then wrote *Kaylee Carter* in magic marker on the front.

That done, he climbed two sets of stairs until he held Sofia's hairbrush. He repeated the process, refusing to let guilt overtake him.

Analyzing the DNA would take longer and cost more this way, but it would be worth it.

TRYING NOT to panic, Kaylee hung up the phone on the kitchen wall and faced Tony's questioning look.

"Well?" he said. "What did Will's cousin say about the car?"

"It was the electronic ignition, just like I expected." She ignored the ache in her chest and relayed the rest of the bad news. "The car also needs to be aligned and won't pass its next inspection without new tires. All told, it's going to cost close to a thousand dollars."

"Did you give Bob the go-ahead to do the work?"

Kaylee looked away. "I might be able to get a lower estimate someplace else."

Tony shook his head. "Bob's as honest as they come and as reasonable. If he says it costs a thousand dollars to fix your car, it costs a thousand dollars."

She blew out a breath. "I don't have a thousand dollars."

"Sofia does."

The thought of asking Sofia for the money turned Kaylee's stomach. It didn't matter that a thousand dollars was an insignificant amount for a multimillionaire. Or that the ring Sofia had given her had probably cost three or four times that much.

"I don't want to ask her." Kaylee cast about for words to explain her reluctance. "I'd hate it if Sofia thought her money was what's important to me."

She belatedly realized she was talking to a man who had accused her of being a fortune hunter. She held her breath, hoping he could bring himself to take her response at face value.

His expression didn't change. "Then what are you going to do about the car?"

She turned her mind to her dilemma. "The service station that towed it has a used car lot, right?"

"That's right."

She made a decision on the spot. "I'm going to ask Will's cousin if I can trade in the Honda for a cheaper car. That way, he'll make money on the trade even after he fixes my car."

Tony started to shake his head even before she finished revealing her plan. "You're already driving an older car. Getting one even less reliable isn't a good idea. You have Joe to think of."

She couldn't deny that Joey's safety was of paramount importance, but she'd be smart. She wouldn't drive the car at night or take unnecessary chances.

"I don't have a choice," she said.

"Yes, you do." His arms uncrossed, and his expression softened. "I'll lend you the money to get your car fixed."

Hope flared in her chest, not only about the future of her car but about her relationship with Tony. He'd understood that she was loathe to accept charity, especially from his stepmother, and provided her with an acceptable solution.

"I'll pay you back in installments," she said, "but it might take a while to repay the entire amount."

"There's no rush." He shrugged. "We can do it any way you like."

Straightening from the wall, she took a step toward him. "Thank you."

"You're welcome."

"I've got your number now," she said, smiling at him. "You're not as tough as you wanted me to believe."

He put a finger not to his lips, but to hers. "Don't tell anybody."

Her smile faded, and she felt the contact down to her toes. Only his fingertips touched her lips, but she relived the feel of his mouth on hers.

It struck her that they were alone. Sofia had called to say she was taking Joe to a movie and wouldn't be home until nearly five o'clock. That was two hours from now.

Her lips trembled, and she knew it would be useless to deny that she wanted him. His girlfriend had stood between them like an invisible shield the night before, but today that girlfriend seemed very far away.

"Kaylee," he said, his voice low and rough, "I need to tell you—"

The "Yankee Doodle" song rang out, signaling that somebody was at the door. She couldn't usually read his expression, but his eyes filled with what could only be disappointment.

"I need to get that." His voice sounded thick with frustration.

She longed to know what he'd been about to say, ached more for his kiss. But she nodded. She slumped against the wall as soon as he left the room, her knees as weak as her will.

The murmur of voices in the foyer alerted her that Tony hadn't turned away whoever had been at the door. Disappointment stabbed at her as she entertained the possibility that he'd had second thoughts about the wisdom of what they'd been about to do. Maybe he even thought he'd been saved by the bell.

Sighing and gathering her poise, she drew herself to her full height and waited to see who their visitor was. An old woman Kaylee had never seen before preceded Tony into the kitchen, but something about her seemed familiar.

She was of medium height with snowy white hair, a face lined with wrinkles and a slightly stooped posture. The woman stared at her with piercing dark eyes.

The eyes, Kaylee decided. It was those remarkable dark eyes that seemed familiar.

"Angela, I'd like you to meet Kaylee Carter." Tony dutifully performed the introduction. "Kaylee, this is Angela Crenna. She's Sofia's mother."

Kaylee's breath caught. Could this be her grandmother?

SOMETHING wasn't right between mother and daughter.

Kaylee reached the conclusion after spending part of a single evening in the presence of Sofia and Angela.

The warmth Sofia usually exuded was missing, replaced by an odd tension every time Angela asked Kaylee a question. Because the questions had been constant, it made for an uncomfortable atmosphere.

"There's something I've been meaning to ask you that's been puzzling me, Kaylee," Angela said.

The four of them—Angela, Sofia, Tony and Kaylee—were outside on Sofia's wide, inviting porch where they'd retreated after Joey had gone to sleep. Tony sat next to Kaylee on the porch swing, and Angela occupied the wicker rocking chair.

Sofia stood, occasionally pacing the width of the porch.

"Do you have to ask Kaylee all these questions, Mother?" Sofia interrupted. "That's all you did during dinner."

"You can't blame me for trying to get to know a young woman who could be my granddaughter."

"You're interrogating her."

"I don't mind, Sofia," Kaylee interjected before the exchange got out of hand. She really didn't mind. Angela had already covered her childhood, her parents and her move to Fort Lauderdale. As long as she didn't ask about Rusty, Kaylee would tell her whatever she wanted to know. "Now what is it you don't understand, Angela?"

Angela leaned forward in the rocking chair. "How could you not know whether you were adopted?"

"I've heard that question before," Kaylee said, giving Tony a significant look.

Tony returned the look and answered for her, all the while keeping his eyes locked with hers. "Kaylee's mother is dead, and her father changes the subject whenever she brings up adoption. He's never confirmed that she was adopted, but it seems like he'd flat out tell her no if that weren't the case."

Surprised and pleased by his response, Kaylee smiled at him. Tony smiled back.

"I should have paid attention to this at dinner, but I didn't," Angela said. "Are you left-handed, Kaylee?"

The connection between herself and Tony broken, Kaylee turned a bemused look at Angela. "No. I'm right-handed."

"Hmm." Angela rubbed her mouth with her own right hand. "What's your bra size?"

"Mother," Sofia admonished, throwing up her hands. "What kind of question is that?"

"You know that big breasts run in our family, Sofia," Angela said. "I can't tell much from that oversized shirt she's wearing. I'm curious to see whether Kaylee got the gift."

"I'm a—"

"Kaylee, you don't have to answer that," Sofia interrupted.

"I don't mind," Kaylee said.

"I'm interested." Tony winked at Kaylee, and her nerve endings jangled.

"I'm a 36B," Kaylee said, "although in some styles I can wear a 36C."

"So you're sort of big-breasted and sort of not," Angela said.

Tony laughed. "If more women looked sort of like Kaylee, the world would be a much better place."

Angela tapped her bottom lip with her

index finger. "How about your period? How old were you when you first got it?"

"Mother!" Sofia cried.

Tony scratched the back of his neck, lightly squeezed Kaylee's shoulder and rose. The porch swing rocked back and forth.

"Okay, that does it for me. I have some work I need to finish up, so I'm going to call it a night and leave the three of you ladies to your girl talk."

He said good-night to Sofia and Angela before his eyes touched on Kaylee and lingered. "See you in the morning."

Kaylee nodded, her gaze tracking him until he disappeared into the house. When she returned her attention to the other two women, she noticed Sofia watching her.

"So when did you get your period?" Angela prompted.

Sofia took two steps to stand between Angela and Kaylee, as though protecting her. "You don't have to answer that, Kaylee."

"Really, Sofia, I don't mind," Kaylee said, cast her mind back to her teenage years and told them.

SOFIA PULLED ON the filmy nightgown and matching robe that her friend Helen Gudzinski, Anne's mother, had talked her into buying at a fancy lingerie store at the mall.

She checked her reflection in the full-length mirror in her bedroom. She was forty-one years old, but genetics had been kind, providing her with above-average height and the build to carry a few extra pounds.

She had to admit the nightgown looked pretty. Sexy, even. Her heartbeat quickened at the thought of Art seeing her in the nightgown, but she doubted that would ever happen after his latest vanishing act.

Frowning, she yanked open a dresser drawer and pulled out her favorite cotton pajamas, which featured clouds on a sky-blue background. Even if Art had been waiting for her in bed, these pajamas were more her style. Within minutes, she'd changed clothes.

The shower in the jack-and-jill bathroom that connected her bedroom to the guest room had stopped running a while ago, which meant her mother was probably in the guest room getting ready to go to sleep. Tony was bunking with Joey tonight.

This was Sofia's best chance to speak to her mother privately. She only hoped Tony didn't intercept her in the hall to try to talk to her about her finances again. Being as quiet as possible, Sofia tiptoed to the guest room door. She knocked softly and waited for her mother's permission to enter.

Wearing a soft, white nightgown, Angela sat on the edge of the bed, rubbing peach-scented hand lotion into her aged hands. "Did you come to say good-night, Sofia?"

Her mother's white hair, which she kept up during the day, fell around her shoulders. The style lengthened her face and made her look every one of her seventy-seven years.

Sofia blinked, an action that seemed somehow appropriate. Time had gone by so swiftly, her mother seemed to have become an old woman in the space of an instant.

"I did come to say good-night, but I need to talk to you, too." Sofia sat down next to her mother on the edge of the bed, silently but clearly conveying this wouldn't be a quick conversation.

The smile disappeared from her mother's face. "I need to talk to you, too, Sofia. There's something I should have told you a long time ago." She stopped, sighed. "But you go first."

Although intrigued by her mother's declaration, Sofia wasn't about to get sidetracked from what she needed to say. "What are you doing, Mother?"

"I'm rubbing lotion into my hands," she said, her face the picture of innocence.

Sofia held on to her patience. Getting a straight answer from her mother had always been next to impossible. "I was talking about earlier tonight, when you asked Kaylee those silly questions about her bra size and when she got her period."

"They weren't silly," Angela said. "Heredity has a lot to do with those things. I thought she might say something that would prove she was Constanzia."

"Is that why you came to visit? To check Kaylee out?"

Angela nodded. "After Tony came to see me—"

"Tony came to see you?" Sofia interrupted. "When?"

"A few days ago. He wanted to know what I remembered about the adoption, but I couldn't tell him anything. Then he told me about Kaylee and how you wouldn't take a DNA test."

"I don't need a test," Sofia said tightly. "I know what I know."

"Still, I didn't think it would hurt to come

and see her for myself. I thought I'd know whether she was Constanzia." The corners of Angela's mouth dipped. "But I didn't."

Sofia's spine stiffened. "So you took it upon yourself to give her the third degree?"

"Can you blame me? If she's Constanzia, she's not only your daughter. She's my granddaughter."

Sofia had been estranged from Angela for years because of her mother's insistence that she give up her baby. They were talking now, but it was an uneasy alliance with things that had been left unsaid boiling beneath the surface. Perhaps, Sofia thought, it was time to let them erupt.

"You talked me into giving up your grand-daughter for adoption," she snapped.

Just like that, in the space of a moment, the subject of which they never spoke was out in the open.

"I did what was best for you and the baby," Angela quickly said.

"You did what was best for *you*. All you cared about was what the neighbors would think if they found out."

"That's not true." Angela had the audacity to look wounded. "You were sixteen years old. You couldn't support yourself, let alone a baby."

"You could have helped me."

"After your father died, I could barely support the two of us on a secretary's salary." She put a hand on her daughter's arm, and her eyes were imploring. "Your baby deserved more than you could give her or I could give her. She deserved two parents who loved her."

Sofia shook her head, not wanting to listen. Constanzia had been her baby. Hers!

"I didn't conceive that baby alone," Sofia said. "She had a father. He could have helped. He and I could have worked something out."

"You can't believe that." Angela placed a hand over her heart, as though pained by her daughter's words. "That boy wanted you to have an abortion."

Sofia thought back to the studious, quiet boy to whom she'd lost her virginity. He'd been her math tutor. And even though they had been the same age, he'd seemed so much more mature than she was.

"Why would you say such a terrible thing?" she said, her hand at her throat. It felt like she couldn't get enough air.

"Because I went to talk to his mother and father when I found out you were pregnant. He was there, too. All three of them wanted the problem to go away."

Sofia shook her head. "No. That can't be true."

"It is true. They kept talking about what a smart boy he was, what a bright future he had and how he couldn't be saddled with a child. Why do you think they moved away?"

Sofia cast her mind back to those dark days after the birth. The teenage boy who'd gotten her pregnant, the one she'd naively thought of as her boyfriend, should have been around to share in their personal tragedy.

"He moved away because his father was transferred to the West Coast." She repeated what she'd always believed.

"His father put in for that transfer to distance his son from what they considered a problem. They were afraid something would go wrong with the adoption and their son would be held accountable for the child."

Sofia wanted to cover her ears and shut out her mother's words, but she couldn't make any of her muscles move. Her mother's story, however much she didn't want to believe it, explained why she'd never heard from Constanzia's father.

"I did what I thought was best," Angela repeated.

For the first time, Sofia saw the situation not from the viewpoint of the child she had been but from the perspective of the mother she had become.

A sixteen-year-old without the support of the boy who had gotten her pregnant. Her mother, widowed, working as a secretary and struggling to stay financially afloat. An impossible situation.

"I believe you," Sofia said, surprised to realize it was true. She reached across the chasm for her mother's hand, which felt thin and frail in her own.

The truce they'd formed when her mother had unexpectedly showed up at Anthony's funeral no longer felt forced. It felt right.

"Is that the something you've been meaning to tell me?" Sofia asked after a long moment. "The truth about Constanzia's father?"

Something flashed in Angela's eyes. She hesitated, then nodded. "Yes. That was it," she said, giving Sofia a watery smile.

But Sofia sensed that her mother hadn't told the truth and that she'd left whatever it was unspoken. She started to call her on it, then thought better of it.

Angela was leaving the next morning after church, and Sofia couldn't risk saying anything that would prolong her stay. Because the more time Angela spent with Kaylee, the more likely she'd be to raise doubts about whether Kaylee was Sofia's daughter.

Sofia's jaw tightened. Her mother had already taken Constanzia away from her. She wouldn't let her take Kaylee, too.

CHAPTER TWELVE

MAY ROLLED INTO June, and life returned to normal for Tony after Sofia's mother left town. Check that. He was living and working in the town he'd left behind. His multi-millionaire stepmother wasn't paying attention to his dire warnings about dwindling fortunes. And he was growing increasingly attracted to the woman who might or might not be his stepsister.

Life wasn't so normal.

Tony had fallen into the habit of eating lunch most days at Nunzio's, where Kaylee no longer tried to get out of waiting on him. At the moment, he was digging into a lunch-time portion of eggplant parmesan while watching Kaylee take a phone call.

She worked the telephone cord with her free hand as she listened, her expression growing more and more distressed. He left his eggplant half-eaten and threaded his way through the crowded tables to the back of the restaurant. He reached her side as she was hanging up.

"I have to go." Her voice was shrill, her eyes wild.

She moved to get past him but he blocked her way, placing his hands squarely on her shoulders. He leaned his head closer to hers so she'd be able to hear him above the din. She smelled delicious, and not only because the scent of Italian cooking permeated the restaurant.

"Tell me what's wrong first." When she didn't answer, his heart seized. "Is it Joe? Is he all right?"

"He'll be fine until I get my hands on him," she said, then moved closer so she was almost whispering in his ear. "Anne just called from day care. It seems he was chasing a little girl around the yard with a snake."

Tony couldn't help himself. He laughed.

She thumped him on the chest. "It's not funny. The girl got to a phone and called her mother. Now the mother is insisting I come get Joey."

"A little girl's fear of reptiles is a ridiculous reason for you to leave work. Especially because it's really busy in here today."

"It can't be helped." Kaylee whipped off her apron, looking ready to take on the world. "We're shorthanded this afternoon, but someone will have to cover for me until I get back."

"Let me go."

Her eyes widened at his offer, but she didn't seem entirely opposed to the idea.

"It makes a lot of sense," he continued. "You're busy. I have flexible work hours, and it's a nonsense crisis."

"Tell that to the mother who's insisting on exiling Joe-Joe from day care."

"Leave it to me to make her see things our way." He wagged his eyebrows. "I'm quite good at talking women into things."

The tension left her shoulders and a corner of her mouth quirked, exactly the reaction he'd intended. "I'll bet."

"I'll take that bet." He released her shoulders, but held her eyes captive. "And later on, I'll show you exactly what I mean."

Her eyes sparkled as she retied her apron.

"You're on, hot shot," she said. "But you'll have a tough time talking me into anything if you can't sweet talk that little girl's mother into dropping her objections to Joe-Joe."

TONY SPOTTED Joe the instant he walked into Anne Gudzinski's back yard. The child sat by himself on a swing, unmoving, his narrow shoulders slumped.

On the open-air deck that lined the back of the house, a frazzled-looking woman with frizzy blond hair gestured expansively to Anne as she talked.

Tony unhitched the metal door latch on the wooden fence. It clanked, drawing Joe's gaze. The little boy's body language changed as Tony came through the gate. He leaped off the swing and came running.

Tony got down on his haunches, preparing to address the boy at eye level. He wasn't prepared for Joe to hurl himself into his arms and hang on.

Tony hugged him back wordlessly, aware by the boy's heaving chest that Joe needed a moment to compose himself. When Joe finally drew back, his face looked pinched and miserable. "Is Mom with you?"

"Your mom's still at work," Tony said gently. "I told her I'd come get you."

Joe's eyes were moist, but no tears fell. "I didn't mean nothing by it, Tony. Honest I didn't. I only wanted to show Kimmy how cool the snake was. And it was just a little snake."

The boy's earnest little face reminded Tony so much of Kaylee that his heart turned over. "I know, buddy."

"You're not mad at me?"

"I'm not happy that you chased a girl around with a snake. But, no, I'm not mad. I understand you didn't do it to be mean."

"I didn't." Joe's lower lip trembled, and it occurred to Tony that the child hadn't expected to find an ally. "I like Kimmy."

Tony ruffled his hair. "I figured that, sport. But next time keep in mind that most girls don't like things like snakes and mice and bugs."

"That's crazy." Joe's tear-filled eyes grew bigger. "Why not?"

"I'm way older than you, buddy, and I'm still trying to figure out why girls are the way they are."

Joe nodded, conveying that he was equally confused.

"I've got to talk to Miss Anne and Kimmy's mother," Tony said. "Wait on the swing until I call for you, okay?"

Joe glanced at the two women watching them from the deck, seeming wary but no longer as fearful. "Okay."

After Joe trudged off, casting backward glances as he made his way to the swing, the two women met Tony halfway.

Anne had been two grades behind Tony in high school, a sunny blond cheerleader who'd been liked by nearly everyone. Her eyes looked apologetic. He'd never seen Kimmy's mother before in his life.

He nodded cordially at both women. "Kaylee couldn't get away from work so I said I'd stop by and see what the problem was."

"I'll tell you what the problem is. The problem is that little hooligan over there…" Kimmy's mother pointed to Joe, whose short legs propelled the swing skyward "…terrorized my Kimmy with a snake."

"What kind of snake was it, ma'am?" Tony asked politely.

"I don't know what kind of snake it was," she sputtered. "Why does that matter?"

"The only kind of snake you'll find in backyards around here are Eastern garter snakes," Anne supplied, then spread her hands about two feet apart. "The one Joey picked up was about this long."

"Garter snakes are harmless," Tony pointed out to the still-fuming mother. "It was probably just as scared of your daughter as she was of it."

"Whether the snake is harmless is beside the point." The tone of the woman's voice spiked. "The point is that your son chased Kimmy around the yard with malicious intent."

"Joe's not my son," Tony said, "and he doesn't have a malicious bone in his body."

The woman glared at him. "If you're not that little delinquent's father, who exactly are you?"

"I'm sorry. I should have introduced you," Anne cut in. "Francine, this is Tony Donatelli. Joey and his mother are, um, friends of Tony's family."

"Donatelli," the woman repeated slowly. Her eyes narrowed shrewdly. "Are you any relation to Sofia Donatelli, the lottery winner?"

"She's my stepmother," Tony said.

Francine put a hand to her head. "Oh, my. The Kaylee you were talking about, isn't she the young woman your stepmother gave up for adoption?"

Tony shuffled his feet, unsurprised at how quickly she brought up the news. "It's a possibility."

"Then that would make that boy over there her grandson." She shook her head. "I can't believe I didn't put it together before now. Well, this changes everything."

"It does?"

"Of course it does," she said with spirit. "I won't be responsible for getting Sofia Donatelli's grandson thrown out of day care."

Tony was about to argue that Sofia's possible relationship to Joe wasn't relevant, then thought better of it. Why mess up a good thing?

"That works for me," Tony said. "Tell you what, I'll have a talk with Joe and tell him to stay away from Kimmy."

"There's no need for that." Francine actually smiled at him. "But I would appreciate it if you had a talk with your stepmother."

A bad feeling gnawed at his gut. "A talk about what?"

"I sent a letter to her post-office box the other day about Kimmy. My daughter's in a Daisy Girl Scout troop of darling little girls. But unfortunately most of them come from families without a lot of money. The girls have worked so hard this year they deserve a reward."

Up to this point, she hadn't taken a breath.

She did now, then her smile turned crafty. "I was thinking you could talk your stepmother into paying for the girls to go on an overnight trip to Cedar Point."

Tony stared, struck speechless by her nerve, but she must have misinterpreted his shock for bewilderment.

"It's an amusement park in northern Ohio," she explained. "I'd be a chaperone, of course."

THE MINUTE Kaylee's final customers left the restaurant, she tore off her apron and headed down the street to meet Tony and Joe-Joe.

Tony had called to leave word that Joey wasn't being exiled from day care after all but that he'd pulled him out early anyway. The two of them planned to "hang out" until she got off work, then meet her at the McIntosh five-and-dime.

The drug store had held onto its name even though prices had risen over the years so that nothing cost as little as a dime. The atmosphere inside the store, however, was straight out of the past.

The focal point was an old-fashioned soda fountain that was a gathering spot for coffee drinkers and ice cream lovers. The long marble counter in front of it contained eight swivel chairs. Tony and Joey sat at two of them, although only Tony's chair remained stationary for more than a couple seconds at a time.

"Hi, Mom," Joey called happily when he spotted her approaching the counter. A chocolate milkshake mustache rimmed his mouth. "Tony bought me a milkshake!"

Her son punctuated the comment by gazing adoringly at Tony, which Kaylee had a hard time faulting him for. Kaylee had only arrived, and she had trouble keeping herself from gazing at Tony in the same adoring way.

She'd thought Tony was handsome when she first saw him, but now that she'd gotten to know him he had so much more going for him than looks.

His character shined through in the simplest of actions, such as the way his hand rested protectively on the back of Joey's chair. He'd put his work on the back burner to handle her problem, but the relaxed set of his shoulders told Kaylee he hadn't minded.

"I can see that Tony bought you a milkshake," she told her son, "but I'm wondering why you got a treat for chasing a girl around with a snake."

Joe-Joe giggled. "That's not why, Mom. Tony got me a milkshake 'cause he likes me."

"And because Joe promised not to do it again," Tony hastened to add. "Isn't that right, Joe?"

"Yeah. Now that I understand how weird girls are."

"Oh, really?" Kaylee cut her eyes at a wincing Tony. "What do you mean by weird, Joey?"

"Tony 'splained how most girls don't like cool things like snakes and spiders." Joey gave her a chocolate smile. "But I told him you did."

Kaylee didn't dare confess that she'd been hiding her distaste for those very things in deference to Joey's affection for them.

"Tony's the best," Joey continued, then added wistfully. "I wish he was my dad."

An uncomfortable silence greeted his comment. Kaylee could have pointed out that Tony was very possibly her son's stepuncle, but thought it unwise to bring up such a complicated family connection to a six-year-old.

"But he's not your father, honey," she said softly, laying a hand on his narrow shoulder.

Joey shook off her hand. "Everybody's got a dad but me. It's not fair."

"Life isn't always fair, sport," Tony told him. "Look at what happened today with the snake. Another boy would never have run away."

"I guess," Joey said, still with that petulant slant to his mouth.

The slapping sound of running feet announced the arrival of a towheaded boy about Joey's age. He approached the opposite end of the counter, with his mother trailing. Kaylee recognized both of them from day care.

"Hey, that's Brandon," Joey said loudly, then yelled even more boisterously. "Hi, Brandon."

Brandon waved back enthusiastically. "Hi, Joey."

"Is it okay if I go sit with Brandon, Mom?" Joey asked.

Not wanting Joey to impose on the family, Kaylee hesitated.

"It's okay with me," Brandon's mother, a plump woman with a sweet face, called cheerfully. "The more, the merrier."

"Go ahead then, Joey," Kaylee said. She'd barely finished extending her permission when he picked up his half-finished milkshake and rushed toward the other boy.

"Won't you join me?" Tony asked, indicating the seat next to him. He looked so tempting she almost felt like he was Adam offering her an apple.

"Please don't feel like you have to stick around," she said. "You've already done enough today, for which I owe you a huge thank-you."

"You're welcome." His dark eyes settled on her, as they did whenever the two of them were in the same room. Excitement skittered up her spine. She was almost used to the thrill. She'd certainly felt it enough over the past week. "But you're not getting rid of me so easily. It's been ages since I bought a girl a soda."

Intrigued at the prospect of finding out more about him, she sat. Her chair was positioned close enough to his that their elbows almost touched. The five-and-dime smelled like ice cream. Tony smelled better, a clean mixture of soap and man.

"Was this a hangout when you were in high school?" she asked.

"Surprisingly, yes. Other teenagers in other towns hung out at fast-food restaurants. But McIntosh teens had the good, old five-and-dime."

She picked up a hint of derision in his

voice. "I take it this wasn't your favorite place to be?"

"You're right about that. I came here every once in a while, but I mostly stayed away." He made a face. "I always thought this place was corny."

"You've got to be kidding." She indicated the old-fashioned atmosphere with a sweep of her hand. A massive mirror hung on the wall behind the soda fountain along with an itemized menu that included custom-made sodas and ice-cream floats. "This isn't corny. This is great. Small-town America at its best."

"That's exactly why I didn't like it."

"Well, I do like small towns," she said. "And if you're serious about buying me one of those custom-made sodas, I'd like mine to be a root beer."

The ponytailed teenage girl working the counter had just served Joey's day-care friend a frothy strawberry milkshake. Tony signaled for her and ordered a root beer for Kaylee and a cream soda for himself. The teen delivered the drinks in frosted mugs, which Kaylee thought made the soda taste even better.

After taking a swallow, Tony set his mug down on the counter. "What did Joe mean when he said he didn't have a father?"

The root beer Kaylee had just swallowed bubbled in her stomach. At the other end of the long counter, Joey erupted into giggles. He was a happy little boy, and she was determined that he stay that way.

"Exactly that," she said. "He doesn't have one."

"Everybody has a father," he countered.

In Kaylee's case, she possibly had two—the man who raised her and the one who'd gotten Sofia pregnant. But Joey's paternal situation was much more clear cut.

"Not Joey. He has me. And that has to be enough." She barely took a breath before continuing. "Now are you going to tell me what happened at the day-care center? When I talked to Anne earlier, she said the little girl's mother was adamant about not allowing Joey to continue there."

Tony didn't answer immediately, and she prayed he'd take her rather strong hint to change the subject. She wouldn't talk about Rusty Collier. She couldn't.

"Kimmy's mother changed her mind after Anne introduced us and she figured out Joe had a relationship with Sofia," he finally said.

Kaylee screwed up her forehead, temporarily forgetting about Rusty. "I don't understand."

"Kimmy's mother won't complain any more about Joe if Sofia pays for her daughter's Daisy troop to go to Cedar Point."

Kaylee gasped. "But that's horrible."

"It's extortion, is what it is."

"You told her no, right?"

His shoulders moved up and down in a silent sigh. "It wasn't my place. As much as I'd like to tell off these people who hit up Sofia for money, I can't. All I can do is suggest to Sofia that she doesn't help."

"Then I'll make the same suggestion." Kaylee shook her head. "I can't believe the nerve of that girl's mother."

"Some people have even more nerve than that." He stirred his soda with a red and white straw, then lifted his dark eyes to hers. "Haven't you noticed that Sofia can't go ten minutes in McIntosh without somebody asking for something?"

"I had noticed," Kaylee admitted.

When she and Sofia had their nails done, a salon employee had claimed her son would be doomed to a life with crooked teeth if Sofia couldn't find it in her heart to pay for his orthodontia.

Earlier this week, a busboy who'd just started work at Nunzio's had begged Sofia for money for his college education.

"The townspeople who approach her are only part of the problem," Tony said. "Has she shown you her mail?"

Kaylee shook her head.

"She changed her phone number and stopped getting mail at the house after she won the lottery. But somehow her post-office box number has gotten around. The letters from young women claiming to be Constanzia have almost stopped, thank God. But she gets mail from all over the state asking for money.

"A few days ago, she got a letter from a mother who said she needed help with medical bills. She claimed her six-year-old daughter was dying of leukemia."

Six years old. The same age as Joey. Kaylee's heart went out to the mother. "Did Sofia help her?"

"She decided to make a couple phone calls first. It turned out the woman was childless."

Kaylee covered her mouth with a hand, shocked by the woman's coldness. "Then it's a good thing Sofia doesn't hand out money to anyone who asks."

"She hands out enough of it," Tony said. "The money will go fast if she doesn't change her ways. She's barely past forty." He shook his head. "You'd think she'd know how important financial security is considering the way things were when I was growing up."

"What do you mean?" Kaylee asked.

He stared down into his drink, as if he regretted saying too much. But then he continued, "I've already told you about my father. Until I got old enough to help out, it was Sofia who put food on the table and kept a roof over our heads.

"She was a waitress before she became a cook. You know as well as I do that a waitress's income isn't steady or reliable."

Kaylee grew silent, mulling over this new information. Tony had effectively told her that he was in McIntosh to make sure nobody took advantage of his stepmother. To make sure *she* didn't take advantage of her.

"I'm ready." Joe's shrill voice came from a few paces away.

Kaylee looked down at her son, surprised she hadn't heard him coming until he'd already arrived. "Ready for what?"

"Ready to go." He grabbed one of her hands and one of Tony's and tugged.

Their drinks finished, she and Tony got to their feet. Kaylee smiled at him over her son's head, and he smiled back. The zing of attraction traveled the length of her body, but theirs was an impossible situation.

Even without his girlfriend in the picture, a great gulf of mistrust existed between them that she wasn't sure could ever be breached. Especially because Sofia stood firm in her refusal to take the DNA test.

As it stood, the only way Tony could believe in her was on faith. Judging by the grudge he continued to hold against his dead father, he seemed to have lost his a long time ago.

TONY ROLLED OVER on the too-soft mattress, punched the too-fluffy pillow and focused on the glowing numbers of the bedside alarm clock.

Almost 2:00 a.m., and he still wasn't asleep. He knew what was keeping him awake, too. Kaylee. She was all the way down in the basement, so he couldn't hear her. But he could sense her.

Something between them had changed today at the five-and-dime and damn if he didn't want to pursue what it was. He wouldn't be able to trust her completely until he had the results of the DNA test in another week, but he couldn't seem to care.

He switched on the light, sat up and futilely searched his night table and the floor near the bed for the murder mystery he'd been reading. Damn. He'd left the book in the living room.

Swinging his legs out of bed, he pulled on a pair of jeans over his boxer shorts. He tramped quietly down the darkened hall, noticing a light shining on the first floor when he reached the stairway.

Somebody else was also awake. His heartbeat quickened. Was it Kaylee?

He moved silently down the stairs, his anticipation growing with each step. He was almost afraid to look into the kitchen and find it empty, but Kaylee sat at the kitchen table bent over a bowl of ice cream.

Her hair was long and loose, and she looked so desirable in the soft light that his pulse quickened and his body hardened.

Trying to keep the mood light, he said, "Caught you in the act."

Her eyes flew to his, so filled with guilt he almost laughed aloud.

"It's not what it looks like," she said. "This isn't something I do every night. Honest."

"Relax," he said, went to the freezer and got out the half-filled carton of ice cream. He scooped some Rocky Road into his own bowl, then joined her at the table. "I happen to think the second-best cure for insomnia is eating ice cream."

"What's the first?"

"Talking about what's bothering you," he said.

Without looking at him, she took another spoonful of ice cream and brought it to her mouth. It seemed to take her forever to finish it. He ate some ice cream himself and waited.

"Remember at the drug store when I told you Joe didn't have a father?" she finally asked, glancing at him over the lip of her ice cream bowl. "That wasn't exactly true."

"I figured that," Tony said.

She grew silent, as though she'd already said all she was going to say. Tony badly wanted to urge her to tell him about the guy who'd fathered Joe, but kept quiet. He couldn't force Kaylee to confide in him.

"His name's Rusty Collier," she said softly. "I met him a few months after my mother died."

She grew silent again, but this time he

prompted gently, "This is when you were nineteen, right?"

She nodded and put down her spoon. "Eighteen. I was pretty messed up. My mother and me, we didn't have the best relationship. She was always telling me what to do, and I was always rebelling."

"Sounds like a typical mother-daughter relationship."

"Maybe it was, but the ending wasn't typical." She blew out a breath and looked inexorably sad. "The morning of the day she died, she and I had a horrible argument. I don't remember about what, but I'll never forget what I screamed at her before I left the house."

She squeezed her eyes tight, as though trying to shut out the memory. When she opened them and gazed at Tony, she looked tortured.

"I told her I hated her. I said that I wished I never had to see her again," she said. "And I never did."

She covered her face with her hands. "I've never told anybody that before. I'm so ashamed of what I said that I'm surprised I told you."

The sexual tension Tony had felt when he

first entered the room faded, replaced by concern for her. He reached out and gently pried her hands from her face. "She was your mother, Kaylee. She knew you didn't mean it."

Her lips trembled. "I'll never know that for sure. The thing is, I thought there'd be lots of time for us to get along." A tear trickled from her eye. "I was a wreck after she died. Then I met Rusty and somehow thought it was a good idea to drop out of high school, hop on the back of his motorcycle and go to Florida."

His hands tightened on hers. "You were eighteen."

"I was stupid. Rusty already had a record when I met him, although I didn't know that. When we got to Florida, the police stopped him for driving a stolen car. It was only dumb luck that I wasn't with him."

"Is that why he went to jail? For stealing a car?"

"And for possession of an unregistered handgun," she said. "Looking back on it, I was fortunate that he was arrested. Otherwise, he might have felt like he had the right to stay in my life."

"Because you were already pregnant," he guessed.

"Another lucky break. Although I didn't think so at the time." Her eyes swam with tears but no more of them fell. "When I found out I was pregnant, I cried for two days. I finally went to a social worker who sent me to a home for unwed mothers. I fully intended to give up Joe-Joe for adoption."

"Why didn't you?"

"I met my friend Dawn. She came up with the idea that we could keep our babies if we helped each other." Kaylee's smile lit up her face, but Tony had already decided the light came from within. "That was the best decision of my life. I can't even regret getting involved with Rusty, because I wouldn't have Joey if I hadn't."

"Does Rusty know about Joe?"

"Oh, yeah." She released a ragged sigh. "That's why I couldn't sleep. Another of the reasons I left Florida was that he was coming up for parole. I worried that he'd get out and come looking for us."

"Did you call the parole board and find out if he got released?"

She shook her head. "I prefer thinking of him behind bars."

"You might have to face him some day."

She shook her head vehemently and

slipped her hands out of his grasp. "It's better for a boy not to have a father than to have one like Rusty."

"Joe might not feel that way."

"Joe's six. He's not old enough to decide what's good for him. That's my job."

He was about to further argue Joe's right to know about his father, but she didn't give him the chance. "Your turn. Why couldn't you sleep?"

She'd changed the subject again, exactly like she had at the five-and-dime. He was trying to wrap his mind around that when she playfully tapped his forearm with her spoon.

"Don't you know how this works? If I tell you my secrets, you're required to tell me yours," she said, and he sensed that she was deliberately making her voice light.

"Required, huh?"

"Uh-huh. It's a version of you show me yours, I'll show you mine. Only in this case, it's I tell you mine, you tell me yours."

She was flirting with him, which he would have enjoyed if he didn't suspect she was doing it to distract him. He decided to let her. She'd opened up to him more than she ever had before. He wouldn't press her. There would be plenty of time to talk about Rusty later.

"Fair enough," he said, then told her the truth. "I couldn't sleep because of Ellen."

The spoonful of ice cream she'd been about to bring to her mouth dropped back into the bowl. Her face was a mask when she asked, "Ellen? Your girlfriend?"

"That's the thing," he said, watching her for a reaction. "Ellen's not my girlfriend anymore. She has an out-of-sight, out-of-mind mentality. Since I'm here in McIntosh and she's there in Seattle, she's dating other men."

Her expression remained unreadable. "So you have insomnia because you don't like thinking about Ellen with other men?"

A logical assumption, but totally inaccurate. The thought of Ellen with other men didn't bother him in the slightest.

"That's not it. I couldn't sleep because I didn't tell you that Ellen and I broke up." He paused. "Or, more importantly, when we broke up."

Lines furrowed her forehead. "When did you break up?"

"Before you and I went to Olney's Orchard."

By the tenseness that settled over her, he

could tell that she understood the ramifications of his admission. The kiss they'd shared loomed between them. The kiss she'd put a stop to because she'd believed he was involved with another woman.

"Why didn't you tell me?" she asked.

"I needed to give you a reason to stop kissing me."

"I had a lot more reasons to stop kissing you than that," she snapped. "You're forgetting that until recently you haven't been particularly nice to me. You still don't entirely trust me. You're probably going back to Seattle any day now. And…" She stopped her rant. Tiny frown lines appeared between her eyebrows. "And I don't understand. Why didn't *you* just stop kissing *me?*"

He swallowed, met her eyes and bared his soul. "Because I didn't think I could."

The wind howled outside the window. The kitchen clock ticked away the seconds. The refrigerator hummed to life, beginning another one of its monotonous cycles.

All of the noise faded into the background. Awareness charged the air. He was close enough to touch her. If either of them moved forward a matter of inches, their lips would meet.

But there were a number of reasons he shouldn't kiss her, just as there'd been that night at the apple orchard.

Tony was having an increasingly hard time believing Kaylee was out to con his stepmother, but he still didn't know if she was Constanzia.

And even with Ellen out of the picture, the life he was making for himself was in Seattle. He'd worked too hard to distance himself from McIntosh to ever consider moving back. Kaylee, on the other hand, had made it clear that she'd like to make her stand in Ohio.

Her top two teeth, the ones with the little gap between them, nibbled her bottom lip. Tony's reasoning fled. He didn't care at the moment about any of the reasons he shouldn't kiss her. He only knew that he couldn't stop himself.

He leaned toward her, his hand cupping the back of her head, gently urging her forward. She came willingly.

He touched his mouth to hers, intending to be gentle and undemanding. But her lips were so soft beneath his, her hand where she touched his cheek so warm, that he increased the pressure.

She opened to him, inviting him to deepen

the kiss, participating in the slide of tongue against tongue.

Desire raced through him, quickening his pulse rate, muddling his mind. He'd tried so hard to deny his attraction that it came pouring out of him, like water from a broken dam.

He didn't only want her in his arms. He wanted her in his bed, where they could enjoy each other through the long, leisurely night.

A flash of light appeared in his peripheral vision, and it dawned on him that somebody had turned on the light beside the staircase. He'd descended the steps in darkness.

With great difficulty, he broke off the kiss. She stared at him, her eyes huge and confused.

"Tony, why—"

He put two fingers against her lips. "Somebody's coming."

She drew back from him, her motions shaky, and combed her hair with unstable fingers. She couldn't do anything about her well-kissed lips or the dazed look in her eyes.

Tony composed himself the best he could and turned his head in time to see Sofia walk into the kitchen. Her hair stuck out at odd angles and dark circles rimmed eyes so bleary he doubted she could see clearly enough to figure out what they'd been doing.

"I guess you two couldn't sleep, either." Her voice sounded tired, as though her insomnia hadn't been from lack of trying. She blinked a couple times and squinted. "Ice cream. Sounds like a good idea to me."

Tony exchanged a puzzled look with Kaylee while Sofia went to the freezer. He was sure his stepmother ate ice cream, but he didn't ever remember seeing her do so. Kaylee seemed equally bewildered. Her chest still heaved up and down, but she seemed more in control than she had been a minute ago.

Sofia sat at the table with them a short while later, shoveling chocolate ice cream into her mouth.

"Are you okay, Sofia?" Tony asked.

"Not really," Sofia said and ate more ice cream.

"Are you worried that Kimmy's mother will make trouble because you said no to that Cedar Point trip?" Tony asked. "Because you were right to say no. You can't give in to people like that."

"I know that," Sofia said. "And I know Anne's a nice woman. She won't let that woman bully her into throwing Joey out of her day care."

"Then what's wrong?" Tony asked, but his stepmother didn't respond.

Kaylee scooted her chair closer to Sofia's. "Tony just got through telling me it helps to talk about why you can't sleep. And you know what? It did."

Sofia didn't look convinced of that. She rubbed her forehead as though her head hurt. "Even if you can't sleep for a silly reason?"

"If the reason's keeping you from sleeping, it's not silly," Tony said.

Sofia glanced from Kaylee to Tony. "I called Art today and asked him to have dinner with me this weekend. He said no."

Tony hated to see that sad look in her eyes and said what he could to erase it. "Maybe he's busy this weekend."

"That's what I thought so I asked him for next weekend." Sofia sighed heavily. "He said no to that, too. He said he didn't think it was a good idea for us to see each other socially."

"But that makes no sense," Kaylee cried.

"It does if you're wrong about how he feels about me," Sofia said. Her ice cream finished in record time, she abruptly got to her feet. "This is stupid. Forget I said anything."

"It's not stupid," Kaylee denied.

"Trust me, it is. My problems are insignificant compared to the ones people write me about every day. If Art thinks we're not right for each other, we probably aren't. This was probably the wake-up call I needed."

Without another word, she turned and disappeared through the kitchen door. Tony turned to Kaylee. She looked as desirable as she had earlier that evening, but some of the things Sofia had said resonated.

Not right for each other. A wake-up call.

Had his stepmother's timely appearance in the kitchen been a wake-up call for him?

The silence stretched between them, neither one of them making a move to finish what they'd started.

"About that kiss," Kaylee began. "I shouldn't have let it happen."

He'd been about to say something remarkably similar to that but her words sliced into him.

"Like you said before," she continued, "there are more reasons than one for us not to get involved."

She rose, placed her ice cream bowl in the

dishwasher and left the room. As he listened to her retreating footsteps on the basement stairs, he felt every bit as rejected by Kaylee as Sofia had by Art.

CHAPTER THIRTEEN

KAYLEE SCANNED a row of books in the fiction section of McIntosh's charming little library, looking for something to read at night that would keep her mind off the unwise attraction she'd developed for Tony Donatelli.

She'd left Joe-Joe in the children's section, devouring a book about a giant mutant lizard whose feelings were hurt by people who went screaming in the opposite direction when they saw it.

Her son's enthusiasm over any book featuring a fish, bird or mammal had charmed the children's librarian, who promised to keep an eye on Joey while Kaylee looked for books for herself.

She pulled out one with striking red letters on the spine and read the back-cover copy. Buried secrets. Brooding stranger. Irresistible attraction.

She shoved the book back on the shelf.

That one wouldn't get her mind off Tony, that was for sure. The "irresistible attraction" part especially resonated.

His admission that he'd let her believe he was involved with another woman to keep her from kissing him should have kept her from kissing him.

She was ashamed that it took Sofia's unexpected appearance to make her stop.

She browsed the rest of the *A*s through *K*s, then turned the corner en route to the *L*s through *Z*s and nearly slammed into another browser.

"Sorry," she said automatically, then realized who she was apologizing to.

Art Sandusky, the man who was breaking Sofia's heart. He was carrying a couple of books, but she wasn't in the mood to give him points for being a reader.

"I'm the one who should apologize," he said with a charming smile. He held up Bill Clinton's autobiography. "I got so absorbed in the back of the book that I didn't look where I was going. Forgive me?"

She was angry enough over what he'd done to Sofia that she didn't want to forgive him, but refusing would be churlish.

"Sure," she said.

He didn't take the hint to move on from her curt response. "I saw your son over in the children's section. He didn't even look up from his book. You're a smart mom to raise a reader."

She nodded her acknowledgement and started to move past him, then stopped. "The last time I saw you was at Nunzio's with Tony and Sofia, remember?"

He seemed surprised by her question. "Of course I do. That would be hard to forget."

"Aren't you going to ask me how Sofia is?"

She could tell by his expression that he hadn't planned on it, but he complied. "How is she?"

"Not good," Kaylee said. More silence. "Aren't you going to ask me why?"

This time, he sighed. "Something tells me you're going to tell me anyway."

He was right. Holding her tongue was an exercise in futility. "She's upset because of you."

His mouth tightened. "Forgive me for saying this, but this isn't any of your business."

Kaylee knew that, just as she'd known she was being too pushy when she'd engineered it so Sofia and Art would run into each other at the restaurant.

She couldn't say for sure why she was pushing so hard. She'd always been rash, but hadn't thought meddling was in her nature. She just knew she wanted to do something positive for Sofia, the way she'd never managed to do for the mother who'd raised her.

"When Sofia isn't happy, it is too my business."

He released another heavy sigh. "Listen, it bothers me that Sofia's upset. But, believe me, it'll be better in the long run that I broke things off before they could get started."

"Why would it be better?" Kaylee pressed. "I know you like her, so don't try to tell me you don't."

He frowned. "If I tell you, will you stop trying to get us together?"

"Probably," Kaylee said, then added, "unless your reason makes no sense."

He shook his head, his mouth forming a half smile. "Oh, my reason makes sense. You're right. I do like her. But I'm not in her league."

"That's not true. I've seen you together. You have similar backgrounds. You live in the same town. You're perfect for each other."

"Maybe that was true before," he said. "But it's not true now."

"Before what?"

"Sofia refers to it as B.L. Before the lottery." His shoulders slumped. "I can read the writing on the wall, Kaylee. I've had a woman leave me before. A year from now, Sofia won't even be living in McIntosh."

"For a smart man, you're incredibly stupid."

His eyes widened. "Excuse me."

"Have you asked Sofia if she plans to move away?"

"Well, no, but money changes people."

"Have you paid attention to her at all?" Kaylee threw up her hands, a gesture she'd probably picked up from Sofia. "Money isn't what's important to Sofia. People are." She paused significantly. "You are."

He didn't appear to know how to respond. Maybe he didn't intend to respond at all. She didn't find out because she felt a tap on her shoulder.

Charlie Marinovich stood behind her, beaming like a lighthouse. "Kaylee! When I saw you go into the library, I had to come over and say hello."

The newspaper office where Charlie worked was directly across the street, with huge glass windows that afforded a good view of the library's parking lot.

"That's nice of you, Charlie," she said, then turned to include Art Sandusky in their circle. "Do you know Mr. Sandusky?"

"Sure do. He's one of the *McIntosh Weekly*'s most loyal advertisers," Charlie said, pumping his hand. "In the market for fresh meat? Look no further."

Kaylee regarded Charlie blankly.

"That's the slogan I use in my ads," Art supplied, then gave that formal little bow she'd seen him execute before. His eyes appeared troubled. "If you'll excuse me, I need to be on my way."

Kaylee wanted to ask him not to go, not because she was feeling particularly warm and fuzzy toward him but because she suspected she knew why Charlie had sought her out.

Since asking for her phone number, the newspaper editor hadn't yet phoned her but he'd stopped at Nunzio's for lunch a few times. Whenever he'd attempted to turn the conversation personal, she'd turned it back.

"I should confess I had an ulterior motive for coming over here," Charlie said.

He was standing much too close, invading her personal space. She got a not-unpleasant whiff of cologne but much preferred Tony's clean scent.

Tony, the thought of whom had sent her to the library in search of books so she wouldn't think about him.

"I wondered if you'd like to go to the movies with me tonight. I'm a huge science fiction fan, and Apple Valley Cinema is showing the classic version of *Planet of the Apes*."

Her impulse was to refuse. She wasn't partial to science fiction or actors dressed as apes, and the only man she wanted to be with tonight was Tony. Who she wasn't going to think about.

But what would it hurt to go to the movies with Charlie? She read hope on his face and was afraid it could hurt quite a bit if she didn't make herself clear.

"I'd like that," she said, "but only if we go as friends and you let me pay my way."

His shoulders slumped but then he recovered and smiled. "I can live with that. But only on one condition."

She tensed, afraid she didn't want to hear the condition.

"You know the woman working the checkout over at Sandusky's?"

Kaylee nodded, puzzled by the question. She knew exactly the woman to whom he referred.

"Her name's Jill, and I would love some advice on how to get her to go out with me," he said. "And not just as friends."

Kaylee laughed, feeling infinitely better about their upcoming trip to the movies. "It's a deal as long as you realize I'm no expert on relationships."

"Then I'll pick you up at seven," he said, the hurt she'd seen earlier already gone from his expression.

Her mood had lightened a little when she went to tell Joe-Joe it was time to check out their books.

Unlike Art, at least Kaylee hadn't broken anyone's heart. It remained to be seen if Tony, by his mere existence, would break hers.

AT A QUARTER PAST seven that evening, Tony walked into the family room where Sofia and Joe were curled up on the overstuffed sofa watching a cartoon lion belt out a tune.

Sofia looked up, her surprise evident. "What are you doing home so early? I thought you were going out with Will tonight."

"Shhh, Sofia," Joe said. "One of the best parts's coming up. The daddy lion is going to rescue them from the evil hyenas."

Without taking his eyes from the screen, Joe took a handful of popcorn from the large bowl on the coffee table and shoved it in his mouth.

Sofia put a finger to her lips, got up from the sofa and ushered Tony away from the television. "Now tell me what happened," she said when they were at the mouth of the room.

"We had an early dinner, then Will ran into an old girlfriend." Tony kept his voice low, although the sound on the television was turned up so loud it was probably unnecessary. "Three suddenly seemed like a crowd."

"You could watch the movie with us," she offered.

On screen, the wicked hyenas were singing about how they wanted to chow down on the lion cubs. Had the movie been showing a month ago, Tony would have fled. But a night at home with Sofia, Joe and Kaylee sounded tempting. He knew she was home because her newly repaired car was parked outside.

He made his voice casual as he asked, "Where's Kaylee?"

"Charlie Marinovich picked her up about ten minutes ago."

His blood felt like it rushed from his head to his feet. "She went on a date?"

"Don't look so surprised, Tony. She's a vibrant, attractive woman. Just because you're not smart enough to ask her out doesn't mean other men aren't."

"Maybe I'm not interested in her that way," Tony said, unable to bring himself to issue an outright denial.

"If you weren't, you would have said so," Sofia said smugly, proving how very well she knew him.

There was no use denying the validity of her observation, so he didn't. "Where did they go?"

"I don't know," Sofia said. "To some date place, I assume."

"Sofia," Joe called. "Something bad's going to happen to the daddy lion soon. If I don't hold your hand, you'll get scared."

Tony glanced into the family room, not at the TV screen but at Joe. He leaned back into the sofa cushions, putting as much distance as possible between himself and the television. His young face was clouded with tension. Sofia saw through him just as easily as she'd seen through Tony.

"I've got to go," Sofia said, her gaze on

Joe, "or I'll miss my chance to have Joey comfort me."

She started back toward the worried-looking little boy, tossing over her shoulder, "Are you coming, Tony?"

Tony voiced the decision he'd made when he found out Kaylee was with Charlie Marinovich. "I'll take a rain check on that. There's something else I need to do."

Ten minutes later, after determining that Kaylee and Charlie weren't at Nunzio's, Tony stood in front of the next most-likely date place. Apple Valley Cinema was a neighborhood theater that had served McIntosh for the past twenty years, showing mainly second-run movies.

Scanning the selections didn't take long. Of the two showing, only *Planet of the Apes* fit into the right time frame. Charlie had picked up Kaylee at around seven o'clock, giving them plenty of time to make a seven-thirty movie.

Tony approached the ticket booth, bought a single ticket from a tired-looking cashier and entered the theater. Only then did he stop and think about what he hoped to accomplish by an "accidental" meeting.

His immediate goal was to stop a romance-

302 ORDINARY GIRL, MILLIONAIRE TYCOON

in-the-making, but he hadn't thought past that. Nothing had changed since he and Kaylee had kissed in Sofia's kitchen. Nothing, that is, except the fact that he wanted her more every day.

The movie was scheduled to have started ten minutes ago so the lobby was empty aside from a few people buying popcorn and candy. The lights would be down inside the theater, rendering it too dark to tell if Kaylee and Charlie were among the moviegoers.

He hesitated, second-guessing what hadn't been a very good idea. What would he say if he ran into them anyway? Fancy meeting you here? Hey, Kaylee, ditch the date and come with me?

"Tony! What are you doing here?"

It didn't seem possible, but that was Kaylee's voice. He turned to see her walking from the direction of the restroom, looking tall and leggy in black slacks and a bubble-gum-pink shirt. She was dressed for a date, one he had no right to horn in on no matter how he felt about her with Charlie.

"I thought I'd see a movie, same as you," he said casually.

She looked right, then left. "Alone?"

"Yep. I had plans with Will but they fell

through." He stuck his hands in his pockets, trying to appear innocent. "How about you? Are you alone?"

She hesitated before answering, or at least he thought she'd hesitated. "I'm here with Charlie Marinovich."

Aware she was watching him for a reaction, he acted as though that was news to him. Feigning nonchalance was more difficult, but now that he was here his plan seemed wrong.

"You better join him then," he said with great difficulty. "The movie's probably already started."

"With the length of coming attractions these days, I doubt it," she said, but then preceded him through the swinging doors into the darkened theater. It felt like a knife twisted deeper into his gut with every step she took closer to Charlie.

But then she stopped and looked at him over her shoulder. "Why don't you join us?"

He swallowed the yes that threatened to spring from his lips. "Charlie wouldn't like that."

"He won't care," she whispered back. "He knows the score."

He was dying to know what she meant by

that comment, but an old lady in the back of the theater shushed them.

"Follow me," Kaylee instructed.

She didn't have to ask another time. He trailed her down the aisle, nodding in the darkness to a surprised-looking Charlie as on-screen a spaceship was crashing into a body of water on an unusual planet.

Tony lowered himself into the seat next to Kaylee and spent the next few hours pretending to be absorbed in a society of apes while trying to put a lid on his attraction.

It was no use.

BARELY THIRTY MINUTES after Joey had fallen asleep for the night, Sofia stood next to his bunk bed gazing at him. She'd tried to last an hour before sneaking into his room for a peek, but hadn't been able to hold out.

He slept with the same abandon he did everything else. His covers were off, his arms flung over his head. His little-boy face, though, was soft in sleep. She wondered if he was dreaming about the lion cub in the cartoon movie that had grown up to be king.

A wave of love hit her that was so powerful it almost knocked her over.

Relationships were what made life worth

living, and love was the glue that kept them together. She'd always known that. Because she had, she should have kept Constanzia with her all those years ago. No matter the cost.

She took another long look at the sleeping child, then softly closed the door. She couldn't do any-thing about the past, but she could hold tight to the present.

She'd do anything to keep Kaylee and Joey in her life, which might not be so hard. Tony no longer seemed to object to Kaylee's presence. She wondered if he'd admitted to himself that he was falling for her, too.

She walked softly down the stairs. Her life, she thought, would be nearly perfect if only Art Sandusky were in it.

Sighing, she opened the door and stepped onto the porch to enjoy the early June weather. She froze at the railing. A man was walking up the sidewalk. The shape of him and the way he moved was familiar enough to stop her heart.

It was Art Sandusky.

She had a moment's fear that her subconscious might have conjured him, but then he spoke in that wonderful low voice of his and she realized he wasn't an apparition at all. "Hello, Sofia."

She stepped back. She'd asked him to dinner for this very night but he'd rejected the invitation. Rejected her.

She felt herself start to tremble, but wasn't sure if the cause was anger or heartache. Pretending she was angry was easier. She crossed her arms over her chest, closing herself off to him.

"The invitation to dinner isn't good anymore, Art." She wasn't sure how she accomplished it, but her voice sounded cool. "Neither do I feel like making you a late-night snack."

He stopped shy of the porch and rubbed his chin. He looked wounded. Sap that she was, she felt awful for having caused the reaction.

"I deserved that," he said.

She tried not to let compassion for him weaken her voice. "What are you doing here, Art?"

"There's no easy answer to that. I guess I'm here to get something straight."

She waited, confused by his appearance, puzzled by what he'd say next.

"When Anthony was alive, he was always talking about the mansion he'd build when he made it big. He never said so, but I got the idea that mansion wouldn't be in McIntosh."

Anthony. Why was Art talking about Anthony? She'd loved her husband, but that chapter of her life had ended. She'd embark on another one, with Art, if only he'd say the word.

"I'm not sure I follow," Sofia said. "Anthony never made it big. You know that."

"Maybe he didn't make it big," Art said. "But you have, Sofia."

"What does that have to do with building a mansion?"

"I'm not expressing myself very well." Sounding exasperated, he ran a hand through his hair. "You probably know that my wife left me. What you don't know is she left me for a job as a flight attendant. She said the lure of other places was more interesting than I was."

"Then she was a fool," Sofia retorted before she remembered she was treating him coolly. She cleared her throat. "What does that have to do with me?"

He indicated their surroundings with an inclination of his head. "This town, it isn't the place for a multimillionaire. Anthony knew that. I figure it's only a matter of time before you figure it out, too."

"Is this your roundabout way of asking me if I plan to move away from McIntosh?"

"I guess it is." He pressed his lips together, looking pained. "I wouldn't blame you. You're bound to get tired of it here, considering all that's changed."

He hadn't moved from his position on the sidewalk. There was some cloud cover, rendering the stars not as bright as they usually were and making it difficult to see his expression.

She walked deliberately down the porch steps and over to his side, intending to make her point very clear.

"I'll tell you what hasn't changed, Art Sandusky. I haven't changed."

"But all that money—"

"No amount of money can change who I am. I've heard too many stories about how money brings out the ugly in people. I'm making sure that doesn't happen to me."

"But the mansion—"

"Was my husband's dream, not mine. He was the one who was preoccupied with getting rich." Sofia poked him in the chest with a forefinger. "How could you possibly think such stupid things about me?"

The corners of his eyes crinkled. Sofia bristled. She was deadly serious, and he was amused.

"What's so funny?" she demanded.

"The apple doesn't fall far from the tree." When she cocked her head in confusion, he continued, "I ran into Kaylee at the library today."

Sofia nearly groaned aloud. After the way Kaylee had manipulated it so Art was forced to have dinner with her the other night, she suspected what was coming.

"She told me that for a smart man, I could be quite stupid."

"She's right, and she hasn't even known me that long," Sofia said. "You've known me for fifteen years."

"Yeah," he said softly, "but I've only let myself love you for two of those years."

Sofia went very still, and it got so quiet that she could hear her own breathing. Still, she couldn't quite believe she'd heard Art correctly.

He closed his eyes, and she watched his chest expand and contract as he exhaled. "I guess I shouldn't have said that."

"Didn't you mean it?"

"Of course I—"

Before he could finish his sentence, she threw her arms around his neck and kissed him. She didn't hear bells, but her entire body hummed, the way it had the other time he'd kissed her.

Art wrapped her in his arms and kissed her back, and that was when she knew she was a very lucky woman.

Not because she'd had the incredible luck to match six of six numbers in a silly game. But because for the second time in her life, she was in love with a good man who loved her back, fulfilling the only dream she'd ever had that counted: to be happy.

FUNNY HOW THINGS had worked out, Kaylee thought as Tony drove her back to Sofia's house.

On the way out of the movies they'd run into Jill, the pretty blond cashier from Sandusky's. Seizing the opportunity, Kaylee had immediately suggested that the four of them get a nightcap at McIntosh's only bar.

It turned out that Jill was a fellow sci-fi fan who'd gone to the movie alone rather than miss it. She'd hit it off big with Charlie. He hadn't minded, or possibly even noticed, when Kaylee accepted Tony's offer of a ride home.

And now the universe had been set right. She and Charlie had started off the night together, but were ending it with the person they'd most like to be with.

Kaylee cast a glance at Tony's strong, handsome profile. It was past time she admitted to herself how strong her attraction had grown, because fighting it was growing more difficult with each passing day.

"I appreciate you driving me h...back." She'd almost said home, but realized how dangerous it was to think of Sofia's house that way. Tony, thankfully, didn't seem to notice her slip.

"Glad to do it. I almost didn't suggest it but you seemed to be pushing Charlie and Jill together."

"It didn't take much pushing. Charlie told me before we went out that he was interested in Jill. And that was before he knew she was a sci-fi buff."

"So that wasn't a date you and Charlie were on?"

"No date. It was two friends going to a movie."

"The friends part," he said, "was that his choice or yours?"

He seemed to strive for a casual tone but didn't quite achieve it. She could tell he was fishing and that the answer mattered. Or maybe that was wishful thinking on her part.

"My choice." She watched him for a reaction, wishing it were daylight so she could pick up the nuances of his expression. She thought she glimpsed the ghost of a smile. "And since we're being honest, I have a question for you. Did you really run into Charlie and me tonight by accident?"

She continued watching his face. He seemed to be struggling with how to answer as he maneuvered the car into the turn onto Sofia's street.

While she waited for his answer, Kaylee's gaze took in the now-familiar scenery. But something in Sofia's yard was anything but customary. Silhouetted against the moonlight, two people were kissing each other as though they never wanted to stop.

"Stop the car!" she ordered. "Now!"

Tony stepped on the brakes, stopping in the dead center of his lane. The street was quiet, with no traffic in front of or behind them.

"Want to tell me why?" he asked after a beat.

"Look in Sofia's front yard." Excitement grew inside Kaylee like helium pumped into a balloon. "That's Sofia and Art." In a softer voice, she added, "I can't believe he actually listened to me."

"You told Art to kiss my stepmother?" He sound-ed puzzled.

"No, silly. I ran into Art at the library and got him to tell me why he was avoiding Sofia. He was afraid she was getting ready to leave McIntosh because she'd won all that money. I told him to wise up and ask her."

Tony released a short, disbelieving breath, but then he smiled. "You're good at this matchmaking stuff, aren't you?"

"I confess I seem to have a knack for it," she said. "Which is why you can't pull into the driveway yet."

"We have to go home sometime."

"But not yet," she repeated.

"So what do you want me to do?"

She indicated the driveway nearest their car, which belonged to neighbors who lived two doors down from Sofia. "Back into the Stewarts' driveway and reverse directions."

He did as she asked, not speaking until they were back on the street heading away from Sofia's house. "Where to? McIntosh is not exactly hopping at night."

She didn't have to think about her answer for long. The destination might even have been in the back of her mind since she and Tony had left the bar together, because it was the only place where they could be truly alone.

"The apple orchard," she replied.

CHAPTER FOURTEEN

TONY UNFOLDED the soft cotton picnic blanket he'd found in one of Sofia's kitchen cupboards onto the cool grass beneath the apple tree, waited for Kaylee to sit down, then simply looked at her.

The glow of the moon shined on her face as she gazed up at him, highlighting the slope of her nose and curve of her cheeks and making her look like some sort of moon goddess.

"You're full of surprises, Tony Donatelli," she said. "I got the impression you weren't wild about the apple orchard the last time we were here, yet you put that blanket in your car trunk."

He lowered himself to sit next to her, finally admitting to himself that there was nowhere he'd rather be and no one he'd rather be with. This place and this woman must have been in his subconscious when he stowed the blanket.

"I like to be prepared for anything when my stepmother's making out with a guy in her front yard," he quipped, deliberately lightening the moment.

She grinned and uncapped one of the bottles of water they'd picked up at the convenience store where Sofia had bought her winning lottery ticket. She tapped her bottle to his.

"Here's to Sofia and Art." Her dark eyes twinkled every bit as much as the stars above. "May he realize money has nothing to do with the value of a good woman."

The moon again caught her in its glow. With her dark hair tumbling down her back and happiness radiating from her, she'd never looked more beautiful.

She tipped back her head as she drank, exposing the graceful line of her neck. None of her actions were deliberately provocative. There was no flirtatious batting of the lashes, no come-hither body language, no suggestive smiles.

Kaylee was just being herself, but everything about her turned him on.

"We should have bought wine or beer," he said. "Toasts seem to carry more weight when alcohol is involved."

"I don't think that's true." A light breeze blew over them, bringing with it the scent of the night and the fresh green grass. She shook her hair back. "I think the most important factor in a good toast is sincerity."

Tony's eyes seemed to clear as he gazed at her. Why had he ever imagined her capable of swindling his stepmother? She looked like everything that was good and pure.

His thoughts weren't pure. His body had been in a constant state of semiarousal since he'd sat next to her during the movie. Now he was fully aroused.

She lay back on the blanket and gazed up at the stars. The apple blossoms were gone and the night temperature was almost balmy. Neither of them even needed a jacket.

"I love everything about McIntosh, but this is my favorite place," she said.

He'd never thought of the orchard as anything special. When he'd worked here harvesting apples while in his teens, he'd daydreamed about leaving McIntosh and never returning.

He stretched out beside Kaylee, then looked from the beauty of her face to the stars overhead. They seemed to be winking, as though the joke was on him.

"You never answered my question," Kaylee said, bringing his attention back to her.

The moon and the stars bathed her in light, outlining her body, making his flare to life. "What question?"

"Did you really run into Charlie and me by accident?"

He could easily sidestep the question. He could tell her that he'd been at loose ends after his plans with Will had fallen through, that he'd gone to the movie theater on a whim.

But there was something about the night that called for the truth.

It might have been the stars, which had transformed an ordinary apple orchard into a slice of Eden. Or the velvety texture of darkness that had made their bottled water taste better than a fine wine.

But in his heart, Tony knew it was neither of those things.

It was the woman.

He propped himself up on one elbow so he could gaze down into her face.

"My running into you wasn't a coincidence." He reached out to touch the softness of her cheek. "When Sofia told me you were with Charlie, I was so jealous that all I could think about was finding you."

Her eyes grew big. "Why were you jealous?"

"You know why," he said and bent down and kissed her.

Because he'd kissed her before, he thought he was prepared for the passion that rose between them. He wasn't.

Maybe it was because the barriers he'd worked so hard to erect between them had come tumbling down. There was no girlfriend to keep them apart, and no niggling doubt festering in his mind that Kaylee was an impostor.

She was everything a woman should be: Good and kind, with a soft heart lined with steel will. He knew of only one other women who possessed all those qualities: Sofia.

They kissed deeply, their arms tangled, their bodies pressed together. If they had been at Sofia's house, they would have had to stop.

But here, in the apple orchard, the cover of night was their privacy.

"I want to make love to you," he said against her lips. "But I'll stop and take you home if you say so."

In answer, she wrapped her arms around his neck and dragged his mouth back down to hers. And he knew with a joyous certainty they wouldn't return to his stepmother's house any time soon.

Just as he knew that the woman in his arms was his stepmother's daughter.

ANGELA CRENNA'S palms were so damp that she dropped the receiver the first time she picked up the telephone.

The angry dial tone blared from the carpeted floor near her recliner. She leaned over to retrieve the phone, her back aching as her arthritic fingers stretched to reach it.

It was hell getting old.

But while Angela's body might be failing, her mind wasn't. She was thinking more clearly than she had in years.

Wisdom, she thought, was wasted on the old. How much more useful it would have been to have that wisdom years ago when Sofia had pleaded to keep her baby daughter.

Angela couldn't turn back the clock, but neither could she keep lying. Not even if it meant losing Sofia's love all over again.

She simply couldn't justify keeping quiet any longer. Not when she could confirm with a simple phone call whether the young woman living with Sofia was really Constanzia.

Nothing was wrong with Angela's memory. She recalled the name of the doctor who had delivered the baby. A family friend had recommended him, and then Angela had struck a deal with the doctor.

Angela would see to it that Sofia handed over her baby on two conditions. The first was that the child go to a loving couple. The second was harder to reconcile with her conscience.

Truly believing that it was best for Sofia to completely and irrevocably sever ties with the baby, Angela had asked the doctor to arrange matters so that Sofia would never be able to track down her daughter.

The doctor had responded by falsifying the original birth certificate. Sofia's name had never appeared. Instead he'd inserted the names of the couple who received Constanzia, enabling them to bypass legal adoption channels.

At the time, Angela had thought the somewhat shady arrangement was in Sofia's best interests. But she hadn't been nearly as wise back then as she was today.

She wiped her palms on her slacks and

painstakingly dialed the phone number she'd gotten from information.

She knew that Dr. Robert Minelli, the obstetrician who'd delivered Constanzia, wouldn't answer. She'd stumbled across his obituary in the newspaper five years ago and knew he'd died of a heart attack. But the doctor hadn't taken the secret of what had happened to Constanzia with him.

Angela distinctly remembered Dr. Minelli telling her she could rest assured the infant girl would go to a loving couple because his wife had made the arrangements. The doctor's wife, now his widow, was still alive.

She completed dialing the number and waited, not entirely sure the ringing she heard was on the other end of the line or in her ears.

"Hello." A mature woman's voice.

Angela squeezed the words out with difficulty. "May I please speak to Mrs. Robert Minelli?"

"This is she. May I ask who's calling?" She sounded cultured and confident.

Angela felt as though she was neither of those things but managed to blurt out a response. "Angela Crenna. I have a daughter named Sofia. Your husband delivered her baby twenty-five years ago."

A pause, then the same authoritative voice. "My husband was an obstetrician, Mrs. Crenna. He delivered a lot of babies."

"He falsified the birth certificate for my daughter's baby. The couple who received her didn't go through a legal adoption. He said you chose the couple."

Silence. It stretched so long that Angela feared the doctor's widow might have hung up.

"Mrs. Minelli?" she asked nervously. "Are you still there?"

No answer. But Angela could hear the other woman's uneven breathing. It sounded panicked. Another few nerve-racking moments passed.

"Why are you calling?" Mrs. Minelli's voice no longer sounded so assured.

"I want to know what happened to my daughter's baby." Angela couldn't bring herself to call Sofia's baby her granddaughter. She'd forfeited that right long ago. "It's important that I know."

"Your daughter. She's the woman from McIntosh who won the lottery, the one who put out the word that she was searching for her birth daughter?" Mrs. Minelli didn't wait for Angela's reply. "Tell me, has anyone come forward?"

"A young woman named Kaylee Carter," Sofia said. "That's why I'm calling. I need to find out if Kaylee could be Sofia's daughter."

"She isn't." Certainty rang in Mrs. Minelli's voice. "The girl you called Constanzia is finishing her residency in a hospital in San Diego."

Angela's heart pounded. Her palms grew damper. For a moment, she couldn't make her vocal cords work.

"B-but how do you know that?" Angela finally asked.

She only paused for a second or two, but it seemed an eternity to Sofia.

"I know because my husband and I didn't find another couple to adopt your daughter's baby, Mrs. Crenna. We adopted her ourselves."

TONY CONSIDERED himself to be a conservative man. He kept his hair short, wore classic clothes and drove a car that had tested well in highway crash tests. He didn't put his money in risky ventures, preferring municipal bonds and money-market accounts to flyers on new stocks.

Nobody who knew him would call him rash, which was why he couldn't be in love with Kaylee Carter. He'd known her for less than a month, had trusted her for less than a day.

What he felt for Kaylee couldn't be love, but it was stronger than lust. Otherwise, he would be focusing on Creature Features rather than worrying about what loving Kaylee would mean to the rest of his life.

Three quick raps on the open door had him swiveling in his chair.

"Good morning, Tony." His stepmother stood in the doorway dressed smartly in one of the outfits she'd bought after winning the lottery. This one was a tailored brown pantsuit. "I'm afraid I overslept. Did I already miss Kaylee and Joey?"

"They left about a half hour ago," he said, looking closer at her. The brown of the pantsuit combined with her dark hair could have made her look drab, but her complexion glowed, her cheeks and lips rosy with color. "You look happy. Any particular reason?"

She crossed the room to his side, leaned down and patted his cheek, the way she used to when he was a young boy. "If you and Kaylee think I didn't see you last night when you turned around in the Stewarts' driveway, you're wrong."

He laughed. "I guess we're busted."

"Except I'm anything but angry. Art told me Kaylee talked to him."

"Talked some sense into him, you mean." He smiled at her, genuinely happy that she was happy. "Are you all dressed up because you're meeting Art for a late breakfast?"

"Not for breakfast. But for lunch and dinner," she said, then giggled. Actually giggled. "He's driving to Cincinnati to meet with a supplier and asked me to go with him. Of course I said yes. I'll probably be home late tonight, but I packed a bag just in case we have to stay overnight."

From the excited flush on her face, Tony would say the overnight stay was a good bet. "Are you leaving right away?"

"I'm leaving home right away, but Art and I aren't leaving McIntosh for a few more hours. I'm going to stop at the restaurant to tell Kaylee about my trip. Then I'm meeting Will."

His eyes narrowed while the wheels in his brain turned. "Will didn't tell me about this last night."

"That's because I just called him. I've decided to buy Kaylee a house. I'd love for her to keep on staying with me, but she and Joey need their own place."

The hairs on the back of Tony's neck stood up. "Did Kaylee ask you to buy her a house?"

"She didn't have to. From some of the things she says, I can tell that owning a home is one of her dreams." She wagged a finger at him. "But don't you tell her about it. I want it to be a surprise."

"Quite an extravagant surprise," he murmured.

"I can afford to be extravagant with the people I love. I just won the lottery." She bent down and kissed him on the forehead. "I'll see you later."

When she was gone, Tony leaned back in his office chair, second-guessing himself for not dissuading Sofia from keeping her appointment with Will.

But what reason could he have given? Sofia had accepted Kaylee as her daughter and Joe as her grandson. Hell, Tony had, too. At this point, the results he had yet to receive from the DNA laboratory would be a formality. He believed that Kaylee was Sofia's daughter, so it shouldn't bother him that Sofia was splurging on her.

It wasn't as though Kaylee had asked Sofia to buy her a house.

A memory of a conversation he'd had with Sofia about his father swam to the surface of his brain. She'd been defending his near constant jobless state by saying that Anthony had never outright asked her to be the one with the full-time job. She'd offered because she'd known he wanted to work on his inventions.

No doubt Anthony Donatelli had dropped broad hints to that effect. But surely Kaylee's comments had been innocent. Kaylee had a guileless quality that reminded him of his father, but his father had been hiding a manipulative soul. The Kaylee he'd come to know wouldn't maneuver Sofia into buying her a house.

Satisfied with his rationale, Tony went to work creating a tropical rainforest with stunning waterfalls and fast-flowing rivers that would serve as a crocodile's habitat. He was so absorbed in his work that he wasn't sure how much time had gone by when the phone rang. He answered it distractedly.

"Tony. It's Angela. I need to speak to Sofia." She spoke so rapidly, her words tripped over each other.

He checked the time on the bedside alarm clock to discover it was nearly noon. Sofia would have set off for Cincinnati with Art by now. "She won't be back until late, maybe not even until tomorrow. Is this something I can help you with?"

"I really need to talk to my daughter," Angela repeated, prompting Tony to give her Sofia's cell phone number. A few seconds later, he heard the faint ring of a phone and followed the sound. Sofia had left her cell phone on the kitchen counter.

"I can't believe this," Angela said after he answered the phone and explained what had happened. She sounded upset. "It was so hard to make this call. I don't know if I'll have the courage to do it again tomorrow."

"You're scaring me, Angela," Tony said. "What is this about?"

After a pregnant pause, she blurted out. "It's about Constanzia."

She preceded to tell him a wild story about how she'd orchestrated an illegal adoption so that Sofia would never be able to contact her birth daughter.

Tony gritted his teeth to stop himself from lashing out. Angela had done a terrible thing, but there was nothing anybody could do about it now except move on. Besides, he sensed that nothing he could say would make Angela feel worse than she already did.

At least her coming clean about what had happened in the past cleared up a few mysteries.

"If the adoption never legally took place," he said, thinking aloud, "it explains why Kaylee's parents never told her she wasn't their biological child."

"Kaylee is the main reason I'm calling," Angela said.

"Of course. You'll want to talk to her and tell her what you found out. You can clear up a lot of questions she has about her past."

"You don't understand." Angela sounded even more agitated. His hands clenched as he waited for her to continue. "Sofia's daughter goes by the name Stephanie Minelli.

"Kaylee's not Constanzia."

CHAPTER FIFTEEN

KAYLEE SPOTTED Tony standing by her car that afternoon when she got off work at Nunzio's, looking tall and dark and loveable.

Her heart, which evidently planned to ignore the conventional wisdom that it was far too soon to even consider she might be in love, gave a happy little skip.

She hurried to join him, her steps as light as her mood. "What a nice surprise," she said when she got within ten feet of him. "I didn't think I'd see you until…"

Her words trailed off when he didn't return her smile. He was leaning against the car, his arms crossed over his chest, his eyes hooded, his expression glum.

Her soaring heart crashed to earth, like a bottle rocket that had been spent.

"What's wrong?" She felt herself grow cold even though the sun shined. "Did som thing happen to Joey or Sofia?"

"They're fine." He straightened, his full height seeming to take him even farther away from her. "I need to talk to you, and I need to do it before you pick up Joe from day care."

He sounded remote, nothing like the man who'd made love to her the night before. She felt her shoulders tense and indicated a park bench across the street.

Her heart pounded as he walked with her in silence across McIntosh's main street. The bench was beside an azalea bush and under a dogwood tree. The bush had been resplendent with red blooms and the dogwood thick with tiny white flowers a few weeks ago, but the blooms were gone.

Their relationship was different, too. She didn't know what had changed between now and last night, but something had.

Once they were both seated, he didn't keep her waiting. His cool gaze rested on her, and he said, "I know you're not Constanzia."

She'd read somewhere that words couldn't stop a heart from beating, but she didn't believe that was true. Hers stopped. And when it started again, the beats came in a slow, painful rhythm.

"Constanzia's real name is Stephanie Minelli. She grew up in upstate Ohio, and she's doing a medical residency in a hospital in San Diego."

Kaylee tried to process the information. If what Tony said were true, Sofia wasn't her mother.

She shook her head. That couldn't be. Sofia was already in her heart, had been since the first moment they met, maybe even since she'd seen her on television.

"Why are you saying this?" she asked.

"I got a call from Sofia's mother this morning. Suffice it to say that she can prove it. You're not Sofia's daughter."

Pain sliced through her, as real as if it had been administered by a knife. Hot tears gathered at the backs of her eyes. Her shoulders shuddered with her effort at holding them back.

She'd already lost a mother once in her lifetime. Logically she knew this was different, because Sofia was still very much alive. But she felt like she was losing her mother all over again.

She needed an anchor, someone who'd take her into his arms and pat her back while she sobbed her pain. She needed Tony.

But it dawned on her that he hadn't offered a single word of comfort. She raised her watery eyes to find him regarding her coolly.

"What do you know about the house my stepmother is buying for you?" His voice was as frosty as his eyes.

She tried to make sense of what he was saying and why he was saying it now, during one of the most devastating moments of her life. A house, he'd said. She shook her head. "I don't know anything about a house."

"So you're denying that you ever told Sofia you dreamed of living in a house of your own?"

Had she said that? Possibly. She and Dawn had discussed the topic ad nauseam when they'd lived together in the crowded duplex.

"I might have said that, but I never meant for Sofia to buy me a house." Her brain had started working again, registering the meaning behind his words. "Oh, my gosh. You're implying that I tried to manipulate Sofia into buying me a house, aren't you?"

He shrugged, but the gesture looked anything but careless. "Do you deny it?"

If last night had meant as much to him as it had to her, she wouldn't have to deny it. He'd trust her enough to believe in her.

"You've got to admit the timing looks suspicious," he said when she didn't answer.

Her brain went into overdrive. He was insinuating she'd done something much more damning than hint that she wanted a house. He was accusing her of having known all along that she wasn't Constanzia.

She'd thought she and Tony had connected last night on a level that was much deeper than the physical. She'd thought he knew what kind of person she was. How could she have been so wrong about him?

She blinked to dry her tears and got to her feet.

"We're not through talking," he said.

"Oh, yes we are." She stalked away, angrier than she'd been in years even though a part of her suspected Tony was distancing himself from her because he was afraid of what had happened between them last night.

Despair rushed upon her like a dark cloud in a storm. In the space of a few minutes, she'd lost not only a mother but the man she was coming to love.

She dashed away a tear, annoyed at herself for letting it fall and incensed at Tony for causing it.

She dug a tissue out of her purse and blew

her nose. She couldn't crumble. She had a son to pick up at day care and a car to pack.

Maybe it was wrong to leave without saying goodbye to Sofia in person, but she couldn't stay in Sofia's house any longer, not with Tony believing what he did.

Later, as she drove away in the packed car with her crying son, she realized she was leaving the only place she'd ever felt like she belonged and faced the cruelest irony of all.

She wasn't meant to be in McIntosh with Tony, either.

"I'M HOME."

The words Tony had been dreading drifted up the stairs to the guest room, where he was working on a Creatures Features problem that paled in comparison to the problem he had to face.

It was Saturday afternoon, more than twenty-four hours since Sofia had left McIntosh for Cincinnati and nearly that long since Kaylee had taken Joe and left for good.

Tony got up from the computer, squared his shoulders and went downstairs to face his stepmother.

He found her in the entranceway kissing Art, who must have carried her suitcase from the car. From the look of it, neither Sofia nor Art was ready for their time together to end.

Tony had felt that way when he was with Kaylee. He shook off the thought and cleared his throat.

The couple reluctantly broke apart, both of them turning his way, neither of them seeming the least bit self-conscious. Sofia looked happier than he'd seen her since his father's death. Her complexion glowed, her eyes shined. Art smiled broadly.

"Did you two have a good trip?" Tony asked unnecessarily.

"It was wonderful," Sofia said and kissed Tony's cheek.

"Wonderful," Art echoed, shaking Tony's hand with a firm grip that Tony had always thought spoke well of him.

"But I've got to be getting back to the store," he told Sofia, clearly reluctant to leave. He gave her a quick kiss goodbye, but their lips clung.

When he was gone, Tony picked up his stepmother's bag and carried it upstairs. She trailed him into her bedroom.

"Where's Kaylee and Joey?" she asked casually when he put the suitcase down on her bed. "Saturday afternoons can be pretty busy at Nunzio's, but she's usually home from work by now."

Here it was, the moment Tony had been dreading. "They're gone, Sofia."

She crossed to the bed, opened her suitcase and started unpacking. "Gone where?"

"I couldn't tell from her note, but my guess would be Texas. Or maybe Florida."

Sofia whirled, her face turning pale. "You mean they left McIntosh?"

He nodded, experiencing the same pang watching Sofia's shocked disappointment as he had when he read Kaylee's goodbye note.

"But why would Kaylee leave?" Her voice wavered.

"You'd better sit down for this," Tony said. She sank onto the edge of the bed and gazed up at him with eyes that were already misty. He would have given anything not to have to break the news to her. "Kaylee's not Constanzia."

He expected shock. Tears wouldn't have surprised him. He wasn't prepared for exasperation. "I know that."

He could barely choke out his next questions. "You do? How?"

"That first night at dinner, when Kaylee flipped her hair back, I saw that her earlobes weren't attached. Constanzia's were. I only held my baby for a few minutes after she was born, but it was long enough to notice that."

Tony cast his mind back, remembering how Sophia had commented on Kaylee's earrings that night. "But I don't understand why you didn't say anything."

"The same reason I refused to take the DNA test. I liked having a daughter and a grandson. But it became more than that. The longer they stayed, the more I loved them. It didn't matter that they weren't related to me by blood, because they were already family." She paused. "I thought you felt the same way."

"My feelings and my duty are two different things."

"What duty?"

"The duty I have to protect you from anybody who tries to take advantage of you," he said firmly.

"Kaylee wasn't taking advantage of me, and you know it."

"What about the house you were planning to buy for her?"

"I told you she didn't know anything about it."

"I'm not convinced of that," he said stubbornly. "But either way, it seems suspicious that a woman having trouble making ends meet suddenly shows up at the doorstep of a multimillionaire."

"I thought you'd gotten past your suspicion of Kaylee when you got to know what kind of person she was." Sofia's eyes narrowed. "Explain something to me. Why are you so paranoid that people will take advantage of me?"

"Because you let your own husband take advantage of you," he retorted.

"I did not!"

"You worked sixty-hour weeks to support a man who dreamed away his days."

"But I didn't mind working. And the fact that your father was a dreamer was one of the things I loved about him. He never gave up hope that one of his inventions would turn out to be the big one."

"But none of them ever did."

"That's because he never could get the financial backing he needed. A little money would have made a big difference in his life. Why do you think I've been backing these ventures people come to me with?"

He was silent as he thought about the kinds of businesses in which she'd invested—a bagel shop, a jewelry-making operation, a small office-supply store.

For the first time in his life he considered that his father might not have been a failure as much as he was a man who hadn't been lucky enough to fulfill his dream.

"That doesn't mean you should spend all your money on others without providing for your financial future," he finally said.

"Now you sound like Art. Over the weekend, he convinced me to put at least half of the money in an interest-bearing account to provide for my retirement."

Tony's respect for Art grew, especially since he'd gotten through to Sofia when Tony hadn't. "How about the other half?"

"I'm going to keep investing in causes I think are worthy, and I'm going to make sure I don't die of boredom. I'm making an offer for Nunzio's, Tony. But I won't be an absentee owner. When I feel like it, I'm going to be one of the cooks."

"But that's…" he groped for a word, "…wonderful."

"Do you really think it's wonderful? You're the one who told me to quit."

"Only because I didn't realize how much you loved working at the restaurant," he said.

"I think it's wonderful that you can do something that makes you happy."

"I only wish you'd figure out what will make you happy," she said cryptically. "Now let me see the note that Kaylee left."

Kaylee had actually left two notes, a curt one for him alone in which she'd promised to send him the money she owed him for the car repairs. She'd left the second one on the kitchen table for Sofia. He pulled it out of his pocket and handed it to her. She hadn't enclosed it in an envelope so he already knew what it said.

Dearest Sofia:
Please forgive us for not saying goodbye in person, but we couldn't stay now that the truth has come out. I pray that you realize I would never deliberately deceive you. I feel lucky to have had you for a mother, if only for a little while.
Love,
Kaylee and Joey

"You haven't asked me how I know Kaylee isn't Constanzia," Tony said when she was through reading.

Sofia dashed away her tears and sniffed. "I

don't need to. I know about the hair samples you sent to that DNA place. I overheard you calling the lab to see if the results were in. I assume they are?"

Tony started, feeling unreasonably guilty even though he'd only been trying to protect her.

"That's not how. Your mother called, Sofia." He paused, knowing his next words would change her life. "She found her, Sofia. Angela found Constanzia."

Sofia stared at him for a moment in disbelief until her eyes welled with happy tears. Tony gathered her into his arms, but he wasn't thinking of the daughter she'd found.

He was thinking of the woman he'd lost, the one he'd driven from McIntosh, the one he feared he'd never see again.

KAYLEE'S PULSE raced as she sat statue still in the once-familiar family room of her father's house.

Her heart had been through the wringer the past few days as she dealt with a triple whammy: the painful after-effects of Tony's distrust, Joey's tears over leaving McIntosh and the discovery that Rusty Collier's parole had been revoked a few days after it had been granted.

And now her beleaguered heart was in for another workout. She was about to come face-to-face with the father she hadn't seen in seven years, the one who hadn't cared enough to come after her when she'd run away to Florida.

She listened to Lilly ask him how his day had gone. It might have been more accurate if her sister had asked him about his night. Paul Carter was a conscientious and hard-working plumber who made house calls at a customer's convenience, day or night.

"It went okay, same as usual," her father answered in his Texas drawl, then asked, "The car out front with the Florida plates, is that Kaylee's?"

"Yeah," Lilly said. "She and Joey got here late this afternoon. Joey's already asleep, but Kaylee's in the family room."

That was Kaylee's cue to get off the arm-chair and go to meet him, but her legs seemed frozen. She clasped her suddenly shaking hands together and waited for her first look at her father in what seemed like an eternity.

His hair had thinned, his body had expanded by maybe twenty pounds and his gait had slowed, but his closed expression when he looked at her hadn't changed.

"I hope it's okay if Joey and I stay here for a few days while I figure out what I'm going to do." When he didn't answer, she added, "If it's not, we can go to a hotel."

"'Course it's okay," he said gruffly.

She half expected him to turn and exit the room, but he sat down on the sofa across from her. She longed for her sister to appear and smooth things over with her cheerful chatter, but Lilly was obviously giving them time alone.

Her father wore jeans and a short-sleeved white shirt embroidered with "Paul Carter Plumbing," the same as she remembered. But of course they weren't the same clothes, just as she wasn't the same bratty teen who'd run away from home.

But how do you go about telling a father who never really knew you that you're no longer the same?

"What were you doing in Ohio?" His voice held no inflection that she could pick up.

She started to invent a plausible reason as to why she could have been there, then changed her mind. She was tired of secrets.

"I saw a news feature about a woman

who'd given up a baby named Constanzia for adoption twenty-five years ago. I went to Ohio because I thought I might be that baby."

Her father's jaw dropped, and the self-control she'd always viewed as formidable faltered. His voice shook. "Why would you think you belonged to someone else?"

She gathered her composure and met his eyes. "Because you change the subject every time I ask if I was adopted. What was I supposed to think?"

He closed his eyes. An unnamed emotion flitted across his face that she thought might have been pain. She expected him to get up and walk out of the room, as he had on the other occasions when she'd brought up the subject.

She waited, bracing herself to see his retreating back. But the only parts of his body that moved were shoulders that heaved and eyelids that opened to reveal eyes that looked tortured.

"I never wanted you to know this." He paused, and she'd never seen him look so vulnerable. "But I'm not your biological father."

He took a deep breath while she struggled to make sense of his admission.

"Your mother was pregnant when I married her," he said, the words seeming to come with great difficulty. "The guy that got her pregnant died of a drug overdose when she was a few months along. I was the friend who was in love with her.

"It was easy to pretend you were mine after you were born. Your mother never told anyone else who fathered you. I didn't want her to give you that damn middle name, but she said she had to."

"Because he was Italian?"

Paul Carter shook his head. "He had dark coloring but he wasn't Italian. She gave you the name because his favorite movie was *The Godfather.* Constanzia was Don Corleone's daughter's name."

The information hit Kaylee like a blow. She'd been named after a character in a movie. Not only that, she didn't have a drop of Italian blood.

If she'd known these facts from the beginning, she never would have gone to McIntosh. Never would have believed she was Sofia's daughter. Never would have fallen in love with Sofia's stepson.

She swallowed the lump in her throat. Everything finally made sense, including the distant way Paul Carter had always treated her and the way he doted on her sister.

"Now I understand why Lilly was always your favorite," she said, her throat thick, "and why you never interfered when Mom yelled at me."

"You're wrong. I didn't have a favorite. And I didn't interfere because I knew your mother was scared you'd end up like the wild guy who got her pregnant. Dead before he'd even lived."

"Is that why she was so hard on me?" Kaylee asked, wonder in her voice and in her heart. "Because she was afraid for me?"

"She loved you. She didn't want you to make the same mistakes as she did."

"But I did," Kaylee said softly. She'd not only gotten pregnant by the wrong man, but she'd yet to tell her son the truth about his father. The same way her parents had never told her the truth.

Her father rubbed a hand over his lower face. "I should have got your mother to ease up, but I didn't want to lose you, either. Not when I loved you from the minute you were born."

"You love me?"

"Of course I love you."

"But I always thought…" She stopped, started again. "I always thought you didn't. You didn't even come after me when I ran away."

"I wanted to," he said. "But then I thought of that saying about how if you love something you should let it go, that if it doesn't come back—"

"—it was never really yours to begin with," she finished.

She stood up, came to sit beside him on the sofa and said, "I'm back, Dad. And I could really use a father."

His lower lip trembled, and he gathered her into his arms for the first time she could remember. A sense of peace filled Kaylee, and she knew she could forgive her parents for not telling her about the boy who'd fathered her.

But she wouldn't be able to forgive herself if she made the same mistake. It was past time to tell Joey about his father.

KAYLEE WAITED until her father and sister left the house the following afternoon to seek out Joey. She found him at the edge of the backyard vegetable garden between the tomatoes and the climbing beans. He had a pail in one hand, a hand shovel in the other.

June afternoons in Houston tended to be scorching, and this one was no different. The temperature was in the mid-eighties and the grass already showed signs of baking.

"What are you doing, Joe-Joe?" she asked when she approached him.

He looked up at her, a smear of dirt across his damp face, his eyes bright. "Digging for worms."

That wasn't surprising. Paul Carter had taken the morning off to get acquainted with his grandson by showing him the joys of fishing. That included digging up bait.

Joey seemed so intent on finding a worm that Kaylee had second thoughts about it being the right time to tell him about Rusty. But realistically she knew there would never be a perfect time.

"I've got something to tell you, Joe-Joe," she announced.

He stopped digging and gazed up at her, his expression hopeful. "Are we going back to Sofia's and Tony's?"

She frowned, amazed at how much his simple question hurt. She wanted to go back to McIntosh every bit as much as he did, probably more, but the difference was she knew they never could.

"This isn't about McIntosh." She crouched down beside him. "It's about your father."

He stopped digging and thrust his lower lip forward. "You said I don't have a father."

Kaylee nearly groaned aloud. She hadn't exactly phrased it that way but understood how he might have gotten that impression. The sun beat down on her, punishing in its heat.

"Everybody has a father," she said and plunged ahead. "Yours is named Rusty Collier."

"Where is he?"

This was the toughest part of all. She'd had to readjust her thinking about Rusty after contacting the state prison system. She'd discovered he'd been sent back to prison fifteen days after he'd been released. The charge was possession of marijuana with intent to sell.

Swallowing her pride, she'd contacted the brother Rusty had lived with for those fifteen days. The conversation with Rusty's brother had been short but not sweet. He'd told her that Rusty hadn't tried to contact her because he had no interest in his son.

Kaylee had thought about it long and hard and decided her newfound knowledge didn't exonerate her from telling Joey the truth.

"He's made a lot of mistakes in his life, Joey. Before you were born, he made a big one. He stole a car, and the police arrested him."

His eyes rounded. "Is he in jail?"

"Yeah, he is."

"Is he a bad man?"

She bit her lip. That was a tougher question to answer. "He's not a bad man, but he's not a particularly good one, either."

"Are you married to him?"

"You know I'm not married, Joey."

"Do you want to marry him?"

"No," she said, wondering where he was going with this.

"If you married somebody else, would he be my dad?"

"Technically he'd be your stepdad."

"You mean the way Sofia is Tony's stepmom?"

"Exactly like that," she said, wishing he hadn't brought up the Donatellis.

"Then you should marry Tony," he said matter-of-factly. "I want him to be my dad."

Shock prevented her from speaking, but her son had no such trouble. "Don't you think Tony would make a good dad?"

An image of Tony and Joey at the soda

counter with their heads together flashed through Kaylee's mind. She had no doubt Tony would make an excellent father, just as she suspected he'd make a good husband.

"Yes, I think he would. But Tony doesn't want to marry me, Joey."

"Have you asked him?"

She hadn't stuck around in McIntosh long enough to ask Tony anything. The thought that he didn't believe in her had cut so deeply that she'd packed up everything and run, just as she'd run from Houston when she was a teenager.

She should have known running never solved anything. She should have tried to understand why Tony was so willing to believe she'd conned Sofia. She should have fought to make him understand that wasn't the case.

She should have told him she loved him.

"No, I haven't asked him," she said.

"Then how do you know he doesn't want to marry you?" Joey didn't wait for her response. "When we go back to McIntosh, you can ask him then."

Her heart leaped at the prospect of seeing Tony, Sofia and McIntosh, but just as quickly crashed to earth.

She was all grown-up now. She couldn't

rashly follow her heart and expect everything to work out.

The belief that she belonged in McIntosh had been a beautiful fiction, even if the pretty countryside with the rolling hills and the rows of apple trees had never stopped calling to her.

After she'd left, neither Tony nor Sofia had tried to contact her. Tony was no doubt back in Seattle, pretending that's where he wanted to be. Sofia was probably getting acquainted with Stephanie Minelli, the real Constanzia.

Kaylee was the fraud.

She laid a hand on her son's arm and told him the sad, inevitable truth. "We're not going back to McIntosh, son."

CHAPTER SIXTEEN

TONY HAD ONLY been back in Seattle for five days, and he'd never heard a quieter silence.

He'd gotten used to working with the door open at Sofia's house, where the occasional murmur of cheerful conversation or Joe's happy shrieks of laughter brightened his days.

The building where he lived was in a busy part of Seattle, with steady pedestrian and vehicle traffic on the street below. But inside the four walls of his pricey condominium, there was only silence.

He could put on the television, turn on the radio or play a CD, but he knew that wouldn't remedy the real problem.

He was lonely.

Lonely for his stepmother. Lonely for Joe. But, most of all, lonely for Kaylee.

For the hundredth time since she'd walked out of his life, he thought about the insinuations he'd made after finding out Kaylee wasn't Constanzia. He still couldn't say why he'd done it, especially when she'd seemed as shocked by the news as he was.

He sighed, wandered into his kitchen and picked up the application for Supersonics season tickets that he'd transferred from his dresser drawer to the top of his stack of mail. He set it back down, although he'd yet to fill out as much as his name.

He thought briefly of returning the numerous calls he'd gotten from his Realtor, but discounted the notion. He wasn't in the mood to hear about the wonderful property that another buyer would snap up if he didn't act quickly.

Calling Ellen had no appeal, either, although he suspected she knew he was back in town through her friendship with the receptionist who worked in his office.

The sound of a doorbell cut through the quiet, both unexpected and unwelcome. Even though he'd admitted to himself that he was lonely, he didn't especially want to see anybody.

The doorbell rang again. He checked the identity of his visitor through the peephole. It was Ellen, looking blond and elegant even with the fish-eye effect.

"Can I come in?" she said when he opened the door. He stepped back to allow her entrance.

He would have greeted her with a kiss as recently as five weeks ago. But five weeks ago, he'd been under the delusion that he wanted to marry her.

"You haven't called." She stated the obvious as she breezed past him to the minibar in a corner of his living room. She didn't seem to expect a response, so he didn't give one.

"Do you mind?" she said, holding up a bottle of gin. When he shook his head, she poured herself a gin and tonic and took a swallow. "I called your Realtor today. She thinks you're avoiding her."

"I am," he said as the reason became clear. "I've decided not to buy a house."

"I see," she said and took another swallow. "I take it you haven't given the go-ahead to expand Security Solutions, either?"

"True again," he said.

She braced a hand on one elegant hip. "So what's her name?"

"Pardon me?"

"Her name, Tony. I sensed you wavering about what you wanted before you returned to that backwater town, but your priorities wouldn't have changed so completely if you hadn't met a woman."

"What makes you so sure my priorities have changed?"

"Besides the house you're not buying, the business you won't expand and the basketball season tickets you haven't applied for? How about the way you dealt with me?"

"You're the one who said you wouldn't wait around."

"True, but I didn't expect you to make me wait. When I told you I wanted to date other men, I thought you'd fly back to Seattle on the next plane. But you said it was all right with you."

It had been all right with him. He hadn't known it then, but whatever had been between him and Ellen had been over before he went back to McIntosh. Kaylee had only driven the point home.

"Her name's Kaylee," he said, figuring Ellen should at least have the satisfaction of thinking she was right.

Her eyes didn't stray from his. "Are you in love with her?"

It was a question he hadn't dared ask himself. He did so now and realized a harsh truth. Kaylee might not have been the reason he and Ellen hadn't worked out, but she was the reason things weren't working out for him in Seattle.

"Yes," he said. "I am in love with her."

Ellen downed the rest of her gin and tonic, then set the empty glass on the counter and walked over to him.

"I had to come over and see for myself," she said.

"See what for yourself?"

She stood barely a foot from him. He could smell her expensive perfume and appreciate the symmetry of her features, but he preferred the way Kaylee looked. Kaylee wasn't as powerfully striking as Ellen, but she was far more attractive.

"That it's over," she said, "and it is."

She kissed him on the cheek, then left.

He stood in the middle of his quiet, empty apartment, finally making sense of it all.

He'd hadn't bought a house or expanded his business or asked a woman to marry him because everything he needed wasn't here in Seattle, after all. Something had been missing in his life. Now he knew what that something was: Kaylee.

The reason he'd lashed out at her after discovering she wasn't Constanzia had nothing to do with not believing in her and everything to do with not believing in himself.

Because he'd been afraid to face the ramifications of admitting he was in love with a woman who was in love with McIntosh.

He rushed to his computer and pulled up one of the travel sites he'd used in the past to book airline tickets. The apology he owed Kaylee would best be delivered in person, where he could get down on his knees if he had to.

He was typing in dates when the phone rang. He snatched up the receiver, intending to get rid of the caller. "Yeah."

"Tony, dear. It's Sofia. I hope I'm not getting you in the middle of anything."

Only in the middle of coming to my senses, he thought.

He took his hand off the mouse, immediately attentive. She'd called him twice from San Diego, where she'd been reunited with the daughter she'd never known. She'd been thrilled with the way the reunion had gone, but Tony had never doubted that Stephanie Minelli would recognize the goodness in his stepmother and grow to love her.

"You know I always have time for you, Sofia," he said. "Are you in San Diego or McIntosh?"

"McIntosh," she answered. "It was tough leaving Stephanie but we're going to see each other again real soon."

"So everything went well?"

"Everything went great." Emotion clogged her voice. "She told me before I got on the plane that she was blessed because now she had two mothers instead of one."

"I haven't met her yet, and I already like her."

"Come to McIntosh this weekend and you will meet her."

"I thought she was finishing up a residency. How did you manage to talk her into coming to McIntosh?"

"I believe it's difficult to say no to your mother when she asks you to come to her wedding." She waited a beat. "So how about it, Tony, will you come to my wedding Saturday afternoon?"

"You're getting married? On Saturday?"

She laughed. "I found an advantage to winning the lottery. If you have enough money, you can make things happen when you want them to happen."

"That's not what I meant, Sofia. I meant this thing between you and Art has happened really fast."

"We've known each other for fifteen years, Tony. That's not fast."

Tony tensed as the old suspicions crowded his mind. Art seemed like a good guy, but money changed people.

"It's too soon," he said.

"Art predicted you'd say that. That's why he insisted on signing a prenuptial agreement. He said it would help convince you that he loved me for me." Her voice grew soft. "I'm not naive, Tony. Art really does love me."

Tony couldn't dispute that, not when he'd seen them together, not when Art had insisted on the prenup. "Then I'm happy for you."

"So you'll come to the wedding?" She sounded hopeful.

"I'll come to the wedding."

"And you'll be nice to Kaylee?"

Tony's hand tightened on the receiver. It hadn't occurred to him that Sofia would invite Kaylee, but of course she would. If not for Kaylee, she and Art probably wouldn't be getting married.

"Has Kaylee said she'll come?" he asked.

"I haven't asked her yet. Frankie Nunzio told me she had him send her last paycheck to an address in Houston, so I know where she is." He heard the hesitation in her voice. "To be honest, I'm afraid she won't come. So I'm thinking of sending her an invitation and plane tickets by courier. That way, it might be harder for her to say no."

Tony's heart thudded as an idea occurred to him. Once it formed, he couldn't get it out of his mind.

"I've got an idea about that courier," he said.

KAYLEE'S RED PEN hovered over the classified section of the newspaper, but so far she hadn't circled any job listings. Several employers had advertised for waitresses, but none of the jobs appealed to her.

She put her elbows on the kitchen table and her chin in her hands. The problem wasn't the jobs. It was her. She and her father were getting along better than they ever had, but she was reluctant to put down roots in Houston.

Not when she wanted to be wherever Tony was, whether that be McIntosh or Seattle or Timbuktu. She sniffed, wondering when she'd arrived at that conclusion. Not that concluding anything made any difference with Tony so very far away.

The doorbell sounded, competing with the sound of the cartoon Joey was watching in the family room. It was a classic ring instead of the strains of "Yankee Doodle" that played at the Donatellis. She missed the patriotic ring.

"I'll get it," Lilly called from somewhere in the house, allowing Kaylee to try to refocus on the classifieds.

She was debating whether to circle an ad for a cocktail waitressing job when her sister walked into the kitchen wearing her lifeguarding T-shirt, very short shorts and a speculative look.

Lilly handed her a manila envelope. "This just arrived for you by courier."

Kaylee took the envelope, which didn't have a return address. Very strange. Neither was the envelope sealed. Even odder.

She dumped the contents of the envelope on the table and picked up a card depicting an apple orchard in bloom. With trembling fingers, Kaylee opened it and read the scripted handwriting: *Sofia Donatelli and Art Sandusky request the honor of your presence at their afternoon wedding…*

Joy burst inside her. She'd been right. Art did love Sofia, exactly as she'd suspected. And they were going to make it official this Saturday.

A folded note had come inside the card. She unfolded it and read: *The only way I'll forgive you for leaving the way you did and not getting in touch is if you come to my wedding. After all, it wouldn't be happening without you. Love, Sofia.*

"Who's Sofia? And why wouldn't her wedding be happening without you?" Lilly asked over her shoulder.

Kaylee refolded the note, wondering how she'd missed noticing her sister had been reading over her shoulder.

"Sofia's the reason I was in McIntosh. She exaggerated about the wedding. The guy she's marrying is crazy about her. All I did was give him a little nudge."

"Sounds to me like it was a big nudge," Lilly said. "What are those?"

She indicated a number of pieces of white paper that had been folded in half. Kaylee picked up the stack, straightened the papers and saw the logo of an airline. She leafed through them, realizing they were electronic plane tickets to McIntosh issued in the names of Kaylee and Joe Carter.

"Somebody really wants you to go to that wedding," Lilly remarked. "Are you going to?"

Kaylee's heartbeat accelerated. Days ago, she'd resigned herself to never seeing Tony again. But here was a second chance to make things right. Tony wouldn't miss his stepmother's wedding. Tony would be there.

Lilly didn't wait for her answer. "Because the courier who delivered the envelope, who by the way is very hot, is waiting outside the door for your answer."

Lilly's revelation penetrated the thick haze of hope that Kaylee had been swimming in. "That's odd. Are you sure?"

"Am I sure that six-foot-something of gorgeous man is standing outside our door? Let me think about that." Lilly tapped the side of her mouth. "Yeah, I'm sure."

Her curiosity roused, Kaylee got up from the table and hurried to the door, nearly knocking over a vase in the foyer in the process. She caught it in her right hand and pulled open the door with her left to see Tony Donatelli.

The Texas sun beat down on him, throwing his handsome face into stark focus and making the fact that he was here in Houston startlingly real.

The breath left her lungs, and for a moment she couldn't speak.

"If you threw that vase at me, I wouldn't blame you," he said. "I wouldn't even duck."

She looked down at her hand, saw that she was still holding the vase and put it down. She swallowed. "I couldn't do that. It was one of my mother's favorites."

He winced. "You're not going to make this easy for me, are you?"

She could barely squeeze the words out. "Make what easy for you?"

"Apologizing," he said and shielded his eyes from the sun. "But do you think I could do it inside?"

"Kaylee, what's going on out there?" Lilly called. "Is the courier somebody you know?"

"What's a courier?" she heard Joey ask. If he was paying attention to what was happening around him, the cartoon must be over.

"Give me a minute," Kaylee called back, stepped outside and shut the door. "Believe me, we'll have more privacy out here."

"It's a million degrees out here."

"The newspaper said the high was only going to be ninety-one."

"We're talking about the weather," he pointed out.

She didn't take her eyes off his face. "What would you rather talk about?"

"What a jerk I was for accusing you of trying to con my stepmother." His eyes looked pained. "I don't deserve your forgiveness. But I'm asking for it anyway."

She looked away from the sincerity in his eyes. "It hurt that you believed I'd do a thing like that."

"That's the thing," Tony said. "I never really believed it, not after I got to know you."

"Then why did you make those accusations?"

"I think partly because you have a quality that reminds me of my father, a kind of hopefulness. I used to think he took advantage of Sofia. I wanted to make absolutely sure you didn't."

"Used to think?" She picked up on the syntax he'd used. "Don't you believe your father took advantage of her anymore?"

"How can I believe it when Sofia doesn't?" Tony ran a hand through his hair. "But, like I said, that was only part of the reason. A minor part, really." He looked her straight in the eyes. "Mostly I was afraid to face the consequences of loving you."

Kaylee's heart pounded. Tony loved her. Her heart started to soar but she brought it back down to earth.

"What consequences?" she asked.

"You love McIntosh. I thought that committing to you would mean coming back to my hometown to live."

"I do love McIntosh," she said huskily, her throat nearly closing, "but I love you more."

No sooner had she spoken the words then he gathered her into his arms, spinning her around right there on the sidewalk in front of her father's house until she was dizzy. Dizzy with love. Dizzy with wanting him.

He captured her mouth in a searing kiss that was as hot as the temperature.

"Remember the spectacle Sofia and Art made of themselves when they were necking in her front yard?" she asked when they drew back for breath. "We're making a bigger spectacle, because it's broad daylight."

"The better for the world to see how much you love me," he said smugly. "You did say you loved me, right?"

"I did." She giggled. "I mean I do. Yes."

"I was so afraid you didn't," he said.

"That's because I tried really hard to keep it from you." She sobered. "That day in the park when you accused me of conning Sofia, I should have talked until I was blue in the face to make you believe I'd never hurt her. I shouldn't have run. I should have told you I loved you."

"And I shouldn't have been a jerk," he said.

"A great, big jerk," she amended.

He grinned. "Will you and Joe come back to McIntosh with this great, big jerk for Sofia's wedding?"

"We wouldn't miss it for the world."

"And after the wedding, do you think you and I can start over?"

"I'll start over with you anywhere you like."

"Anywhere?" he asked.

"Anywhere," she agreed.

"Then how about if we start over in McIntosh?"

She drew back in his arms, the better to study his face. "But you hate it in McIntosh."

"I hated it. Past tense. But then I saw the town through your eyes," he said. "There's something magical about an apple orchard in the middle of the night when you're with the woman you love."

The memory transported her to that night they'd made love, but she couldn't let it cloud her thinking, not when this was so important. "But how would you spend your days if we lived in McIntosh?"

"I told you about the friend who's my right-hand man in Seattle, right? Nick's perfectly capable of running—and expanding—Security Solutions with occasional consulting help from me."

"Occasional? That doesn't sound like it would be enough to keep you busy."

"It's not," he said. "The rest of the time I'll design educational video games for children. Joe's been helping me with the one I'm working on now. It's called Creature Features."

She cocked her head. "Why didn't I know you were designing a video game?"

"Because I never thought of it as anything other than a hobby before now."

"Are you sure?"

"Very sure. I'm even confident I can get you your old job back." He winked. "I have an in with the new owner."

"Are you telling me that Sofia bought Nunzio's?"

"She did," he said. "She needs somebody

to help her run the place, and I have it on good authority she's going to offer the position to you. She also has a position open for grandson. I think Joe might be able to fill that one."

Kaylee studied his eyes. "Are you sure, Tony? I meant it when I said I'd go anywhere with you. I don't belong in a place. I belong with you."

"I meant it," he said. "Those tickets to McIntosh, they're one-way. If I've learned anything since meeting you, it's that home is where the heart is. And you have mine."

Kaylee flushed with pleasure, then pulled his mouth down to hers for another lingering kiss in full view of anyone who might be watching.

"Hey, Kaylee." It was Lilly's voice, coming from the porch. Kaylee hadn't even heard her come outside. "Why are you kissing the courier?"

"That's no courier," she heard Joey shout. "That's Tony."

Joey whooped and came running at them full tilt, exhibiting utmost confidence in Tony by executing a flying leap into his arms.

Kaylee had to say this for the man she loved. He had good hands.

KAYLEE'S EYES were so misty that anybody would have thought it was her wedding day instead of Sofia's.

"You look gorgeous," she told Sofia, blinking back happy tears while she fussed with a sprig of baby's breath in the older woman's dark hair.

They were in the vestibule of the little stone church in McIntosh where Sofia and Art were to be married in about ten minutes.

Sofia wore a simply cut tea-length gown of cream silk. Kaylee's dress was a pale yellow. The third woman in the room, who wore pastel orange, stepped back and snapped a pre-ceremony photo of Sofia and Kaylee, then dashed a tear from under one of her dark eyes.

"Now I understand why I cry whenever I'm happy," said Stephanie Minelli, who'd been given the name Constanzia by her birth mother. "It's an inherited trait."

"But I'm not the one who's crying," Sofia pointed out. "Kaylee is."

Kaylee exchanged a watery glance with Stephanie, then broke into a reciprocal grin. She supposed at first glance they looked like they could be related, but Stephanie had

374 ORDINARY GIRL, MILLIONAIRE TYCOON

rounder features, bigger breasts and lighter, straighter hair. She was also left-handed.

"Are you absolutely sure you didn't give birth to two daughters?" Stephanie asked Sofia.

Sofia looked from Stephanie to Kaylee. "I feel like I have two daughters, and that's what counts."

Kaylee blinked, determined not to surrender to happy tears and ruin her eye makeup. Sofia had been wonderful since the moment she'd returned to McIntosh.

She'd forgiven Kaylee for running off without saying goodbye, dismissed as nonsense any thought that Kaylee had been trying to scam her and then revealed an incredible secret: she'd known almost from the beginning that Kaylee wasn't her biological daughter.

Because they'd shared a strong connection from the start, it had been difficult for Kaylee to refuse when Sofia asked if she'd be her maid of honor. That privilege, Kaylee had told Sofia, should go to Stephanie.

"There's no rule preventing me from having two maids of honor," Sofia had said.

That's exactly what she'd done. Stephanie had arrived on a flight from San Diego last night with her adoptive mother, a matronly woman with blond hair and a warm smile. Mrs. Minelli was inside the church now, sitting next to Angela Crenna. Kaylee thought Sofia and Angela still had things to work out, but for the most part Sofia seemed to have forgiven her.

A knock sounded on the door, and the wedding planner stuck her head inside the room. "Are you ready, Mrs. Sandusky-to-be?"

Sofia smiled. "That depends on whether my stepson has things back under control."

"If you're talking about the toad the ring bearer had in his pocket, your stepson convinced him to take it outside," the wedding planner said.

Kaylee smiled. "That's my son, for you."

"And mine," Sofia added. She drew herself to her full height. "So let's go do it."

Kaylee held the door open. Stephanie left the room first. Sofia started to follow her, then stopped. She held up her bouquet. "At the end of the day, this will be yours."

"You can't be sure I'll be the one to catch it," Kaylee said.

"Oh, I'm not going to throw it. I'm going to hand it to you," Sofia said. "If I can't have you for a daughter, I want you for a daughter-in-law."

Kaylee's throat clogged with emotion. She followed Sofia out to the vestibule. It was time for Tony to take his place at the altar next to Art, but he winked at her en route and whispered in her ear. "You're going to marry me next, you know."

She nodded, because she did know that. She also knew she'd been right after all.

Here in McIntosh, with Tony and Sofia, was where she truly belonged.

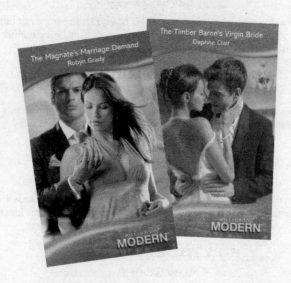

His passions were as tempestuous as his temper…

Even though Kate Whittman was young and inexperienced, she wanted moody Texas rancher Jason Donovan more than anything. But he offered her only brotherly protection.

So Kate pursued another fantasy – becoming a successful New York fashion designer. But just when it seemed that her fairy tale was coming true, fate brought her back to Texas. And to Jason.

Available 1st May 2009

www.millsandboon.co.uk

M&B

THE ROYAL HOUSE OF KAREDES

Two crowns, two islands, one legacy

Volume One
BILLIONAIRE PRINCE, PREGNANT MISTRESS
by Sandra Marton

Wanted for her body – and her baby!

Aspiring New York jewellery designer Maria Santo has come to Aristo to win a royal commission.

Cold, calculating and ruthless, Prince Xander Karedes beds Maria, thinking she's only sleeping with him to save her business.

So when Xander discovers Maria's pregnant, he assumes it's on purpose. What will it take for this billionaire prince to realise he's falling in love with his pregnant mistress…?

Available 17th April 2009

Three Latin males, brothers, must take brides…

Let these three sexy brothers seduce you in:

THE RAMIREZ BRIDE
by Emma Darcy

THE BRAZILIAN'S BLACKMAILED BRIDE
by Michelle Reid

THE DISOBEDIENT VIRGIN
by Sandra Marton

Available 1st May 2009

www.millsandboon.co.uk

IN HIS POWER...
AND IN HIS BED?

Featuring these three passionate stories:

Desert Prince, Blackmailed Bride
by Kim Lawrence

The Marcolini Blackmail Marriage
by Melanie Milburne

Dante's Blackmailed Bride by Day Leclaire

Available 17th April 2009

2 FREE

BOOKS AND A SURPRISE GIFT!

We would like to take this opportunity to thank you for reading this Mills & Boon® book by offering you the chance to take TWO more specially selected titles from the Superromance series absolutely FREE! We're also making this offer to introduce you to the benefits of the Mills & Boon® Book Club™—

- ★ FREE home delivery
- ★ FREE gifts and competitions
- ★ FREE monthly Newsletter
- ★ Exclusive Mills & Boon Book Club offers
- ★ Books available before they're in the shops

Accepting these FREE books and gift places you under no obligation to buy, you may cancel at any time, even after receiving your free shipment. Simply complete your details below and return the entire page to the address below. You don't even need a stamp!

YES! Please send me 2 free Superromance books and a surprise gift. I understand that unless you hear from me, I will receive 4 superb new titles every month for just £3.69 each, postage and packing free. I am under no obligation to purchase any books and may cancel my subscription at any time. The free books and gift will be mine to keep in any case.

U9ZED

Ms/Mrs/Miss/Mr .... Initials ....
BLOCK CAPITALS PLEASE

Surname ....

Address ....

....

.... Postcode ....

Send this whole page to:
UK: FREEPOST CN81, Croydon, CR9 3WZ